Callum Fox
and the
Mousehole
Ghost

Callum Fox
and the
Mousehole
Ghost

AC HATTER

Woodside White Books

Callum Fox and the Mousehole Ghost Copyright © AC Hatter

Woodside White Books
First published in 2014

Cover design by JD Smith
Designed and typeset by JD Smith

British Library Cataloguing in Publication data available.

Paperback ISBN 978-0-9929319-1-9
Ebook ISBN 978-0-9929319-0-2

www.achatter.co.uk

Printed in Great Britain by TJ International Ltd, Padstow, Cornwall

For Paul, Cameron, Caroline,
and all my family with love

Chapter 1

Friday 25ᵗʰ July 2014

Callum hoisted his rucksack up onto his shoulder — he was good to go. He double-checked the Paddington Station departures board. With a flurry of orange on black his train was confirmed.

'Right,' said Mum, fumbling in her purse for her Oyster card. 'All you have to do is stay on the train till the last stop. Grandad will meet you at the station. Are you sure you don't mind doing this on your own?'

'Don't worry,' Callum replied, flicking his fringe out of his eyes. 'What can go wrong?'

Mum shook her head and led the way, expertly manoeuvring through the constant stream of morning commuters.

There was a muffled tannoy announcement that Callum couldn't make out. Mum let out a cry of 'That's yours!' and broke into her ineffective 'mum jog'. Callum lengthened his stride and kept pace with her easily enough. By the time they reached his train she had slowed right down and was puffing and panting.

'I'm going to miss you so much,' she said, giving him an enormous hug. He pulled back — he wasn't a kid any more.

'Miss you too,' he whispered, trying to sneak on board before she could embarrass him any further. It didn't work. She grabbed hold of his T-shirt and caught him off-guard with a smacker of a kiss. He could have sworn that a girl walking past with a pink tartan holdall laughed out loud.

'Send my love to Nana, and remember Grandad's heart's in the right place, he's just... well, he's just Grandad... You're only there for six weeks. Don't let him get to you.'

'What do you mean, "Don't let him get to me?" What do you think he's going to do?' Callum hopped onto the train and stood in the doorway. 'Come on, Mum. What do you mean?'

'Goodbye,' Mum called out. 'Have a great summer, and remember I love you.'

A shrill signal sounded and a red warning light blinked on and off above the carriage door. But he hadn't said goodbye properly. He wasn't going to see her for six weeks — they'd never been apart that long. He thrust his arm out to wave a last goodbye — at exactly the same time as the doors slid shut.

'Argh!'

Somehow Callum managed to get his right arm trapped between the heavy duty rubber seals of the automated doors. Man, it hurt. He pulled and tugged but his arm wouldn't budge. He felt the carriage shudder and heard the creaking of the train as it prepared to move.

'You can stop waving now…' Mum shouted.

'Open the door!' Callum yelled, banging on the glass. 'Open the door!'

Mum leapt forward to hit the door open button but it wasn't needed. A sensor somewhere kicked in and the doors sprung open and then closed again, giving Callum just enough time to pull his throbbing arm back in. He cradled it against his chest, whilst back on the platform Mum slapped her forehead in despair.

'I'll be all right.' he called to her, but the train was already pulling away.

Callum rubbed his sore arm and went to find his allocated seat. There was only one other passenger at his table — the girl who had seen his mum kissing him goodbye. It really was turning out to be one of those days.

He guessed she was around his age, twelve or thirteen, possibly a little older, girls always looked older. She had deep copper-coloured hair, cut short and spiky, and she was reading a book called *The Smart Girl's Guide to Hunting, Shooting and Fishing.* She glanced up to acknowledge him as he stowed his rucksack on the overhead luggage rack, but she didn't say anything. Instead she raised her book higher, forming a barrier between them. Subtle, he thought, checking his reflection in the window, in case any of Mum's lipstick had been left on his face. Great! He rubbed off the tell-tale pink smear on his cheek and sank down low in his seat.

He took out his mobile and sent texts to his mates, reminding them he was going to be away for the whole six weeks and telling them he hadn't been allowed to bring his Xbox. They couldn't believe it either. He updated his Facebook status to 'missing in action' and then later added 'injured during a bust-up with the train door.' He was perfectly happy, plugged into his phone listening to his music and playing with his apps.

The train rocked from side to side. Whenever Callum looked out the window the view was the same. Farmland, farm animals, farm buildings. Green... green... more green... patch of mud... green.

Around Exeter he stood up and tried to get his rucksack down. The rack was pretty full and he had to manoeuvre the other bags to get to his own. They all started shifting around and he couldn't support them. The redhead's tartan pink holdall slipped and fell. He thrust his injured hand out to catch it, but missed. It landed on the table with a heavy thud, knocking over her can of Fanta, which poured its luminous contents everywhere. She glared up at him.

'I'm sorry,' he spluttered, clearing up the mess as best he could with a crumpled napkin. She produced a packet of tissues and finished the job for him.

'Thanks,' he said. 'Do you want me to get rid of those?' He held out his hand, offering to take her sticky tissues to the bin. 'I'm Callum,' he said, but she ignored him and his hand was left hanging in no-man's land for a moment too long. She made a small pile out of the wet mush on the corner of the table. He added his soggy napkin to it, and she sighed heavily.

'Are you getting off soon?' she asked.

'No; not till Penzance. I'm meeting my grandparents

there,' he told her. 'Well, that's the plan. I don't know how I'm going to recognise them though; I haven't seen them since I was two.' He knew he was going into too much detail but his mouth kept going. 'Family argument, usual kind of thing. My mum's going to be away all summer, with her job; so I'm staying with them…'

The girl cut him off mid-sentence. 'Well aren't you the modern day evacuee?' And with that she raised her book and went back to her reading.

What!

A modern day evacuee!

As if!

Chapter 2

Monday 4th September 1939 - Operation Pied Piper

'I told you, Mam, I told you. I ain't going.' Jim shouted over the uproar of the station, the screech of the steam trains and the yells of the other kids. He didn't care if every other kid in London had agreed to be evacuated; he hadn't, and that was that.

'I ain't doin' it,' he shouted again, before his voice cracked and he buried his face deep in the folds of his mam's red coat, wrapping his arms round her waist and holding on as if his life depended upon it. 'You can't make me. You can't!' The brass buckle of her belt poked him in the eye — it didn't bother him, he'd take a black eye any day if it meant he could stay at home instead of getting on that train and going off to… well, wherever it was going.

Mam stood her ground while the crowds rushed round them, jostling and knocking into the two of them.

'You can't stay, Jim — it ain't safe,' she smoothed down his messy black hair and leant over to kiss the top of his head. He nuzzled in even closer, filling his lungs with the familiar smell of honeysuckle perfume and home cooking. Somewhere behind him he heard a shrill whistle and a cry of 'All aboard.'

'You got to go,' Mam said, forcing him to stand up straight and handing him the battered old suitcase. 'Keep yourself out of mischief, you hear? Mind your Ps and Qs — and have a bath every week, whether you need it or not — all right?'

He nodded, but he couldn't talk anymore because all his words were bunged up behind the big lump in his throat.

'There you are! Jim. Mrs White. Mrs White. Over here.'

They'd been spotted. And there was only one person he knew who hollered like that — his teacher, the dreaded Miss Fitter. He looked up to see her heading straight for them, using her clipboard to beat her way through the hordes of labelled children. 'Come on, hurry up. All our lot are on the train already.'

He grabbed on to his mam even tighter.

'They'll take good care of him, Mrs White. There's nothing to worry about,' the teacher sounded reassuring, but Jim wasn't daft; he'd heard the grown-ups talking about this evacuation — no one knew where the trains were going or who would be looking after the children when they got there.

'Don't want to go,' he said, so quietly that he didn't think she would hear.

But she did. 'That's enough of that,' Miss Fitter snapped, grabbing his thin arm and yanking him towards her. 'Now, say goodbye to your mammy.' She bent down low, so his mam wouldn't catch what she said: 'Did you hear the radio yesterday? Did you? We're at war, Jim. At war! We'll all be doing things we don't want to do — for some time! So, you can do your bit by getting on this train and getting out of London — understand?'

She stood up again and smiled at Mam. 'Goodbye, Mrs White. Jim'll write home as soon as he's settled and he'll confirm his new address. Won't you, lad?' She yanked Jim hard so it seemed as if he'd nodded.

Everyone else was on the train. He knew he didn't have any choice. He grunted a muffled goodbye to his mother as Miss Fitter tightened her grip on his arm and pulled him away before he could change his mind. He stumbled after her, fighting to hold back the tears.

Mam's smile was weak, as was her wave. 'Be a good lad, Jim. Be a good lad.'

Miss Fitter dragged Jim onto the train and shoved him into a small compartment. It was crammed full of kids but he didn't know any of them. There were a couple of older lads laughing, probably at him and a large group of girls whispering and giggling. Miss Fitter had to squash three youngsters up to make room on the bench for him, then she thrust her face so close to his that he could taste her breath. 'Not another word out of you, do you hear me? You'll set the others off.' He thought he was going to be sick.

She prised his fingers off the small case and stowed it on the luggage rack high above his seat. 'That's very light,

Jim. I hope you've packed enough — there's no knowing how long you'll be away. Don't you believe anyone who says it'll be over by Christmas. They said that last time and look how long that went on for.'

Jim hung his head. Not home by Christmas? 'Thought I'd be home sooner, Miss,' he said. She ignored him.

The group of girls nudged one another. The tallest put her hand up, like she was still in class. 'Miss Fitter, where we goin'?'

'Away dear. You're going away.'

'What kind of a bleedin' answer is that?' the girl whispered to her friends, who all started giggling again.

But Jim didn't find it funny, not at all.

Jim heard whistles blowing and the shriek of a steam engine. 'Well, jolly good luck everyone,' Miss Fitter announced to the whole compartment. 'I'm sure you'll have a wonderful time — wherever you end up. And you'll be in safe hands, far away from Hitler's bombs.' Then giving them all one of her best phoney smiles she stepped back onto the platform, slamming the train door behind her.

Jim pressed his nose to the window and searched the crowds of mams and dads. There she was, a bright red blob amongst all the greens, greys and blues. She had her hankie out and was wiping her eyes. She was crying! She was actually crying! Jim hadn't ever seen his mam cry before. His world shook. He couldn't leave her like this. He had to go back. He had to get off this stupid train and get back to his mam.

Bang, bang, bang! Whistle! Bang! All the train doors were being slammed shut one by one.

Everyone ran to the windows, pinning him into his seat. He pushed himself up to his feet and elbowed his way through. 'Ger out me way!' he screamed, kicking a couple of the boys in the shin when they refused to move.

'Stop your shovin',' barked one of bigger lads standing in the doorway.

'But I've gotta geroff,' he cried, squeezing himself right up against the door. All around him kids were shouting their goodbyes and everyone on the platform was roaring and waving. Jim fumbled to find the handle.

The train jolted forwards and started pulling out.

There was no inside handle. He had to lean out of the open window and reach down to the one outside — but his arm wasn't long enough.

'Oi! What you doing?' The older lad cried as the train picked up speed. 'It's too late…'

Jim knew he was right. They were moving too fast. He gave up and let his arm trail out of the window. He wouldn't be able to get back to her, not now, not ever. He leant out into the wind and screamed.

'Mam!'

But Mam's red coat had already disappeared from sight and his voice was lost amid the roaring and hissing of the steam engine.

Chapter 3

Friday 25th July 2014

Callum's train powered on across Dartmoor, speeding through smaller and smaller stations without stopping. He looked around the carriage, desperate for something to do. He was hot, sweaty and bored.

He got up to visit the loo. The tiny cubicle smelt foul and the floor was sticky. When he tried to leave the bolt refused to slide back, holding the door firmly in place. His pulse quickened. It was like the walls were closing in on him. He knew the feeling well — claustrophobia.

He examined the lock again. It secured a folding door that should have opened as he pushed it. He tried shoving it with the bolt in place but this really jammed the lock. He leant against the back wall of the cubicle and tried to push the bolt hard with both hands and then one foot. Nothing. He smothered the whole mechanism with soap. This made a mess of him, the lock and the door. Still nothing.

The voice of the tannoy boomed into the tiny cubicle, 'Next station Penzance.' That was his stop! He could feel his heart pounding in his chest and his breath started coming in short sharp bursts. He wasn't going to be able to get out before he had to get off the train — he was going to be locked in the loo forever!

'Help! Help!' He hammered on the door, hoping someone in the carriage would hear him and rush to his rescue.

No one came. He flopped back onto the toilet seat and held his head in his hands. He tried to control his breathing. He'd always been claustrophobic. Mum said Grandad was too. If he ever got out of here alive he could ask him about it.

There was a polite knock on the door.

'Is someone in there? Are you OK?'

'No! I'm stuck! Please help!'

'I think the door opens the other way, if you pull it towards you...' Callum recognised the voice. It was the nameless redhead, it had to be her.

He pulled the door towards him, slid the lock back and holding his head high he opened the door and left the cubicle. He'd been right. It was her — dragon girl.

'Yes, I thought it opened inwards,' she said smartly.

'Looks like it does,' he replied, removing a stray piece of toilet paper from his hair and marching back to his seat.

He could hear her giggling behind him. He was desperate to spin round and demand to know what her problem was. But he didn't.

It wouldn't be long till they arrived in Penzance. Then he'd be able to get off this awful train and as far away as possible from the horrible girl. If he ever came to Cornwall again he would take Mum up on her offer to drive him. Even being stuck in the car with her listening to Radio 2 for hours on end had to be better than this.

He took several long deep breaths and plugged himself back into his phone. He made a mental note to disinfect the ear-piece, his hands and his whole head as soon as he got to Grandad's. Then he engrossed himself in his music and apps, until the phone's battery ran out and his Angry Birds were cut off mid-chirp. He tutted to himself.

Soon the train started to slow and another muffled announcement was made; apparently Penzance was 'the end of the line.' That had an ominous ring to it.

The redhead started packing away her stuff but Callum didn't move. He was worried about how he was going to identify his grandparents. What if he presented himself to a couple of strangers who turned out to be mad, or worse — mad and evil and ended up kidnapping him?

What if they had forgotten he was coming? Grandad Bob was eighty-two and Nana wasn't much younger. People that old forgot things all the time, didn't they? And what if Grandad was there but he 'got at him' like Mum had said…

The train slowed down. The other passengers stood and hurried to the doors. When it came to a complete standstill the redhead got up, nodded to Callum, and moved gracefully to the exit. Pretty soon he was the only person left on the train. He couldn't put it off any longer. He grabbed his rucksack and went to find his grandparents.

There were no obvious eighty-year-olds on the platform. Callum hung around waiting for the crowds to clear and within five minutes the station was almost empty, except for some railway station staff chatting over by the ticket booth, the red-headed girl and, Callum assumed, her red-headed mother.

The girl's mum was short, plump and homely. They were having quite a bad argument, loud enough for Callum to hear every word.

'No way, Mum... I don't want to...'

'But it must be him.' The woman spun around and stared at Callum. 'Excuse me, are you Callum Fox?'

His mouth fell open — he clamped it shut again.

'I'm Linda,' she said, walking over and smiling. 'Your grandparents asked me to pick you up when they realised you'd be on the same train as our Sophie — no point all of us coming out to meet you both. We live in Mousehole too. Come on, bring your bags. The car's over here.' She shot a warning look at her daughter. 'And you!'

Sophie seemed to be very unimpressed.

Callum's cheeks flushed red. 'Thanks. That's kind of you,' he said. But he was thinking: how embarrassing; just how embarrassing.

Was there no escape from this girl?

Chapter 4

Monday 4th September 1939

'Form a line. Come on now. Yes, you!' The uniformed woman in charge of the billeting waved her papers at Jim. 'Stop lurking at the back there, we need to see all of you.' He shuffled forward, scraping his boots on the stone floor until he fell in line with all the other kids standing to attention on the platform of the Penzance Railway Station.

It was even worse than he'd imagined. There was no one here to look after him and no home to go to. Instead, all the 'vacees' were being put on display, like a load of tatty old veg on a back-street market stall. And overseeing it all was the bossy billeting lady, marching up and down, shouting, 'Roll up, roll up. Take your pick, all fresh today, brothers and sisters — two for the price of one.' Oh, she thought she was so funny.

And the people doing the picking were a rough lot, miserable old men and even more miserable looking women. Jim caught a great big scary farmer sizing him up —checking him out for farm work. Jim thought the man was going to ask him to trot round in a circle, to check he weren't lame. Bleedin' cheek!

'Too scrawny by half,' the farmer growled and moved on to the older boy standing on Jim's left.

Jim started to shake. He didn't want to be picked, but he didn't want to be left on the platform neither. And if he was chosen did he have to go with that person, even if he didn't like the look of them?

As it worked out it didn't matter because he wasn't picked anyway. The older lads were chosen first, then the pretty girls. After an hour or so of standing around, Jim and a dozen other no-hopers were still left on the platform with no homes to go to.

'That's it. All the rooms here have gone,' the lady called out, drawing a sharp line across her notes. 'We'll have to try somewhere else to home this lot. Come on; I want this finished tonight.' And with that she ushered Jim and the others down the platform, past all the chosen children who were laughing and chatting with their new host families and out into the cold. 'Smug gits,' Jim muttered to himself.

The wind hit him hard as he left the station building. It swept in off the sea and knocked them all for six. The station was right on the very edge of the harbour, 'Blimey, it's a miracle the trains don't fall into the sea!' one girl shouted.

Jim had never seen anything like it in his life. The water stretched as far as you could see and it growled up at him, slapping its waves against the harbour walls and filling the air with a horrid fishy salty smell. The moon cast narrow slivers of silver across its black rolling surface. Another girl gasped and the boy in front of her said, 'Cor, would you look at that? Ain't that somethin'?' All the city kids ground to a halt, spellbound by the ocean. The billeting lady had to shout to get them moving again. They dragged their feet across the seaside car park and climbed up into a waiting bus.

Penzance had been quick off the mark with its blackout — it was dark in the town and darker still when they left the houses behind. Jim's head was too heavy to hold up and his eyelids kept closing. When he did glance out the window there was nothing to see and it didn't help him feel any calmer.

None of the kids talked, but once he heard a girl crying and it made that lump in his throat rise up again. He struggled to push it back down and strained to listen to the billeting officer and the driver. He hoped they would give him a clue about where they were going and what was happening, but they were talking quietly and very fast and their accents were so strange that he couldn't understand a word.

The bus bounced along, turning this way and that, heading down narrower and narrower winding roads, with great high hedges towering above them. Overhanging branches scraped at the bus's windows. With no notice at all they swerved sharp left and slowed to a stop at the end of a long and rutted driveway.

'What's 'appening?' asked a girl sitting behind Jim, wearing thick glasses and a thin coat.

Before anyone could reply the billeting lady barked,

'Stand up at once,' and they all leapt to their feet. The dim lights of the bus illuminated a small yard and a tired house. A brighter light shone from the door when it opened, then shut off again as it closed. The bus driver cut the engine and Jim listened to the crunch of footsteps on gravel. His breath stuck in his chest.

A woman clambered aboard and stood up the front talking to the billeting officer. She was old. Jim didn't want to be with anyone that old. She could be a blooming witch.

'Take your pick, they're no great shakes,' the billeting officer said and the old witch squinted down the bus and pointed straight at Jim.

He froze.

'The girl with the specs,' she said. 'She looks no trouble.'

It wasn't him! Thank goodness. The girl sitting behind Jim let out a small cry and stumbled to the front.

Jim wiped his brow, surprised how hot he felt. He watched the girl follow the old woman off into the dark, pressing his face to the cool window. The night swallowed them both and then they were gone.

There was no way on *earth* he was going off into the dark like that. He stared at the billeting officer. If she couldn't find a family for him she'd have to put him back on the train and send him home — wouldn't she? His hopes soared. Yeah, that was all he needed to do — make sure he didn't get picked. He crouched ever so low in his seat and stayed there, hiding whenever they were asked to stand, pretending he wasn't there, until everyone else had been chosen.

He listened as the driver congratulated the billeting officer on having sorted out 'all them brats.' The engine choked to life and they pulled away again. I've done it, he thought. I've only gone and done it.

'Wait! I've a name on my list that hasn't been ticked off. One of the little blighters is still here.'

Jim's stomach fell. He threw himself back to the floor and tried to bury himself under the seat in front.

'Jim White, where are you? I know you're still here!'

He held his breath as she marched down the aisle, checking each and every row for her stowaway. He could hear her coming closer and closer. A hand grabbed his collar and snatched him up. 'You need your bum whacked, you do, Jim White. What am I going to do with you?'

'Send me home, Miss?'

She laughed and said something rude that he wished he hadn't heard, then shouted back to the driver.

'Got one more. Any ideas?'

'You could try Mousehole,' he replied, pronouncing the place *mow-zaul*; where the *mow* rhymes with cow and the *zaul* with Paul; Mow-zaul.

'If we have to,' she called back, pushing Jim into his seat as they lurched forwards. Jim grabbed his suitcase and held it close to his chest, staring into the dark outside the window.

They stopped at the edge of another blacked out village. The billeting officer grabbed Jim by the arm, pulled him off the bus, across a narrow road and up some steep stone steps to someone's front door.

Jim sniffed, there wasn't going be any choice for this lucky lot he thought to himself. And no bloomin' choice for him either.

The billeting lady held him tight by the arm and banged on the door, then she turned to look at him in the moonlight, took out her hanky, spat on it and started wiping his face.

'Ger off me!' He knocked her hand away. That kind of thing was bad enough when Mam did it!

'Don't you be so cheeky,' she hissed. 'You just concentrate on standing up straight and doing what you're told — right?'

Jim braced himself. This was it. He could hear heavy footsteps clumping towards the door. He felt his knees beginning to go. The horrible billeting lady yanked him roughly to her, pulling him behind her skirt. He was happy to hide. He listened as the door creaked open.

'What do you want?' It was a woman's voice. She didn't sound very pleased to be disturbed in the middle of the night, that was for sure.

'It's your duty to 'ave him,' the billeting officer snapped, and without any introduction or explanation she whipped Jim out from behind her and shoved him hard across the threshold. He stumbled over a doormat and fell into the dark house.

Behind him the door slammed shut.

Chapter 5

Friday 25th July 2014

The doors of Linda's battered old Land Rover rattled when they slammed shut. 'Don't worry,' Linda shouted over the noise of the engine. 'No one's fallen out yet.'

They juddered out of the car park and into the packed streets of Penzance. It wasn't the picturesque seaside resort Callum had been expecting; it looked pretty much the same as any other town but with more pirate-themed pubs. And it was so full of tourists that Callum suspected the whole place could erupt at any moment in a giant volcano of caravan parts and fish heads.

Linda was chatting away, checking Sophie's teacher had escorted her across London and that she had been alright on the train. Turns out it had been Sophie's first solo train journey too. Callum had to have a little smile to himself — she wasn't quite so full of herself now.

Linda had a gentle country tone to her voice, not a heavy accent, more of a sing-song rhythm to the way she spoke. She drummed her fingers on the steering wheel while they were stuck in traffic and explained how she had bumped into Callum's nana in the Post Office-cum-General Store that morning.

'She's so excited about you coming down. She was telling me all about it and when she said what train you'd be on, I said, "That's the same one our Sophie's on!" and I offered to pick you up. Save your grandad a trip out. Of course she leapt at it, because no one feels safe when Bob's driving these days,' she laughed an infectious, carefree laugh. Everything started moving again and the Land Rover lurched forwards.

'It's very kind of you,' said Callum.

'Oh, it's no problem. Mousehole's a small place; we all look out for one another. Everyone's really close... well, not so much your grandad, but you know what he's like.'

She wasn't making Callum feel any less worried. He hung his head and wished he'd discussed this more with Mum before agreeing to come down here.

Sophie coughed deliberately in the back seat — Callum had almost forgotten she was with them. Their families obviously knew each other, so he decided to have one last go at being friendly. He twisted round to talk to her.

'I wish I'd realised you knew my grandparents when we were on the train.' He said. 'It's such a coincidence, isn't it? Us sitting at the same table, all that time, not talking, when we had so much in common, but didn't realise.'

'I knew,' she sniped. 'You *had* to be the prodigal grandchild.'

Ouch — she was harsh! How could she have known? And what did 'prodigal' mean anyway? Surely she was winding him up. He turned away, vowing to ignore her for the rest of the journey and for his entire stay down here. She was awful.

'Sophie!' Linda scolded, glaring at her daughter in the mirror.

Callum straightened up in his seat and flicked his long fringe out of his eyes. They rode the rest of the way in an uncomfortable silence.

After driving some distance south along the shoreline, Linda slowed down, swerved straight across the road and drove up a sharply sloping track, no wider than the Land Rover itself. Callum gulped. If anything had been coming the other way they would have smashed it to smithereens. He clutched at his seat belt.

One side the road looked down to the glistening blue sea and the other faced up a steep grassy hill. The houses along here were all very different. Most were old, but a couple were ultra-modern with massive sheet glass windows making the most of the spectacular view. Two or three of the larger ones had plaques outside identifying them as bed and breakfast establishments. All were on the right hand side of the track as the Land Rover sped past and all were nestled into the steep hillside at varying distances from the road. The gardens were filled with bent and battered palm trees that might had been blown inland from somewhere with a more reliable climate. Callum thought this was exactly how Cornwall should look and he started to feel a little more positive about his summer here.

The road levelled out and Linda pulled up alongside the garden of an old grey bungalow. It had a lean-to conservatory running along its front, with sun-faded wicker furniture facing out to sea. He could see his grandparents getting up out of their chairs and coming to the door.

'You will be careful here, won't you?' Linda asked, giving him a concerned smile. Was that meant to help put his mind at rest? Why would she be worried for him? Callum opened his mouth to ask her what she meant but as soon as he had both feet on the pavement she shot off down the road quicker than a Formula 1 car leaving a pit stop. She couldn't get away from him and his grandparents quickly enough.

He turned to face the bungalow. His Nana was hopping from foot to foot and waving wildly at him, Grandad stood with his hands buried deep in his pockets, tapping his foot in a staccato rhythm on the concrete of the path.

Callum waved back. Too late now, he thought, pulling his rucksack up onto his shoulder one last time and climbing the steep slope up to his grandparent's bungalow. And as he did he was surprised to feel a single freezing cold shiver run slowly up and down his spine. He wasn't sure what Linda had meant about him 'needing to be careful' here, but something at the bungalow felt wrong. Very, very wrong indeed.

Chapter 6

Monday 4th September 1939

It was dark inside the house, as dark as it had been outside. Jim could hear someone huffing and puffing. He pressed his back hard against the door; if it had been open he would have made a run for it. There was a rustling, a click, and then a low light flickered on, giving off a faint yellow glow which cast long shadows over the uneven walls.

'Let's be seeing you then.'

She was a huge woman in an enormous dressing gown. 'I'm Mrs Fox,' she said, in a sing-song kind of an accent. She towered over Jim and bore down on him with an outstretched hand.

He stood rooted to the spot, gripping hold of his battered old suitcase.

When he didn't take her hand she used it to mess up his hair. 'You can call me Ma, everyone does. And how old would you be then?'

He couldn't talk; he just stared up at her.

She answered for him. 'I'd say you were six or seven. That'd be the same age as our Bob. Yes, I think you looks seven.' Jim nodded and to his relief she seemed pleased about that. 'And what shall we be calling you?'

'Jim... Jim White,' he whispered, overcome with relief. She seemed friendly, and she had a boy his age, and he knew he was going to be all right.

Ma smiled, 'Well, Jim White. I'm very pleased to meet you. It's late, so let's get you up to bed. Leave your case down here — we'll unpack that in the morning. You can meet Bob then too, and my Walter. Come on, up you come,' and she started up the stairs, signalling to Jim to follow. 'And don't you be fretting none,' she said, turning back to him; 'you're with the Foxes now...'

Chapter 7

Friday 25ᵗʰ July 2014

'Oh Callum!' Nana cried. 'It's so good to see you. Hasn't he grown, Bob? Hasn't he grown? Have you seen the boy's feet! Will you look at those feet? Oh he's going to be so tall; he's going to be a true Fox. Your mum must be so proud! We're so proud!'

Nana was short, stout and had a killer grip. She pulled Callum into a bone-crushing hug — he didn't think she would ever let him go.

'Let's see you then, boy,' boomed Grandad. 'Jean, put him down, he's turning blue.'

Nana loosened her grip and Callum fell away, stumbling into his Grandad. The old man regarded him intently. Callum stood up a little straighter and stared back.

Grandad was massive; at least half a metre taller than Nana. He was broad and strong where she was curvy and cuddly. Nana exuded warmth, while Grandad was as cold as steel; and sad, there was no other word for it, just sad. Callum thought he looked like a man who had known disappointment, whereas Nana looked like a woman who had known cake.

Nana beamed up at him. 'And he's got the Fox nose.'

Callum studied his grandad's face. He had pale blue eyes, the same colour as Callum's, and a huge bobble on the end of his nose. Callum's hand moved instinctively to the end of his own nose. Grandad's massive red and blue hooter grew in size as Callum watched. A family nose — the horror of what was to come!

Nana asked if any one fancied a nice cup of tea, and scurried off to the kitchen without waiting for a reply, leaving Callum to follow scary Grandad into the living room. Callum managed to trip over his rucksack on the way and warranted a 'careful lad' rebuke from Grandad. It didn't bode well.

The inside of the bungalow was very brown. Like it had been last decorated in the 1970s and then maintained as a museum piece ever since. There was a large, faded brown velour settee with two matching armchairs and a collection of assorted orange cushions. Dark wooden book cases and coffee tables filled every other available space and they were all piled high with books, magazines and old fashioned china ornaments. A large threadbare rug could be seen in between the small gaps left in the furniture.

'Your Nana and I made that,' said Grandad, easing himself down onto the settee, 'a few years after we were married. We sat every evening with it on our knees surrounded by boxes of wool; and between us we made that rug. We worked one side each and met in the middle.' He smiled to himself. 'It kept us warm because we didn't have central heating. You have it so easy today — you've no idea what real cold is.' He paused, studying the rug. 'It's blooming awful, isn't it? I hate the thing, but your nana likes it.'

Nana joined them, wobbling in with a tray of four rattling tea cups and all the tea essentials. She sat herself down at the opposite end of the settee. They were like a couple of mismatched bookends. Callum wasn't sure if he was meant to sandwich himself in between the two of them, but as he couldn't think of anything worse he flopped down on to one of the armchairs, which he found had a very comfortable pull-out leg support. He yanked the lever back and forth, shooting the leg rest in and out. Grandad didn't seem to approve of that either.

'Why the extra cup, Nana?' Callum asked, wondering if there was anyone else in the house.

'For you silly,' she said handing him a dainty cup and saucer.

At home Callum would have sooner drunk dirty dish water than a cup of tea. It was a real wrinklies' drink. But he could tell his grandparents had high expectations of him and it appeared that that included him being an accomplished tea drinker. He filled his cup with as much milk and sugar as he thought it polite to take and then promptly burnt his tongue on the hot sweet drink.

They sat in an uncomfortable silence.

'Thanks for sending Linda to get me,' he said.

'Interfering witch,' Grandad muttered. 'You got my text message then?'

'No, nothing at all.' Callum hadn't expected Grandad to own a mobile, let alone know how to text.

'Well, how did you get the message to go with Linda then?' asked Nana, putting the tea pot back on the tray and covering it with scone shaped tea cosy that said *Cornwall hearts the cream on top.*

'Well, she offered and you weren't there.'

'Where's my text message gone then?' shouted Grandad, slamming his arm down so hard on the sofa that Nana shot up in the air. Callum almost jumped out of his chair too – was Grandad accusing him of lying? 'Took me ages to type the darn thing,' the old man continued, 'with those stupid little keys; designed for a six year old girl. I tell you! That's their target market! Six year old girls! And I couldn't get the blasted thing to send — had to go all the way into the harbour to get a decent signal.'

Callum's ears pricked up. 'What's the signal like round here?' he asked, patting his pockets for his mobile without even realising he was doing it.

'The TV's fine,' Nana replied, adding a third spoonful of sugar to her own cuppa. 'We've got a massive aerial on the roof.'

Callum took another sip of his tea — it really was gross. 'No. I meant the phone signal?'

'The phone works too,' she replied. 'There's one in the hall and one in the kitchen. You're not going to be calling your mum all the time, are you? What with her in Africa. That could be pricey.'

'No, no. I mean the mobile signal. Is the mobile phone signal any good?'

Grandad clicked the TV on to an antiques programme

and then ignored it. 'You'll be bloomin' lucky to get any signal here at all. I've got a mobile in case of emergencies, but it's a complete waste of time and money. It only works in the harbour and how often do I have an emergency there? Doesn't make any difference to me though, no one ever calls me and you're the first person I've ever tried to send a text to.' He pulled out a mobile the size of a house brick and threw it down on the table for dramatic effect.

Callum was horror-struck. This could be a disaster of epic proportions. Perhaps Grandad was exaggerating. Perhaps a different provider would be better. Callum decided he wouldn't panic until he had conducted his own tests. This was the twenty first century after all; everywhere had a signal these days — didn't it?

'Do you have wi-fi?' he asked, assuming that he could use that to contact the outside world, if absolutely necessary.

Grandad finished his tea and put his cup and saucer down. 'Not in my house, lad. Oh no, not in my house. I don't want any of those infra-red x-rays zapping round here. We have to protect the few brain cells your nana's got left.'

Surely he was joking. 'You don't mean that, do you?' he asked.

Grandad leant forward in his chair. 'Are you questioning me, lad? Are you? Are you saying I don't know what's best for your nana?'

Good grief, Callum thought, he's completely mad!

'But you have got a PC here, haven't you? Or a laptop or something connected to the internet?'

'Course not,' Grandad snapped. 'And if that's all

you're interested in you can bleedin' well run off back to London like your mother did!'

Callum's mouth flopped open.

'Oh, for goodness sake Bob, please don't.' Nana was up on her feet and waving her finger at Grandad. 'Why do you have to be so confrontational all the time?'

But Grandad couldn't stop himself, and he and Nana launched into a full scale row. Nana said she didn't like Grandad's attitude and blamed him for pushing Angela away. Grandad said he'd done nothing wrong. It was all Angela's fault, and he accused Nana of being a couple of sandwiches short of a picnic.

Callum couldn't get away quickly enough. He hated hearing them talk about his mum like that. He looked around the room, searching for an escape route, and as he did his attention was caught by a six inch porcelain figure of a mother and child. It sat on the top shelf of the teak bookcase and then, without any visible prompt, it started to wobble — all by itself. No one had touched it and there wasn't a breeze or a draft. It wasn't so close to the edge to be in a perilous position, but it fell. Or rather it launched itself off the bookcase across the room and dropped, hitting the corner of the coffee table and smashing into a million tiny pieces.

'Now look what you've done,' Nana screamed at Grandad.

'How? How on earth do you think I did that, woman?'

Callum did a double take.

What had he got himself into?

'I'll go and get the dustpan,' Nana sighed as if flying ornaments were an everyday occurrence in the Fox's household. 'Come on, Callum. I'll show you to your room on the way. Let's leave the miserable old horror to himself,' and grabbing hold of her grandson's arm she dragged him to the door.

'Don't apologise for me,' Grandad shouted after her, emphasising his point with a very loud fart.

Nana hurried Callum out of the room, tutting as she went, and for the second time that day an ice-cold shiver ran slowly up and down his spine. There was definitely something very, very wrong in the Fox's bungalow, and it wasn't only the lack of internet.

Chapter 8

Tuesday 5ᵗʰ September 1939

'This is Jim, the evacuee that arrived last night,' Ma announced as Jim crept into the kitchen on his first morning in Mousehole. The room was small and busy and smelt of fried food. Jim hadn't realised how hungry he was until Ma handed him a plateful of bacon and eggs and a cup of steaming hot tea.

'Have a seat, lad. Don't be shy.'

In the warm light of the morning Ma didn't look anywhere near as scary as she had the night before. She was beaming from ear to ear and cooking up a feast.

'This is Walter, my husband. And that there, that's my Bob.'

Jim had never seen a man as huge as Walter. He was dressed for the sea, in a thick knitted jumper with a black cap set low over his forehead, and under it was a great ruddy bauble of a nose and a thick bushy beard.

'Thank you most kindly for 'aving me,' Jim stuttered,

trying his very hardest to be as polite as he'd promised his mam he would be.

Walter brought his fist down on the table in a crescendo and howled. "'Thank you most kindly!" Ma, we got royalty in the house! Did this one come down from Buckingham Palace?' His whole body rose and fell with laughter. Ma and Bob joined in too, turning Jim into a quivering wreck, slopping his tea on the floor and struggling to hold his plate up.

He couldn't understand what he'd done wrong. Mam had told him to be polite. He was being polite. Ma scooped the cup and plate out of his hands and placed them on the table. She sat him down on the bench next to her son and gave her husband a playful slap for making fun of their guest.

'Don't mind Dad,' the boy whispered. 'He has to be that loud to be heard on his boat. You'll get used to it. I'm Bob by the way, Bob Fox.'

How could he get used to it? Everything here was so different. He watched in silence as the family chatted their way through breakfast, teasing each other, laughing and banging the table as often as not so that every plate rattled. It sort of reminded him of his Mam and Dad back home, before his dad was called up, before he put on that rough green uniform and left. But this family was so much bigger and noisier.

When Ma had finished eating she assigned the boys jobs for the day. 'Bob, I said you'd go up to Thornham Farm. Take Jim with you. An extra pair of hands won't go amiss.' She explained to Jim, 'Most of the men round here have been called up, you see, and Old Mr Thornham, he's got a large farm with fields all the way from Treen to Penlee. He'll be ever so grateful for your help, especially as its harvest time, isn't that right, Bob?'

Bob choked on a bit of bacon rind and Walter had to slap him hard on the back to stop him retching. Jim hoped the big man was careful; he could have flattened young Bob. Ma didn't seem worried. She congratulated Jim on the size of his appetite and then sent the boys up to the farm.

The Foxes' home was at the end of a row of whitewashed fishermen's cottages, with grey slate roofs and brightly painted doors. The road sloped down to a busy harbour teaming with boats and people. They were so close to it that Jim could taste the sea in the air. 'Can we go see?' he asked.

Bob shook his head. 'Nah. We can't be late. Thorny'd have our guts for garters, come on.' Jim had to run to keep up with him as Bob charged off uphill.

'Is that the school I'll go to?' he asked, as they passed a large new school building.

'Yeah, but not till after harvest. No one expects you to go to school when there are crops in the fields. Why would they?'

Jim couldn't believe his luck.

Ma had been right; he and Bob were exactly the same age, although Bob was much taller and broader. He looked a lot like his dad, but without the beard, and the bobble on the end of his nose wasn't red and veiny — yet.

Soon the lane opened out into a farmyard full of bits of broken ploughs and crates upon crates of cauliflowers. Mr Thornham came out to see who had arrived and didn't seem at all pleased to find Bob had bought a friend along.

'Who's this?' he grunted to Bob.

'He's a 'vacee, Mr Thornham. He's staying with us and Ma's sent him up to help.'

'Did she,' the old farmer grunted, pointing to a pile of empty crates and sacks, and then he sent the boys up to the top field to pull cauliflowers all day. Not long after they had started, Jim began to wish he had been at school after all — he didn't think his back and arms would ever be the same again.

They stopped for lunch when the sun was at its highest, sitting down on a grassy mound at the edge of the field and taking in the view. They could see right out over Mousehole harbour and all the way across the bay to a castle-topped island that Bob called St Michael's Mount. 'That's the prettiest thing I ever seen,' Jim said.

Bob grunted, 'You ain't seen much, then.'

'You know the farmer?' Jim asked, folding up the paper his bread and butter had been wrapped in and stuffing it back into his pocket in case Ma needed it again.

'Yeah, old Thorny.'

'If he owns this farm and everything, why's he so miserable?'

Bob's mouth was full of bread, and crumbs sprayed out as he spoke. 'Dad says it's 'cause they won't let him be a lifeboatman. Everyone round here wants to be a lifeboatman. But you can't be if you ain't at sea the whole time. Old Thorny's a landlubber all right and always will be; that's what Dad says.' He gazed out across the sea and before adding, 'and his wife died last year,' as a bit of an afterthought.

Jim recalled how big Bob's dad was. 'Is your dad a lifeboatman?'

'He certainly is,' Bob grinned. 'He's the skipper. And I'm going to be a lifeboatman too when I'm old enough. Dad says so.'

It was hot up in the top field. The boys kicked off their boots and lay back on the long grass.

'What the hell are you two good-for-nothin' wastrels doing, lying round on my time? Do you think this is some kinda holiday camp?'

The boys jumped to their feet to find Old Thorny marching up the field towards them, shouting, swearing and waving his hoe. They got straight back to work. At the end of the day they were rewarded for their efforts with a selection of freshly picked cauliflowers and a clip round the ear for not having worked harder.

Chapter 9

Friday 1ˢᵗ August 2014

Callum had been staying at his nana and grandad's for a week.

It felt like forever.

In that time he had been forced to watch sixteen episodes of *Antiques Roadshow*, nine episodes of *Cash in the Attic* and twenty one episodes of *Bargain Hunt*. He had established that Nana couldn't cook for toffee and indeed couldn't cook toffee — she had tried to make some, but now Callum was missing a back tooth that he very much hoped was the last of his baby teeth and not one of his proper grown up molars.

It was mid-morning and he was in the garden, sat astride the top of the shed. It was the highest point on the property that Callum could reasonably get to and he was still searching for a mobile signal. There was nothing — not even a single bar. He wondered how long he could leave his Facebook account inactive before he was declared dead. Possibly some of his friends were already posting touching obituaries for him.

The rickety old shed was made of splintered wood panelling. Its triangular roof was covered in places with a coarse grey felt that had the texture of sandpaper and flapped in the breeze where it was coming loose. He stood up, spreading his weight as much as he could. He raised a hand in the air and waved the phone in all directions. Was that a bar? Was it? He looked again. Yes!

No. Oh no!

He was losing his balance, his feet were beginning to slip. He caught the ridge of the roof between his knees — a millisecond before it slammed into that part of his body he really didn't want crashing into the ridge of a splintered roof covered in sandpaper. But when he thought he had saved himself, his foot slipped again.

'Arrgghh!'

'There you are, Callum,' said Grandad walking up the sloping garden carrying a book under one arm. He didn't seem in any way surprised to see his grandson falling off the roof of the shed.

'Nana's making a cup of tea and *Bargain Hunt's* about to start. You coming in? It's Tim Wonnacott today.'

Callum stared up at the clear blue sky from the comfort of the bush that he'd landed in — if he *never* saw another antiques programme it would be too soon. He staggered back to his feet. He couldn't stay here a moment longer. He had to get out.

'No thanks, Grandad. I think I might go out.'

When he'd first arrived, Grandad had spoken about getting a mobile signal at the harbour. It was time to go out exploring. He ran back into the bungalow, scooping up his wallet and shouting to Nana that he was going out.

'Do you want a cup of tea first?' she called after him.

He pretended he hadn't heard her, tip-toeing down the hall quickly and making for the front door.

His bid for freedom wasn't missed by Grandad, who had no intention of letting Callum escape so lightly. The old man threw his hardback book at Callum and it struck him square across the back of the head with a thud.

'Don't ignore your nana, you ignorant little upstart!'

Grandad was a good shot.

Callum rubbed his sore head and bent down to pick up the book; *Flying with the Luftwaffe*. It was clearly much referred to, the spine was damaged through being read so much (or thrown so often) and it fell open on the page about the Focke-Wulf FW 190.

'Sorry, Grandad,' he said, giving the book back to him. Grandad snatched it out of Callum's hands. Mum had told him to remember he was a guest in Grandad's house, humour him and don't let him 'get to you'. That was proving more difficult than Callum could have ever imagined.

'No tea for me, thanks Nana,' he shouted back towards the kitchen, still rubbing his head and finding an egg-sized lump. 'I'm going out. I'll be in the harbour; I want to see if there's a signal there for my mobile.'

'Haven't you given up on that yet?' Grandad demanded, launching into another full scale lecture on the dangers of mobile phone technology. 'It'll fry your brain... you'll lose the ability to communicate... it'll most likely prevent you from fathering children... you play the music too loud on that thing, it'll make you deaf… don't walk around with your headphones in, you won't hear the traffic coming…' he took a long and deep breath and finished with '…and for pity's sake, if you are going out, put a belt on your trousers or they'll be round your ankles by the time you get to the end of the street!'

'Uhh-huhhh!'

As a compromise Callum promised he'd only use one earpiece while he was walking along busy roads, and when Grandad went to find a belt he made a run for it.

Finally out on the street, he breathed in the freedom and set off in what he assumed was the direction of the harbour, relieved to be out of the house and away from his grandparents.

He sauntered along, happily listening to his music (with just the one earpiece in, as promised) and looking at the space on his phone where the bars of signal used to be. Nothing yet. The road soon began to slope downhill and that felt about right. He followed the path until Cliff Road met up with The Parade and then St James Place, from where he could see the harbour.

It soon became clear how Mousehole had got its unusual name. The harbour was perfectly round except for a small gap that had been left open, like a mouse's hole, to allow boats free and easy passage in and out while keeping the rough seas and storms at bay. It nestled in a natural amphitheatre of greenery. The village itself was made up of a maze of cobbled alleyways and narrow roads with terraces of tiny cottages, all with slate roofs and whitewashed walls, radiating out from the central harbour. It appeared unchanged since the times when men had fished and women had scrubbed door steps.

The circular appearance of the harbour was exaggerated by thick and heavy walls made of huge chunks of grey rock. They branched out into the sea to create a perfect ring of protection for the village's fishing boat fleet. The tide was on the way out, or maybe on the way in, Callum couldn't tell. Either way the water was low and it exposed the full and impressive height of the harbour walls. A ring of seaweed-covered sand stretched out for twenty meters between the elevated harbour road and the sea, leaving many of the boats beached and listing to one side or the other, waiting for the tide to return and give them back some dignity.

It stank of fish here too, like it had in Penzance, but with less salt and vinegar. Callum wondered if all seaside villages smelled as bad. It was a pity, because otherwise the place would have been all right, small and with nothing at all happening, but all right — in an old-fashioned kind of way.

His music was definitely losing out to the sounds of the seagulls, so he twisted his second earpiece in place and pumped up the volume.

The harbour walls were broad enough to act as an overflow car park, and he could see Linda's Land Rover parked up there. He looked more closely. He wasn't sure, but he thought he saw a shock of red hair, casting a fishing rod overhand from the far side of the wall into the sea. Was that Sophie? He set off in the opposite direction, just in case.

He glanced down at his phone and watched with delight as a bar of signal appeared, then a second, then a third and then blip, blip, blip, loads of text messages, missed call details and Facebook notifications poured in.

Yesssss!

He gave a triumphant flick of his fringe and without taking his eyes of his mobile he stepped into the road.

Wham! He walked straight into the path of an oncoming ambulance.

One minute there's no one but Callum anywhere. He's in his own little world with his music and his unbridled delight at being reconnected with the outside world; the next minute he's bouncing off the front of an enormous great green and yellow chequered truck and reading the rather unnecessary label ECNALUBMA right up against his nose.

Time slowed down. He spun through the air in slow motion and as he did he could see the horror on the ambulance driver's face. He saw the paramedic in the passenger seat brace herself with outstretched arms pushing hard against the dashboard, her mouth hanging open in a silent scream. There was a deafening thwack, and he hit the road.

Then nothing; nothing at all.

Chapter 10

**Wednesday 6ᵗʰ September 1939
— September 1940**

Jim and Bob went back to help old Thorny every day until the harvest was in. In the spring they helped with planting and a year later they brought that harvest in too.

Working on the land came naturally to Bob. He really was a mini version of his dad. Jim loved being outdoors too but he never lost his scrawny, townie look, despite all the pulling of vegetables and Ma's best attempts to feed him up.

Ma was so worried Jim didn't have enough meat on him that she knitted him a bright green sleeveless jumper and insisted he wore it all the time. Jim was never without that green jumper, and he was never without Bob. The two of them went to school together, worked on the farm together and got into trouble together.

They spent their evenings and Sundays building a go-kart in the back yard and when it was finished it was big enough to carry them both. It had brakes, bumpers and a proper steering wheel, not just a piece of string tied to the wheels like some boys made do with. They finished it off with paint they 'borrowed' from the new lifeboat station up at Penlee. 'Blimey, it ain't 'alf grand.' Jim said, wishing his mam could see it. And as they swooped down Foxes Lane to the harbour on their wonderfully smart navy and bright orange go-kart no one could miss them.

'Watch out,' they cried as they flew down the hill. 'Here we come!'

Chapter 11

Friday 1st August 2014

Callum woke as if from a deep sleep. He didn't even have the strength to open his eyes. Where was he and why did he felt so fuzzy?

'Did anyone see what happened?'

'You hit him! That's what happened!'

'Thanks!'

He could tell he was lying on something hard, something like a surf board, laid out flat in the middle of the road, looking up at the blue summer sky.

'Did you see how he landed?' asked the voice in charge.

'Badly! Fell on his head — I saw it all from inside my shop.' It was a woman's voice. Two women?

Callum could feel someone prodding him. Feeling for a pulse? Checking his neck?

'On his head you say? Anyone know him?'

He hurt everywhere. His whole body throbbed and

his head was swimming. It felt as if his brain had broken free from his skull and was oozing out across the road. He knew he was surrounded by people and he suspected he'd just made a public spectacle of himself. Then, as if things weren't bad enough already, he could hear Sophie's voice loud and clear above the general din, giving all his personal details to goodness only knew who. Oh joy!

'Yes. Yes. I know him. His name's Callum Fox, he's staying up on Cliff Road with Bob and Jean Fox, he's their grandson.'

'Sophie,' Callum whispered.

'He's trying to talk! Stand back, stand back!' There was a kerfuffle and a woman lowered her ear to catch his faint words. 'What is it, Callum?'

'Sophie,' Callum whispered again and he felt movement at his side as Sophie was pulled into Callum's field of vision, close enough to catch his feeble words.

'Callum, I'm here.'

It was a struggle to speak, his throat was too dry and his voice sounded like someone else was speaking for him, from a long way away.

'Sophie — where's my mum?'

'Africa. Callum, your mum's in Africa,' she took Callum's hand in hers. 'Do you want me to get your grandad?'

Callum let out a sigh of monumental despair. A wave of pain engulfed him and clutching Sophie's hand, he passed out again.

When Callum came round again, he and Sophie were in the ambulance speeding down Cornwall's narrow lanes with the sirens wailing. Callum was strapped to a back board and that was secured to a stretcher, which in turn was fixed to the middle of the ambulance. The ride wasn't exactly smooth and with every bend in the road and every jolt over a pot hole Callum's whole body hurt — a lot!

He couldn't see much of the ambulance. He was strapped down too tightly to look around. He stared up at the clinical white ceiling, trying to make sense of everything. He remembered glancing up from his phone and seeing the ambulance heading straight for him, and he remembered the awful sense of inevitability as he realised there wasn't time to get out of the way. How stupid. How embarrassing. Mum was going to kill him. Grandad… He closed his eyes.

'He can't be too badly hurt — we weren't going that fast. We were on our way back to the hospital after a false alarm; it's not like we were rushing to a 999 call or anything.' Callum strained to hear the paramedic talking to Sophie. 'He'll be fine. I don't think his injuries can be that bad. All his vitals are OK and there are no obvious fractures or lacerations. He's got a few grazes. You know, a bit of road rash, but I can't see anything major wrong. He's mostly in shock.'

'Yeah — well he would be,' Sophie said. 'Did you see the way he fell? He sort of took off and spun through the air, then landed on his head. It was like when you hit all the pins when you're bowling and they fly up and spin round and then crash down. That can't have done him any good.'

The paramedic sighed, lifted up one of Callum's eyelids and shone a torch straight into his pupil; the bright light hurt and he flinched and moaned. The paramedic was delighted at his reaction, and repeated everything she had already told Sophie, trying to soothe Callum's nerves and reassure him that everything was going to be all right.

Sophie had squeezed herself into a small seat at the back of the vehicle and the paramedic encouraged her to talk to Callum. She was prattling along helpfully with comments like, 'How could you have been so moronic as to not see an enormous luminous yellow ambulance?' and 'This is even more impressive than you getting locked in that loo on the train.'

After ten minutes of her harping on about what an idiot Callum had been, the kind paramedic suggested it might be even more supportive if she didn't say anything at all, and to everyone's relief Sophie shut up.

A red blanket covered Callum from his neck-brace down, but he still felt cold, so very, very cold. He struggled to look around but he couldn't. The paramedic apologised and tightened his straps further, explaining that she'd once seen a passenger slide on to the floor while going round one of Cornwall's sharp hairpin bends.

The paramedic was warm and comforting and every time she took a reading from one of the machines, or treated him, she explained what she was doing and why. Callum put her kindness down to guilt — after all she had run him over in the first place. He wondered if she was this sympathetic to everyone in her care and hoped she was. She held Callum's right hand and stroked it. Sophie and the paramedic's conversations played fleetingly on the edge of Callum's awareness, but it was something else, or someone else, that was the main focus of his attention.

There was someone else moving around to the left of his stretcher. They wouldn't stand still. It was dead annoying. Who was it? Another patient? Perhaps someone who had already been in the ambulance when it had hit him?

Just strap yourself in, he wanted to say. You're making me giddy. The ambulance was rocking wildly from side to side but the other patient was just wandering around, even though the paramedic had tied Callum down to within an inch of his life.

He couldn't get a good look at this other person because he wasn't able to move his head and his eyes kept closing. It was a relief when they were closed, everything hurt less. But when he opened them, there he was again — and now he could tell it was a boy — short and scrawny, with matted black hair. He could have been anything from ten to twelve and he was off-the-scale scruffy. He wore a hideous green hand-knitted jumper; frankly, he was in a right state.

'Come on, Callum me lad. Hold on, boy. Come on, stay with me. Stay with me.' The boy wasn't talking to Callum, more to himself. His accent was cockney but there was a bit of Cornish in there too. It wasn't a good mix.

Why didn't the paramedic tell him to shut up? He was talking complete nonsense and it was really winding Callum up. He closed his eyes again and the pain eased.

The ambulance rocked and the paramedic tightened

her grip on Callum's hand. He opened his eyes. The boy was still there, saying the Lord's Prayer, then crying: 'Callum, Callum, please hold on.' Why on Earth didn't she tell him to shut up? He just didn't stop. 'Come on, you're a Fox; Foxes are survivors!' Callum's head was bursting.

Now the boy was resting his hand on Callum's arm; he had a feather-light touch that was cold and damp. It sent shivers through his whole body.

Callum forced his eyes to stay wide open and looked straight at the paramedic. 'Get him away from me,' he croaked.

'Who?' asked the paramedic.

'Him!' Callum tried desperately to nod or motion to his left hand side. 'Him!'

'The driver?' Sophie asked.

'No!' Callum's voice was weak. Why were Sophie and the paramedic being so dense?

'His heart rate's gone through the roof,' said the paramedic.

'Oh God, Callum, please be all right,' cried Sophie.

'Come on, Callum. You're a Fox. You can pull through. Do it for Bob.' The boy started stroking Callum's face with his ice cold dirty fingers.

'Get him off me!' screamed Callum. 'He's touching me — get him off!'

'No one's near you, Callum. No one's touching you,' Sophie sounded panicked.

'He's stroking my face! Get him off!' Callum's head was ready to explode. Why weren't they doing anything?

'No one's touching you, Callum,' the paramedic said calmly.

Callum turned his head as much as he could. 'Who the hell are you? What are you doing in my ambulance and get your filthy dirty hands off me, you freak!'

The boy's mouth fell open and his elfin face turned even paler. It was as if this were the first time he'd ever been spoken to like that. Perhaps even the first time he'd been spoken to at all. He backed away.

'You can see me!'

Callum stared at the boy, at his scruffy hair and his foul green knitted vest. 'Who are you?'

'I'm Jim. Jim White, I'm a friend of your grandad's,' his voice trailed off as he backed further and further away — and then he was gone.

Callum let out an enormous sigh, relieved that the crazy boy had gone. He was so tired. He couldn't keep his eyes open. What had the boy said? That he was Grandad's friend? Get real!

The temperature in the ambulance began to warm up and Callum relaxed, drifting... drifting... and the pain began to ease.

'His heartbeat's coming down,' the paramedic announced, 'and his temperature's returning to normal.'

Callum felt muddled and tired, so very tired. Everything was fading.

It was only later, when the ambulance pulled up to the open doors of the West Cornwall Hospital, that Callum woke and had a moment of clarity so vivid it startled him. How had Jim left the moving vehicle? While it had been speeding through the winding Cornish roads between Mousehole and Penzance, with its sirens wailing? It hadn't stopped and the doors hadn't opened — but Jim had most definitely left.

And, how had he got in it in the first place?

And who was he?

And it was at that point that Callum became absolutely, uncontrollably, hysterical.

Chapter 12

Friday 1ˢᵗ August 1941

The pale yellow envelope rested on the Foxes' kitchen table, propped up against the teapot. It had been delivered just under an hour ago by the Mousehole postmistress. Jim stared at the spidery handwriting. Dad? Was it about Dad, or his mam? Oh God no, not his mam.

Mrs Vincent next door, she'd had one of these a couple of months ago. The Foxes still heard her wailing from her side of the front room wall most evenings. Her cries for her Tom — they were unbearable. Ma said it was made worse because she weren't gonna get his body back — not ever. There was talk of a memorial, but nothing would happen until after the war, and that weren't gonna be any time soon.

'You'll have to open it,' Ma said as gently as she could, her hand squeezing his shoulder. 'You need to know.'

But he couldn't. It was as much as he could do not to scream and scream and scream. Eventually, without discussion, Ma took it from him, opened it and read out loud:

POST OFFICE TELEGRAM
    1ˢᵗ August 1941
    Priority CC — Master Jim White
    Fairey Aviation, Middlesex
    Regret to inform you that your mother Ada White has been killed whilst working at the Fairey Aviation Factory North Hyde Road during day time air raid Thursday 31ˢᵗ July 1941 **stop** *the entrance of the factory's air raid shelter hit directly by a bomb* **stop** *3 killed* **stop** *any further information received will be immediately communicated to you* **stop** *Records Telex Ruislip*

Jim hung his head; he could see her red coat, hear her last words to him as clear as if she were in the room. 'You can't stay, Jim — it ain't safe.' The words just went round and round in his head. He should have stayed with her. He should have. If he'd been there he'd have saved her. At the very least she might have been at home, with him, instead of at the factory. And anyway, if London hadn't been safe enough for him, why oh why had his mam been allowed to stay? But he didn't feel nothing, not yet. Not angry, not sad, not nothing. Just numb. He was so very very numb.

And then it came, as Ma's hand squeezed his shoulder tight. The NO was slipping up his throat, getting bigger and bigger. All the emotion boiled up and out of him and he couldn't control it.

'Nooooo.' Ma Fox lifted him off the ground and clasped him tight to her chest. She held him as he let out gut wrenching sob after sob and then it was out. 'NOOOOO.'

'You're one of us now, my boy,' Ma told him. 'You're one of us.'

Jim didn't speak for two weeks.

Bob stayed with him the whole time; they were most often up in the fields, occasionally down by the sea. Bob physically held him up when he needed it and talked nonsense to him when there was nothing sensible left to be said.

'I'll be all right now,' Jim announced at the end of the third week.

'Yes. We will be,' Bob agreed.

And they were.

Chapter 13

Friday 1st August 2014

By the time Callum's stretcher was wheeled into Accident and Emergency he was off the scale hysterical. He passed through triage at record speed — not because of the extent of his injuries, but because everyone wanted the boy making that awful noise out of the way.

'Sophie, where did he go? Where did he go? How did he get out?'

Sophie held his hand tight and ran alongside him. 'I don't know what you're talking about,' she repeated again and again until a reassuring junior doctor politely shut the door on her, taking Callum into a quiet room 'for observation.'

'Where's Sophie gone!' Callum screamed, 'Everyone's disappearing!'

He was given an array of painkillers and tranquilizers and gradually everything seemed less worrying — until there was talk about cutting his jeans off; he wasn't having that — they were his best pair!

After his X-rays, and with his best jeans thankfully still intact, Callum was wheeled to a busy mixed ward and helped into a funny smelling hospital bed next to the nurses' station.

'I've called my mum,' Sophie told him, perching on the edge of his bedside chair. 'She's on her way in with your grandad and nana.'

Callum groaned, 'Great!'

A tired-looking doctor came over to see him and drew the flimsy blue curtains around his bed. She suggested Sophie wait outside but Callum begged for her to stay. She introduced herself as Dr Akbar.

'Knocked over by an ambulance, eh?' she said, poking around on the back of his head.

When she had worked over every bit of his head and neck she stood back, produced a pen from her white coat and scribbled hastily on his hospital notes. 'You've been quite lucky.' She told them. 'Usually with RTAs — that's Road Traffic Accidents, we are dealing with multiple lacerations — that's cuts, and severe fractures — that's broken bones. You don't have any of those.' She tried to smile. 'But the ambulance hit you at quite a speed and you fell on your head. Your system's gone into shock. The paramedic and the A&E team have both reported you being incoherent. That might be an indication of a greater problem — it's too early to say.'

'What kind of problem?' Callum and Sophie asked, at exactly the same time.

'It's possible that you have concussion... or some other form of brain injury. We'll do an MRI scan tomorrow, then we can be clearer.'

Brain injury! Callum didn't hear anything else she said. Sophie put a reassuring hand on his arm. He couldn't even look at her — he knew he would burst into tears if he did.

Dr Akbar shone another ridiculously bright light into Callum's eyes, peering in so closely that she may as well have crawled right inside his head. She gave a non-committal grunt and left, muttering something about needing more scans, a coffee and some sleep.

'I wasn't incoherent, was I?' he asked.

'Not much more than normal,' Sophie told him. 'You kept shouting "Get him away from me, get him away from me." Then you kept saying "Where's he gone." No pleasing some people.' She gave him a warm and reassuring smile.

The colour rose in his cheeks and for a moment his complexion almost returned to normal. He was about to tell her that he hadn't been at all incoherent — he'd just wanted that weird boy to leave him alone, but the sound of Grandad's voice cut through the quiet of the ward.

'Callum! Callum! Where's Callum?' A foghorn couldn't have been any louder.

Sophie stuck her head out from between the curtains. 'Over here Mr Fox.'

'It's all of them,' she warned, as Grandad, Nana and Linda descended, pushing their way into the tiny curtained cubicle, forming an unruly ring of spectators around his bed.

Nana was crying, Linda appeared agitated and Grandad Bob looked like he was about to lunge for the first ambulance driver he could find.

'I'm so sorry…' Callum mumbled.

Sophie jumped out of the chair and offered it to Nana, who collapsed into it.

'It's good to see you in one piece,' said Linda, filling a silence that everyone feared Grandad would explode into. 'Sophie, I think you and I should go get a coffee — leave Callum to have some time with his grandparents.' Sophie didn't seem so sure, and Callum definitely wasn't, but a sideways glare from Grandad had Linda grabbing Sophie by the arm and pulling her out.

'See you later then,' Sophie called as she and her mum backed out, leaving Nana and Grandad to start their interrogation.

They wanted to know everything.

Callum recounted exactly what had happened, leaving out only a few minor details; for example the bit about walking into the road with both earpieces in and listening to really loud music while reading text messages on his phone. Consequently he may have left his grandparents with the distinct impression that the ambulance had materialised out of nowhere and mounted the pavement in order to knock him over. He felt a little bad about this, especially as Grandad immediately started working on a list of people he was going to complain to and a whole catalogue of improvements he was going to insist on for the next ambulance drivers' training course.

Grandad picked up the clipboard from the bottom of Callum's bed and read it with interest. 'I tried to call your mother,' he said, without taking his eyes from the notes. 'On the mobile, when we were on our way here.

But I couldn't get a signal... Proves exactly what I was saying, doesn't it? What's the point of having a "phone-for-emergencies", if you can't even use it in a genuine emergency?'

Callum had to agree, he had no energy to do anything else.

Nana said they would call Mum as soon as they got home, and that started Callum crying. He knew Mum would be so worried. By now she would be deep in the heart of Mali with her eco-research buddies. She probably wouldn't even be able to call him.

Uncomfortable with his grandson's tears, Grandad went to talk to Dr Akbar, leaving Nana to find Callum a tissue and soothe him as best she could.

'Getting run over by an ambulance,' she said, 'that's considered very lucky round here. No one else gets the paramedics on the scene so quickly. You're like your Grandad, you are. He's very lucky too.'

Callum rolled his eyes — some kind of luck that is!

Nana stroked his hand. 'Linda told me that the Polish lady from the Post Office-cum-General Store told her you were on your phone when you were hit. Were you calling for an ambulance?'

Callum smiled. Sometimes his mum was a bit of space cadet; she must have got it all from Nana.

Grandad returned clutching a pastel green flowery hospital gown and bringing news that Callum wouldn't be coming home with them tonight. Dr Akbar wanted to observe him for a little longer and he had an MRI scan booked first thing tomorrow.

Callum's heart sank.

'Look on the bright side,' suggested Grandad. 'At least you'll get better food in here.' Nana gave him a playful slap and Callum had to smile. They weren't all that bad.

'And they're going to move you to a room on your own, around the corner, so that'll be good.'

'Oh that's lovely,' agreed Nana. 'I wonder if it'll have a kettle.'

There was a knock on the curtains, one of those lame knocks where someone shouts 'knock-knock,' because you can't just walk into a curtained-off cubicle without announcing you're coming in.

Linda poked her head in. 'Jean; we're heading back home, do you want a lift?' She passed a goodie-bag to Callum. Linda and Sophie had excelled themselves by nipping into the hospital shop and picking up a toothbrush, toothpaste, cans of drink, packets of biscuits and quite a bit of chocolate. It was thoughtful of them and Callum was very grateful.

'Better than grapes any day,' he told them.

Nana and Grandad decided they would go with Linda. Callum didn't want them to, but he didn't have the nerve to say so. There were lots of emotional goodbyes, Nana gave him a horribly wet kiss and Grandad patted him so hard on the shoulder that it sent a wave of pain through his whole body.

Nana followed Linda and Sophie down the ward while Grandad stood a moment longer with his hand resting on Callum's shoulder. 'Got to go now, son,' the old man said. Callum thought he'd wanted to say more, but he didn't, or he couldn't.

'You will come back first thing tomorrow, won't you?'

Grandad nodded, pulled the curtains aside and left. Callum listened to his receding footsteps as he left the ward. The doors banged closed behind him.

Callum had never missed his mum so much in his whole life. Why, oh why, had she taken the African project and sent him down here on his own? She should have known something like this was going to happen. Possible brain damage, being left in hospital all on his own. He let it all wash over him. He lost whatever self-control he had left and cried and cried and cried.

Chapter 14

Saturday 2nd August 2014

The dim green lights on the hospital clock glowed 03.14 when Callum woke. He was groggy and thirsty. It took a while to remember where he was, why he was there and consequently why everything ached so much. He was grateful for being in a room of his own and fumbled on the bedside cabinet for the light switch.

'It's on the bed controls,' said a vaguely familiar voice from across the dark room.

Callum's whole body took an involuntary leap. He had presumed he was alone.

'Who's there?' He drew the bed sheets up around him. The room was cooler at this time of night and the hospital sheets weren't as warm as a proper duvet.

He couldn't see anyone but a voice came back at him. 'It's me, Jim. You saw me in the ambulance. I'm your grandad's friend. You do remember — don't you?'

Chapter 15

Tuesday 8ᵗʰ August 1944

Ma stood at her range stirring rabbit stew. She added a little more salt. 'That's the last of this batch of bunnies. Can you get me some more?' she asked.

The boys were engrossed in a game of cards, but Jim heard her. 'No problem Ma, we'll do it tomorrow, soon as we're done at the farm.'

There was a loud knock on the door and all eyes turned instinctively to Walter's empty seat. Since he'd been away in the Navy, unexpected visitors late in the evening were a worry. Ma reassured them with a nod, wiped her hands on her pinny and headed down the hallway. The boys stopped their game and listened.

'Mr Thornham, what a pleasure.'

'What's he want?' Jim whispered. Surely he wasn't here to complain about their work again? He hadn't mentioned anything when they'd left the farm an hour ago.

The farmer followed Ma into the kitchen, the noises of his service issue boots reverberated throughout the tiny house. He was decked out in his Home Guard uniform, with his gas mask and first aid kit slung in opposite directions across his chest marking an X where his heart would have been — if he'd had one.

He took off his cap, folded it and tucked it under his arm. 'I saw light comin' from your windows last night — AGAIN!' His voice was unnecessarily loud for such a small room. 'Mrs Fox, you'll be well aware that there is **still** a night time blackout across this country. We may well have the Nazis on the run, but we can't be taking any chances. Jerry planes were spotted over Plymouth last week. I won't have you risking our safety. I'll report y' first, I will.'

Ma raised a quizzical eyebrow. 'Bob, hop up and adjust the blackout curtains in the front room, will you?'

Bob threw down his cards. His chair scrapped against the slate floor tiles as he pushed it away from the table.

Ma gave Old Thorny one of her disarming smiles. 'John, if you tell me there's a problem you know I'll fix it. Now come and have some dinner with us. Everything's calming down, so why don't you stop a while and eat?'

Jim crossed his fingers under the table. Please say no. A meal with Old Thorny, could there be any worse form of torture? To his relief the old man refused, made his excuses and went to leave. On his way past Jim he leant down low to whisper in his ear.

'Five o'clock tomorrow morning, lad, you and your monkey — and don't be late. I want t'start the top field. There's rain coming, I can feel it in me bones. I want everything in the barns before it's ruined. Understand?' He made it sound like a top secret military mission.

Great, thought Jim, cauliflowers at dawn.

He nodded and with that the old man stormed out, slamming the front door hard behind him for good measure.

Bob burst back into the kitchen. 'Who does he think he is, marching in here like he owns the place?'

'He's making the most of being in the Home Guard,' said Jim, packing away the cards. 'The war's all but done. Nothin's going to happen now and he knows it. He'll be out of that uniform by the end of the year and then no one's gonna have to listen to him issuing his stupid orders ever again — except for us!'

'He's bleedin' loved wearing that uniform,' Bob complained to Ma. 'He prances round with his twelve bore shotgun like he's the last bleedin' line of defence between Hitler and the rest of the world. He's been ready to save us from the Nazi invasion since the day the Home Guard was desperate enough to let him in. And now he's beside himself that the war's nearly done and he ain't seen any action in the strategic stronghold that is…' Bob paused for dramatic effect '…Mousehole harbour!'

The boys laughed.

'Don't you be too rude' Ma scolded. 'It's his farm that puts the food on our table.'

Jim smirked, picking up his knife and fork and looking longingly at the simmering pot of stew on the range. 'Yeah, but I bet you're glad he didn't ask you where that meat came from.'

Ma joined in with their laughter as she swung

the pot to the table. She served out great ladles full of Thornham Farm's best poached rabbit stew and the three of them agreed it tasted all the more delicious for being off rations.

Chapter 16

Wednesday 9th August 1944

Old Thorny had been right about the weather; it had been lashing down all morning and Jim and Bob had a heck of a job getting the day's crop harvested and into the barn. But they'd done it, and what was left of the wet afternoon was their own. It was time to go poaching.

The boys were soaked through when they reached the fields above Penlee Point, high above the coast road and the new lifeboat station. They hunched their shoulders against the wind and stayed as close as they could to the large hedgerow that split Old Thorny's land up here into two fields. It made no difference; it was shockingly cold for an August day and the wind was so wild they had to shout to one another to be heard.

'Can you hear that?' Bob yelled, putting a hand out to catch hold of Jim. 'Listen!'

Jim concentrated hard, and beneath the sound of the torrential rain he could just about make out the faint noise of a plane. The visibility was so bad he couldn't see it at first, and when it did emerge from the clouds, it wasn't at all what he had been expecting.

'That ain't one of ours is it?' Bob shouted.

'Nah, it's a Focke-Wulf FW 190.' Planes were Jim's passion and he knew it was a single seater, single engine, very German aircraft — pretty near to a Spitfire, but with a less sexy name. It had two machine guns and two cannons. But none of that was firing as it flew towards land, so low that it nearly touched the top of the waves.

'What do you make of that?' Bob yelled.

'It ain't right. Can't you hear it? I reckon the engine's broke.' Jim's words were blown out to sea. He followed them, mesmerised by the struggling plane. 'What do you think it's doing 'ere anyway?'

The plane moved surprisingly slowly, spluttering and gurgling through the heavy rain, leaving a trail of black smoke. As it neared the land it veered towards them and pulled its nose up high in one last attempt to gain enough height to clear the steep bank.

'It's comin' for us,' Bob cried out, throwing himself to the ground.

'Don't be stupid.' Jim yelled back, leaning into the wind. 'It ain't got anywhere near enough power. It'll hit the lifeboat station, or the bank. It'll never make it up here.'

The plane began to climb. It missed the lifeboat station by a whisker and started up the bank towards the boys' field.

'Ger down y' idiot' Bob screamed. But Jim couldn't move, he was spellbound. With Bob yanking at his leg he stood there as the plane climbed higher and higher up the bank. So low that its belly tore through branches and greenery, leaving gaping holes in its wake. It crested the bank and skimmed the bushes at the foot of the field, whirring and splattering and ripping its way through everything in its path. It was huge now and heading straight for him.

Finally he came to his senses and screaming he threw himself to the wet ground, flattening his body into the soggy grass next to Bob. He shielded his head with his hands and tried to protect his ears from the near deafening noise and the immense rush of hot air. The undercarriage skimmed the top of their hedge, showering them in a barrage of twigs and muck — it must have missed them by less than six feet.

Then it came down, no more than thirty yards from where they lay, with an almighty thud. It slid across the sodden ground on its belly, creating a cacophony of noise and a mass of ripping metal and churning mud. It only stopped when it slammed into a tree at the far end of the field.

Neither Jim nor Bob moved. Would it explode? Even rain this heavy wouldn't be able to douse the flames if the fuel tank went up.

The tree the plane hit groaned as the aircraft shuddered.

Jim rose up onto his elbows and twisted round. The plane dropped unevenly to one side, the metal letting out a long and painful screech. The fuselage was pretty much intact but rested at a precarious angle, supported by its propeller, which wedged itself into the trunk of the old oak tree. Smoke from the engine filled the air. Trapped under the low cloud-base and whipped up by the wind, it created a ghostly mist around the crash site.

Then there was silence.

'Bleedin' heck!' cried Bob, about a dozen times, staggering to his feet.

Jim got up too, his mouth hanging open, his hands still gripping either side of his head. Planes never flew over Mousehole, certainly not German fighters. But here they were — the first on the scene at a FW-190 crash!

Bob stumbled towards the aircraft.

Jim wasn't sure that was such a good idea. 'Hang on mate.' He caught hold of Bob and tried to stop him. 'Hold on! There could be a German in there!'

'Yeah, it didn't fly itself, did it?'

Jim held on tighter to Bob, slowing him down, trying to think.

Bob had an answer for everything. 'Don't worry, he's probably dead.'

Jim couldn't have wiped the grin off his friend's face if he'd tried. 'I dunno,' he said, scraping the mud from his hair and clothes. 'The cockpit looks all right to me. He could of survived.'

But Bob was champing at the bit. 'Even better! Let's get him!'

'Hold on, let me think.' Jim took a firmer grip on Bob's shirt and struggled to slow him down. 'Give me a minute, all right! We need help… If Old Thorny's round 'ere he'll be up in a minute with his shotgun, even he couldn't of missed that.'

Bob pushed Jim's hands away. 'And what if he was at

the farmhouse? He'll have no clue what's going on and we are up here, on our own, with Jerry — and he'll have a gun, I bet you anything he's got a gun.' Bob stabbed the air aggressively in the direction of the plane. 'We've got to get him, before he gets us!'

'What with?' Jim yelled at him. 'A rabbit wire? Shut up and let me think.'

The rain was easing off and they could at least hear each other now. But Jim couldn't slow Bob down by talk alone, the daft beggar would rush in without thinking. But this wasn't a game — this was real.

'Oh don't be so pathetic,' Bob complained. 'Nothings ever gonna happen if you hang around waiting for the bleedin' Home Guard. That's our German in there; let's get him before anyone else turns up!'

'Idiot! You're gonna get us both killed.'

'Nah. What can a dead man do anyway,' Bob sidestepped as Jim tried to catch hold of him again and legged it up the muddy field towards the plane. 'Come on!' he called.

Jim followed, but he didn't think it was a good idea — not at all!

Chapter 17

Saturday 2nd August 2014

'Do you remember me?' the intruder asked again.

Did Callum remember? Did he?

His mind was so fuzzy. He remembered Sophie in the ambulance and the nice paramedic. Had there been a boy too?

Yes.

Yes, he did remember a boy. He'd been talking, going on and on about a load of old nothing and being generally annoying. But what was he doing here, in Callum's so called private room?

Then Callum remembered how the boy had disappeared from the ambulance, without it stopping and without the doors opening; a shiver ran down his spine. This was not good.

'Well — Do y' remember me or not?' he asked again. 'I'm Jim, Jim White. Bob's friend. Your grandad's friend — remember?' There was urgency in his voice that spoke of raised stakes and serious consequences.

The voice was getting closer. Callum scuttled backwards up the bed, pulling his hospital gown more tightly around him and wishing he'd slept fully clothed instead of giving-in to the nurses and putting on the backless flowery monstrosity. This was not the thing to be wearing if he was going to be coming face to face with a nutter — or worse.

'Well did y'? Did y' see me in the ambulance?'

'Yes — yes I did — all right! You were in the ambulance. I remember, OK!'

Callum's eyes were growing accustomed to the dark. He could just about make out the boy. He was dressed like a street urchin from a Victorian pantomime. It was definitely the same boy from the ambulance — scruffy with a foul green knitted jumper.

'Straight up? You saw me? And you can hear me!'

'Yes, of course. Du-uh! Otherwise I wouldn't be talking to you, would I?'

'Well I'll be damned!' the boy said, genuinely delighted with this development. 'Now that's something.'

Callum didn't think it was anything to be excited about. On the contrary, he thought it was pretty damned scary. He sat up straighter in the bed, struggling to get a grip on the situation. This was going to be tricky, given that he was in bed, in the dark, with his bum hanging out of the back of a hospital gown.

'So?' he asked, as calmly as he could. 'What were you doing in the ambulance this morning?' Keep him talking, Callum thought to himself. That might diffuse the situation — it's the kind of thing they tell you in self-defence classes. Try to keep them talking until someone hears and comes in to see what all the noise is about. 'Umm… Were you already in the ambulance when they knocked me over?' Callum forced himself to be as conversational as he could. 'Were they bringing you in to hospital because you'd had an accident too?'

'No!' Jim sounded surprised at that idea. He moved out of the shadows and stood near the bed. 'No. I was up at the bungalow, with Bob — obviously. And you said you were going down to the harbour and I could tell Bob was real worried you'd get lost or something. So I thought I'd follow y' down there and check everything were OK, y' know.

'And it was a darn good thing I did, because by the time I got there you were already being loaded into the back of a bleedin' ambulance!' Jim buried his hands deep in the pockets of his shorts. He looked sincere — but it didn't make any sense.

'Of course I got in the ambulance with you,' he carried on. 'There weren't no way I was going to let you go off on your own. I was panicking and I knew Bob would be beside himself. He'd want me to stay with you — I knew he would.'

What was this weirdo talking about! There hadn't been anyone else at the bungalow when Callum had left it this morning, barely fifteen minutes before the accident. How could this boy possibly have got there between Callum leaving the house and getting knocked over?

There was no doubt he sounded sincere, but come on!

Callum thought through the possibilities logically:

1. Jim was some local nutter who'd seen the accident and fancied a ride to hospital

2. Jim had taken the hobby of ambulance chasing to a whole new level

3. Grandad had a freaky stalker and now he was stalking Callum too

4. This was all in Callum's mind, he'd had a tough day and taken a lot of medication and he was due for a brain scan tomorrow. Perhaps the Doc had been right after all…

5. Jim really had seen the accident, he really was a friend of Grandad's and it was all straight up — but if that was the case, why was he dressed like a walk-on part from *Oliver Twist*, with prehistoric long shorts and a totally gross vomit-green hand knitted sleeveless jumper — in August?

Well he could rule out option 5, as that was clearly the least likely.

Callum was desperate to get the light on and then get out of the room. He frantically ran his hands up and down the bed searching for the control panel. He found a wire and followed it to a plastic box the size of a TV remote. He started pressing buttons at random. His legs began to rise, his head followed suit but despite his best efforts, he couldn't find the button that prevented him from being folded fully in half like a taco shell.

He carried on indiscriminately pressing buttons, by a stroke of pure luck hitting the 'nurse call' button, the 'cancel the nurse call' button and then the 'nurse call' button again, until finally a nurse arrived just as Callum hit the bedside light button and a small circle of yellow lit up the floor where the top of the bed should have been and threw a pale golden glow into the rest of the room.

'Good grief, Callum — are you in there?' the nurse cried, finding Callum's bed folded up neatly for storage, with him trapped inside. She retrieved the control unit and returned the bed to a horizontal position.

Callum surveyed the room looking for Jim. There was no one there other than himself and the rather stern nurse and as he checked out all the dark recesses of the room he heard the door click shut. Had Jim gone?

'Sorry. I wanted the light on,' Callum tried to explain. 'Jim was freaking me out and I sort of panicked.'

Callum was hot and sweaty and freezing cold, all at the same time. His heart was racing and his head was thumping. The nurse took his temperature and measured his heart rate. She was so concerned by the speed of his pulse that she re-set her fingers to take it for a second time.

'Who?'

'Jim — Oh I don't know,' it was all so fuzzy. 'He was in the ambulance when I came in and then he was here, a minute ago — IN THIS ROOM!'

'When?' the nurse asked calmly, giving up on taking his pulse and pulling his medical notes out of the holder at the bottom of the bed and flicking through them instead.

'A minute ago, when I woke up.'

'Visiting hours finished a long time ago Callum. It's three in the morning. No one visits at this time of night, and no one except you is up or out of their bed — if they were, they'd have me to answer to!'

Callum didn't doubt for one minute that this nurse would stop most patients walking around at night. She was big-time scary. But Jim had been here — Callum knew he had.

'I'll go and get you some more medicine; calm you down a bit,' she announced, placing his notes on the bottom of the bed and strutting out.

'She scares the bejeezus outta me,' said Jim, stepping out of the shadows and moving swiftly to the bed to study Callum's notes.

Callum nearly jumped out of his skin.

With the bedside light on Callum got his first proper look at his stalker. Jim's clothes were indeed old fashioned, but not *Oliver Twist*, Victorian London old, only unfashionably old. He had a small elfin face, with a mop of pitch black hair, cut short very badly. He was untidy and unwashed. Frankly, he looked a mess.

'What are you doing here? And what do you want with me?' Callum asked.

'I'm trying to work out what happened here today.' Jim told him, glancing up from Callum's medical notes. 'I mean, I'm trying to work out exactly what happened to you today — medically. Because you can see me now, but you couldn't see me before the accident. And no one ain't ever seen me before.'

Now, if Callum had been brighter or perhaps even a little bit calmer, he would have thought through what Jim had said and the two of them could have worked on this conundrum together. But Jim wasn't catching Callum at his best and so the part of the speech that Callum focused on was: "I'm reading your medical notes." Which was in no way as interesting as the other comment: "no one else has ever seen me before." But then people do stupid things under pressure.

'You can't read my notes!' Callum protested.

'Course I bleedin' can,' Jim snapped back. 'You let Bob read them.'

For Callum this was the last straw. Jim was getting way too personal — those notes could say anything. And if Jim knew Grandad had read them earlier, he'd obviously been watching him all day long. It was bad enough that Jim had been at the accident and that he'd climbed into the ambulance with him. But he must have been hanging around the hospital all afternoon too, lurking behind the curtains, spying, listening, like some kind of psycho killer in fancy dress.

'Leave my notes alone!' Callum screamed at him. 'Get out. Get out! You freakin' weirdo.'

Jim was getting angry too. He threw his arm down onto the bed to swipe all the notes to the floor. But his massive strop resulted in just one solitary piece of paper fluttering alone across the room. Even more frustrated by this, Jim stormed out.

'I 'ate hospitals anyway! I shouldn't never of bovvered coming!'

Seconds later the nurse hurried back in with a tray of medicines and tablets for Callum. She complained about the fuss he was making as she gathered up the notes that were lying on the bed. Noticing the lone sheet of paper that had fluttered down to the floor she bent over and picked that up too.

'Goodness, how did *you* manage to get this one all the way over here?' she asked.

'I didn't,' Callum said quietly. 'Jim did.'

'My oh my,' said the scary nurse, approaching with a very strong sedative. 'You did get a nasty bump on the head today, didn't you?'

Chapter 18

Wednesday 9ᵗʰ August 1944

The plane looked even bigger close up, and very German. Bob clambered up on to the wing and strained to see into the cockpit.

'Is he alive?' Jim called up.

'If he is, he's out cold… I can't reach the canopy.'

Jim walked round the aircraft. There had to be a way for the ground crew and pilots to get in and out. Sure enough, he found a hanging foothold on the far side of the plane.

'Over 'ere,' he shouted. Bob jumped down and raced round, grinning from ear to ear.

'Well done!' he cried, slapping Jim hard on the back. 'Outta the way then.'

Bob pushed Jim aside and pulled himself up on to the wing, he was in just the right position to reach the canopy. After quite a lot of tugging and even more cussing, the canopy lid slid back.

'Cor! You should have a look in 'ere,' he shouted down, leaning into the open cockpit.

Jim stood with one foot in the stirrup, not knowing what to do. He desperately wanted to see inside the plane, but what about the German? There was a real life bleedin' German in there! He felt sick to his stomach, there was no way he could go any closer.

'I can't shift him!' Bob called down, pulling at the unconscious pilot.

'You taken off his straps? He's probably in a harness.'

Bob leant in further.

'Yeah, that's it.' He climbed in and started fumbling with the pilot's straps. Jim pushed himself up higher on the foothold to get a better look but his view was blocked by Bob's backside.

'He's heavy,' Bob shouted, heaving at the pilot's dead weight until he finally succeeded in pushing him up and over the rim of the cockpit. Jim jumped out of the way as the German's body slid down the side of the plane like one of Old Thorny's sacks of cauliflowers and landed in a crumpled mess at Jim's feet. Bob jumped down beside him; he was barely able to control his excitement.

'You killed him!' cried Jim.

'Have not! Look — he's breathin' and everythin'.'

They stared down at the German's limp body. Jim had expected the Nazi to be a great strong brute of a man, but instead he was short, weedy and unconscious.

'This is gonna be a walk in the park,' Bob declared. 'We'll drag him down to the harbour, hand him over as our very own prisoner of war. We'll be heroes, mate — bloomin' heroes.'

Jim wasn't so sure.

'Let's move him before he comes to.'

The boys took an arm each and set off hauling the body across the wet field. The German wasn't large, but it felt like they were dragging an elephant through the mud. The longer it took the more Jim started to worry. What if the pilot regained consciousness? Would he and Bob be able to stop him killing them both? What if there was a second plane? Shouldn't they be sheltering in case there was an attack?

And Jim couldn't get over the fact that he was actually touching a real live Nazi. It was exciting and terrifying all at once. He kept changing his grip on the German's arm because he wanted to hold on to the pilot's flying jacket and not touch his evil skin. Everything about the German turned his stomach. He slowed up, his mind racing so much he couldn't go on. He let go and the German dropped into the mud. He put his hands on his knees, trying desperately to slow his panting breath. What on earth did they think they were doing!

'Oi,' complained Bob. 'Why y' stopped?'

Jim wanted to explain himself... but he couldn't. What could he possibly say to Bob about how he felt? Instead he said nothing, but he kicked the German so hard that he rolled onto his back, with his unconscious, mud covered face upper most. Both the boys drew in closer to get a better look at him. He really was very young, even younger than Cecil, the lad from the village who had been called up a couple of months ago on his eighteenth birthday. He was wearing a beige flight suit, topped with a heavy black leather jacket complete with huge German badges — symbols of the enemy he was and the evil he had done. Bob pulled off the man's flying helmet and a mop of strawberry blond hair fell out, stained red. Jim swallowed hard, trying to hold down the vomit.

'You alright?' asked Bob again.

Jim couldn't hold it in any longer. 'Do you think… Do you think… Could he …?' He kicked the German again, just in case. It could have been him who dropped the bomb on his Mam — it could easily have been him.

Bob stopped him with an outstretched hand. 'No way mate. No way. Couldn't be. Look at him.' Bob pointed to the German's face, forcing Jim to stop and think about it properly — the pilot really was very young.

'That was three years ago. Look at this one. He ain't been flying anywhere near that long. See? He's weedy. Three years ago I bet he were still at school. This could have been his first flight. Probably was. I mean, he's young, he's a terrible pilot, he's got to've been miles off course and that was a hell of a crash.'

But Jim wasn't so sure. Even if he wasn't the actual pilot that had dropped the bomb on his Mam's factory, he had dropped other bombs, he must have — or at the very least he'd been planning to. They should leave him here, in the filthy muddy puddle, go get Old Thorny and let him shoot the bugger.

But instead here they were, him and Bob, dragging the knocked out Nazi across a field like some sort of giant rabbit they'd trapped for Ma's pot, or the ultimate addition to Bob's shrapnel collection.

'I can't do this.' Jim wanted to explain but he couldn't.

What was the point? Nothing he could say was going to stop Bob. He was having the adventure of his life.

'Come on,' Jim pleaded. 'What if he wakes up?'

Bob scratched his chin. 'Yeah, all right. That would be a problem...He's got to have a gun somewhere.' Bob started systematically patting down the German's body. 'If we can get his gun we've got the upper hand.'

Jim reluctantly agreed. But the German had nothing on him.

'It'll be in the plane,' said Bob, glancing back. 'You stay here and guard him. I'll go get the gun, then we'll drag him down the village and if he comes round on the way we shoot him. Right?'

Right? Jim was about to say he still wasn't sure, but Bob had already started jogging back to the plane.

'Don't take your eyes off him,' Bob called over his shoulder. 'And if he starts comin' round kick 'is 'ead in!'

Jim paced around the unconscious German, stopping near his head in case any more kicking was required. He studied the pilot. Bob had been right — there was no way he was any older than eighteen. Jim had seen a newsreel in Penzance that said Hitler was running out of men and that the Luftwaffe was having to send younger and younger lads up in planes. This one couldn't have been much older than he was. Jim poked him with his foot. He didn't react.

He looked up to check on Bob, who'd reached the plane and was swinging himself up and into the cockpit. Jim watched him rummaging around in there for ages. Oh hurry up, you daft beggar, he thought to himself. What are you doing in there?

The delicate balance of the plane must have been disturbed by Bob moving around in it because with another massive screech of wood and metal, the propeller freed itself from the oak tree and the right hand side of the plane crashed to the ground. It made a horrid screaming, clanging sound and the whole plane landed flat on its belly.

As it fell the canopy over the cockpit jolted forward and slid neatly shut.

Jim started walking back towards the plane. Bob stopped looking for the gun and started searching the cockpit for the handle to open the lid instead. It looked like he had found something and Jim could see him struggling with it, pulling at it harder and harder. Bob peered out at Jim and raised a hand in a gesture of 'what do I do now?'

Jim ran as fast as he could; the distance Bob had covered so quickly took Jim forever, and as he ran he saw Bob's face fall — the lever he had been pulling had come off in his hand! Bob held it up for Jim to see and they both stared at the useless piece of metal. He dropped it and started desperately trying to push the canopy open with his bare hands.

Jim skidded to a halt next to the plane. What was that smell? Petrol! Oh God, that final fall must have ruptured the fuel tank! It was going to explode after all, with Bob stuck inside.

He had to get Bob out.

NOW!

Aviation fuel was everywhere, running across the searing hot metal of the broken plane. Jim could see flames starting to lick at the propellers. He raced round to the foothold. Everything was happening so fast, by the time he got there the flames had engulfed the engine at the front.

Bob had seen the danger too and was beating his fists on the inside of the canopy, his face transformed into a deathly scream.

Jim pulled himself up on to the wing and fumbled with the canopy. He'd watched Bob open it earlier but he hadn't had a clear view. He searched for a lever, a handle, a catch, anything that would open it up — he couldn't find a thing. His fingers glided over the glass without taking any hold. It was hopeless.

He pressed himself up against the glass. Bob and he were no more than half an inch apart, screaming at each other through the canopy lid. The cockpit started to fill with smoke and to Jim's horror Bob stopped banging and sank slowly out of sight.

Jim screamed and screamed.

The heat coming off the plane was beating him back. He knew he had to get Bob out, but he didn't know how. Then something grabbed him from behind and threw him to the ground. He landed square on his back and looked up at the sky.

He was going to lose Bob!

He staggered up to try again.

But he didn't need to. The German pilot was standing on the foothold, pulling back the canopy and lifting Bob's limp body up and out of the plane. He didn't throw Bob to the ground like Bob had thrown him; instead he carried the boy down like a baby in his arms.

'*Schnell! Schnell!*' the German shouted.

Jim spoke no German, but he didn't need to — Quickly! Quickly!

Jim ran from the burning plane as fast as he could, with the German close on his heels carrying Bob in his arms.

When they reached the far end of the field the flames touched the fuel tank and with a mammoth eruption the whole plane turned into a white-hot ball of fire. The flames lit up the dark afternoon sky like a beacon and sent foul thick black smoke high and wide in a giant mushroom. The explosion must have been seen and heard for miles around.

Against the backdrop of the flaming plane and with searing heat at their backs, Jim and the German, still carrying the unconscious Bob, raced down the steep wooded hillside towards the shelter of the nearest building — the Penlee Lifeboat Station.

Chapter 19

Wednesday 9th August 1944

Jim darted across the road to check the coast was clear. He knew he couldn't afford to be seen — not with a German pilot who had an unconscious boy draped across his shoulders. He had to get them all out of the way as fast as possible so that he could check on Bob and work out what he was going to do with the German.

The road was clear, so he gave the thumbs up to the pilot, who staggered out from behind a tree, struggling under Bob's weight. But Jim had to be grateful — he wouldn't have been able to lift Bob out of the plane or carry him all the way to safety. Bob was big for a twelve year old.

Jim led the way down steep stone steps that had been cut roughly out of the rock to the side door and sanctuary of the lifeboat station. The solid building held an unusual position; if you didn't know it was there you'd miss it. It nestled into the cliff face beneath the level of the road so that only the tip of the roof could be seen by passers-by. But Jim knew exactly where it was, and he knew the door would be unlocked. It always was, in case of an emergency. And as far as Jim was concerned, this was most definitely an emergency.

He pulled the door open and led the German in. As he shut it behind them the clanging of a fire engine's bell rang out on the road above. 'That was bleedin' close,' he said, more to himself than to Bob or the German.

Jim collapsed against the door and looked around. The lifeboat station was a glorified boat shed. It didn't have a floor; instead it had a raised walkway on three sides of the building that enabled the lifeboat men to walk around the boat. The walls of the shed were hung with nautical maps, call-out records and dozens of pegs on which the crew hung their uniforms and cork lifejackets. Through the small gap between the boat and the walkway he could see bare rock and an open drop down to the sea.

The boathouse was high above the sea, and in order to reach the water the lifeboat had to be pushed out of the bright red doors at the front of the station and then slide down a steep iron slipway straight into the waves. He and Bob had often watched the boat being launched, with Bob's dad Walter at the helm. It was really something special. But all the crew had long since gone off to war and the boat hadn't been called out since Dunkirk.

It wasn't warm in the lifeboat station and it wasn't always dry, but it was away from all the people heading up to the crash site and it was the best thing that Jim could come up with at the time. He bolted the door and dragged himself round to the far side of the building, where the pilot was on his knees laying Bob down.

Jim ran a hand over Bob's forehead; he was cold and covered in a thick layer of black soot. His breathing was laboured, and when he did take a breath it rattled. 'Come on Bob,' he whispered and shot a pleading look at the German.

The young pilot had already pulled Bob from a burning plane and carried him to safety; surely he could finish the job by bringing his friend back to life — was it too much to ask? He couldn't hold back his tears any longer. 'I ain't gonna lose him, am I? I can't. I just can't.'

'Wake him up then,' instructed the German.

Jim stared at the pilot. He hadn't expected him to speak any English. And he certainly hadn't expected him to start issuing orders. Bleedin' Nazis. But deep down Jim knew he was right. He couldn't just sit there, watching Bob slip away. He had to do something.

He started by rocking Bob from side to side and speaking softly to him. 'Come on Bob. Open your eyes, mate. Come on.'

'*Nein. Nein.* Like this!' The German pulled Bob's unconscious body into a seated position and shook him so vigorously that he might have woke him even if he'd already been dead. 'You!' he shouted, thrusting Bob towards Jim.

Jim wasn't sure. Could shaking the living daylights out of his friend really help? It didn't seem right. He'd never heard of roughing someone up if they were suffering from smoke poisoning. But then again he didn't have any better ideas, and the German hadn't put a foot wrong so far — as long as you didn't count invading most of Europe and reducing London to a pile of rubble. So Jim took hold of Bob by the shoulders and started to shake him.

'Bob. Bob. Wake up.'

Nothing.

Jim took a tighter grip of his upper arms and threw Bob around as hard as he could. He slapped his face one way and then the other. He was a dozen times more vicious than the German had been. He wasn't going to allow Bob to die, not like this, not now. On and on he went, shouting and shaking and slapping and crying until his voice was hoarse and his arms were throbbing.

Just when Jim thought he couldn't do anything more Bob took a massive gulp of air, spluttered smoky spit everywhere and opened his eyes wide.

'Ger off me!'

Jim let go. 'Thank God... Thank God... I thought you were a goner.'

'*Wunderbar! Wunderbar!*' roared the German, clapping his hands loudly above his head, then slumping back against the wall in quiet satisfaction.

Bob spun round, took one horrified look at the Nazi and passed out again.

'He will be all right,' the German declared and rested Bob's head on his lap, smiling a broad and genuine smile and stroking Bob's hair, like you would a young child or a pet.

Jim had to laugh out loud. What must this look like, with the three of them slumped against the wall of the lifeboat station, hiding out behind the boat? They looked like three old friends. But how could they be?

This German, with his eagle and swastika badges, he symbolised everything that Jim hated — everything that everyone Jim knew hated. But then he had saved Bob. He didn't have to, but he had. You couldn't take that away from him, and then he'd just bought Bob back from the dead again with this breathing thing. Jim's head spun.

'Günter Neumann,' said the German, extending a hand to Jim, who leant forward to accept it after only a fraction of a delay.

'Günter Neumann,' Jim repeated out loud, surprised he was able to get his tongue around such a foreign sounding name — it really was very German.

'Jim. Jim White and this is me mate, Bob Fox.' He wasn't sure if he was doing the right thing. Guilt settled deep in the pit of his stomach. He had given his name, and Bob's, to a German. Was that all right? He half suspected he could be shot for less.

'Well done, Jim,' said Günter. 'Today you have saved your friend and me. *Dankeschön* — Thank you.'

Did he really mean that? What was he up to, this Günter Neumann? Was he luring the boys into some kind of Nazi master plan to invade the south west coast of Cornwall? Was Jim already a traitor? Was Günter an enemy agent? Would he end up killing him and Bob to hide his tracks?

Günter wiped some soot from Bob's face. The young pilot didn't look evil. He just looked glad to be alive. And there was no doubt that he'd saved Bob's life — twice. When they'd been up at the plane he could have run off easily enough, leaving Bob stuck under the canopy and Jim clinging to it, trying to get Bob out. And, by saving

Bob, Günter had also saved Jim. If Jim had to make a decision, here and now, based on everything he had seen so far, his gut told him to trust this Günter Neumann.

Bob stirred and jerked awake. His eyes flew open wide and then went wider still, it must have been the shock of finding his head resting in the lap of the pilot. Jim and Günter's hands flew out in perfect synchronization, with speed and precision, and together they clamped down firmly over the boy's mouth. But even through both sets of hands Bob let out a scream so loud that it could have been mistaken for a fog horn.

'Arrrggghhh!'

Chapter 20

Saturday 2nd August 2014

When Grandad and Nana arrived at the West Cornwall Hospital the following morning Callum was beyond desperate to go home. He was sitting on the edge of his bed, dressed and ready to go, the flowery hospital gown slung in a heap in the corner of the room and his dirty trainers placed strategically on the floor next to his bed.

Dr Akbar came into the room and spoke quietly to his grandparents. 'I've already talked to Callum about this, but I would like to discuss it with you too. This morning's scans were all clear, there doesn't appear to be any brain injury that we can identify, which is obviously all good. However, Callum is exhibiting signs of PCS, Post-Concussion Syndrome.'

Nana looked alarmed and the doctor explained. 'His brain took a massive jolt in the accident yesterday; he's going to have headaches, he may experience dizziness, he may become light or noise sensitive, he might get restless or aggressive and suffer from mood swings, that's all perfectly normal following an impact to the head. It's likely to carry on for at least a few weeks, might be longer.'

Callum knew what all this was about. Dr Akbar and the nurses were putting all of last night's drama down to this PCS, Post-Concussion Syndrome thing. He didn't. He knew exactly what had happened in here last night — and it wasn't anything to do with PCS, light sensitivity or mood swings.

'OK. Heady, dizzy, sensitive, emotional and aggressive. How will we know if that's the PCS or just Callum being a teenager?' Grandad asked, without any irony at all.

Dr Akbar raised an eyebrow.

'No seriously,' said Grandad. 'How will we know?'

'PCS is more extreme.' The doctor explained. 'For example, last night Callum was screaming about having an intruder in his room. I can assure you there was no one in here, but Callum was very upset. He wouldn't believe us when we reassured him, and he remains convinced that someone broke in here at three in the morning. I understand that he wants to go home with you, but I think it would be better all round if he stayed in for another night, so we can be here if he has anymore… hallucinations.' She let the word 'hallucinations' hang in the air.

Callum despaired. Jim had been here as much as Grandad, Nana and Dr Akbar were now. He certainly wasn't seeing things. He'd know if he was — wouldn't he?

'I'll let the three of you discuss it,' said the doctor, backing out of the room.

Callum couldn't get the words out fast enough.

'Please don't make me stay here. I'm fine. I know I am — please let me go home. Please.'

'I'm not sure,' said Nana, 'what about this TCP business?'

'PCS!' Grandad corrected her. 'Look here, what's all this about you seeing someone in your room?'

Callum's head was pounding. He would've liked to flick his long fringe out of his eyes, but he daren't. Everything felt so hazy. But despite that, he was clear-headed enough to realise that if he started talking about seeing people, especially people that no one else could see, he could end up stuck in this stinking hospital for a very long time.

'It was nothing,' he lied. 'It was a bad dream, that's all. I want to go home. I feel fine — honest.'

Grandad seemed to be supportive, although Callum suspected it was most likely because he didn't want the aggravation of having to visit the hospital again.

'If you do come home, remember Nana isn't there solely to run around after you. She won't be at your beck and call whenever you feel a bit under the weather. If you're not well, you stay here, OK.' He said it with all the warmth of the polar ice cap.

'And if you do come home I don't want any childish behaviour. I'm stating for the record: I won't be having any of that sensitivity, restlessness, aggression or moodiness, not when you're under my roof. Is that clear?'

'Crystal,' Callum replied, relieved to have secured his pass out of hospital. He flicked his fringe out of his eyes without thinking and winced as the movement sent another wave of pain through his head.

'If that hurts,' Grandad said, 'maybe we should have that fringe of yours tidied up. Nana can do that at home, she's got everything she'd need.'

'Are you a hairdresser, Nana?' Callum asked.

'No darling,' she beamed. 'But I used to shear the sheep up at Thornham farm.'

Chapter 21

Saturday 2nd August 2014

Callum got his way, and by lunch time he was back at the bungalow. As he walked through the door the phone rang. It was Mum. She had called for an update and was thrilled to speak to Callum in person.

Most of the call was spent with Mum lecturing Callum on how to cross roads safely — as if he needed such advice! She said she wished she was there to look after him and he wished she was too, but he didn't say so because he didn't want her to worry. It sounded like she was having a fabulous time. She was making good progress with her work and was delighted to report that she already had the tribe's people recycling their old loincloths into tea towels.

She said she regretted not taking Callum with her and asked him if he wanted her to speak to the team leader about him coming over to join her. He reassured her that he would rather be in Mousehole with Grandad and Nana even after the accident, Nana's cooking and everything, than suffer the embarrassment of seeing her bond with the Dogon tribeswomen through the medium of dance.

All things considered it was a good call and Callum hung up glad he'd spoken to her, thankful that he wasn't in Africa himself and happy to be back in the safety of his grandparents' home.

He made his way into the living room and found Grandad already ensconced on the brown settee, watching *Antiques Roadshow*. The old man was thoroughly enjoying seeing some poor loser on the telly discover that his prize Ming vase was a worthless fake. Callum flopped into the armchair next to him, relieved that everything was back to normal.

Nana bustled in with her tea tray, the usual cracked teapot and four china cups chinking together as she wobbled her way in and set the tray down on the coffee table. Jim followed her in and waited for her to take her seat. He squeezed himself in between the two grandparents and seemed perfectly at home.

Callum creamed; loud, long and hard.

Jim was in Grandad's house!

There was no escape.

Grandad and Nana stared at him.

'Are you OK, dear?' asked Nana.

'Told you we should have left him in the hospital,' Grandad muttered.

'Look…' Callum shot his arm out and pointed at Jim. Nana and Grandad looked at the empty space between them on the settee and on seeing nothing turned back to Callum, puzzled.

'Everything all right, dear?' asked Nana, passing Grandad a cup of tea. Her arm and the cup passing effortlessly through Jim's crossed legs.

Callum closed his eyes tight and then opened them again, blinking to try and rid his imagination of this nonsense. But nothing changed. It didn't look to Callum as if Jim was a hallucination or a figment of his over-excited imagination. It looked like Jim was sitting there on the settee as real as Nana or Grandad.

Callum eased himself up and out of the armchair and backed away.

'Keep calm, lad,' Jim advised, pulling his attention away from the TV. 'I reckon if you scream again, they'll have you back in that hospital quicker than you can say 'ghost'!"

Callum's mouth flopped open in a silent yell. He backed himself slowly up against the living room window. Cold sweat formed on his forehead and he felt beads of it run down the side of his face. He stood there paralyzed as the three of them sat opposite him, watching the TV as if Callum's world wasn't really spinning out of control and heading for a disaster of epic proportions.

Grandad and Nana sipped their tea. All perfectly normal. All perfectly A-OK Grandad sat back, relaxed, and Nana picked up the newspaper and started the crossword. It was obvious that they had no idea Jim was there at all.

But they must have done, because Nana had poured a fourth cup of tea and placed it on the coffee table between her and Grandad. Jim sat forward, warming his hands on it. He didn't pick it up or move it at all, and the cup stayed motionless on the coffee table. But if Nana couldn't see him, why had she poured it?

Callum stood frozen to the spot in the corner of the living room.

Jim spoke calmly to him. 'As I said to you yesterday, Callum, I'm a friend of your grandad's. There's nothing to be scared of and nothing for you to worry your pretty little head about. It would be good if you took a breath though — you've gone blue.'

Callum had indeed stopped breathing. He took a large gulp of air, accompanied by an 'eek' sound that Grandad heard. 'I know, shocking price for that piece of tat, isn't it?' he said, assuming that Callum was commenting on the badger-shaped door knocker on the *Antiques Roadshow* that seemed to be worth more than Grandad thought it had any right to be.

Callum started edging himself around the living room, with his back pressed hard to the wall. 'I'm going out' he stuttered.

Grandad let out a grunt of acknowledgement.

'Make sure you're home before tea,' Nana called after him. But he didn't hear her. He was already out of the door and half way down the road to the harbour, screaming all the way.

Chapter 22

Wednesday 9ᵗʰ August 1944

It took all of Jim and Günter's strength to stop Bob running for the hills screaming. Günter sat astride him, pinning him down, while Jim went over the story again and again. As Bob took it on board, his struggle lost some of its intensity, until eventually the tirade of abuse and punches trailed off into an occasional slap and a few dirty looks.

'So basically, if it weren't for Günter, you'd be pushing up the daisies,' Jim concluded, sitting back on his haunches, not knowing what else he could say. 'Come on, mate, get a bleedin' grip. You owe this man your life. The least you can do is stop being so darn rude to him.'

Bob coughed up another load of soot and glared the German.

Jim was disappointed. Why couldn't Bob share the camaraderie that he and Günter had felt when they were escaping from the exploding plane? Jim understood

Bob's fear and loathing of all things German. He felt the same himself, and he didn't feel any different having met Günter. But Günter had saved their lives. Jim wasn't thinking of him as a Nazi, more as a real person, different from Hitler and all the other Germans, but that was proving difficult to explain to Bob.

Jim retold the story again, stressing all the times that Günter could have run off but hadn't. How he'd saved them both from the fireball, carried Bob to safety and shown Jim how to revive him. Finally, some common sense broke through Bob's thick skull and he raised his hands in an act of submission. Jim gave Günter the nod and calm was restored to the lifeboat station.

'So, what do we do now?' asked Bob, leaning back against the boat, exhausted.

'What d'y' mean?' asked Jim, thinking that the worst was over, Bob was all right and they were all safe.

Bob didn't seem to think so. 'Well, we can't go home looking like this!'

Of course he was right. The fire had left them both covered in soot and Bob's clothes in particular were little more than smoked-out old rags. There was no way they could saunter back down to the harbour and act like nothing had happened.

'You're right.'

The boys started batting ideas around. They couldn't go home looking like this; they couldn't stay here indefinitely; the Home Guard would be out there searching for Günter; would anyone have noticed that they were missing already?

Their banter was quick and laced with their Cockney/

Cornish dialect and Günter struggled to understand. '*Sprecht ihr Deutsch?*' he asked hopefully.

'WE CAN NOT GO HOME LOOKING LIKE THIS,' shouted Jim, with that wonderful British assumption that if you say anything slowly and loudly everyone will be able to understand it, regardless of whether or not they speak English.

'*Ich verstehe nicht* — I don't understand'.

'WE' said Jim even more slowly and with exaggerated pointing at his blackened face and clothes, 'CAN NOT GO HOME LOOKING LIKE THIS.' He waved his hands with a flourish in the style of a mime artist talking to a village idiot.

'*Nein*, you can't,' Günter agreed.

Jim laughed out loud at his new friend's excellent English, but Bob looked like he was about to thump him. 'Look mate. Do you speak English or not?' he demanded.

Günter laughed. 'A little. But slower please. *Mein Vater*, my father, an English teacher, before…'

'Good,' said Jim, not wanting to get sidetracked. 'So what we gonna to do about getting home? We can't trot on home like this and say we was out playing and then all our clothes got blown up in an accident that had absolutely nothing at all to do with the plane crash. No one's gonna believe that. And Bob's not gonna be able to shift that cough even if we do manage to tidy ourselves up.'

'Whatever we do,' snapped Bob, 'he ain't comin' with us.'

Jim had to agree. He couldn't see them turning up at the Foxes' cottage and saying to Ma "Oh, by the way we've found this German. Oh don't worry about all that Third Reich business, this one's a good bloke."

Bob carried on: 'Besides, Old Thorny'll be pacing the streets searching for the missing kraut. He'll have his shotgun. We can't be caught with him; we'll be shot for treason.'

'*Ja, ja,*' agreed Günter. 'I will surrender.'

Surrender? Should he? Jim looked to Bob, they were both worried.

Was that fair? He'd saved Bob's life, was it fair to let him turn himself in to their Home Guard — Old Thorny, the shotgun wielding nutter...

'No way,' said Jim firmly. 'Not to our Home Guard. He'll shoot you on the spot, before you could say anythin'.'

Bob had to agree. 'You can't. He's mad — and we owe you. You're going to have to stay 'ere.'

Günter scratched his chin. 'Here?'

'Yes' said the boys in unison, and that settled that.

'But what we gonna do about Bob and me looking like we was in the plane when it exploded?' Jim was thinking aloud again.

A wide smile spread across Günter's face. 'The plane — go back to the plane.'

Bob must have thought the German hadn't understood the problem. 'What with Old Thorny up there and the fire brigade and probably half of Mousehole and worst of all Ma!'

But Günter was adamant. '*Ja, ja.* You have to, because you look like this,' and he waved his arms up and down the boys smoke-damaged clothes.

Jim understood. 'He's right. We've gotta be found at

the crash site, or they'll know we was there and that we ran off, and that'd start a whole heap of questions that we really don't want to have to answer!' He jumped to his feet. 'Come on Bob! If we're found up there, we can say we was near the plane when it exploded. We could have been knocked out and lying unconscious in a ditch ever since — I mean you practically 'ave been. It's the only way we can explain the state of us. Then, when they asks us about it, we deny all knowledge of anythin' and say we don't know nothin'!'

Günter nodded vigorously. Jim had no idea how much of what he'd said the German understood, but at least he realised that the boys couldn't stay here and had to go back up to the plane.

The idea of going back up there was too much for Bob. 'You've got to be joking, mate. I can't.'

Jim took a deep breath. 'You have to. We have to. We'll say we was near the explosion and it knocked us out cold and when we came to we couldn't remember anythin'. It'll work, trust me — just look gormless.'

Bob did.

'That's right,' Jim laughed. 'Act normal, and say you don't know what's happened. Got it?'

Bob shrugged. 'Got it.'

'We'd best get up there straight away, before too many people turn up.' Jim offered Bob a hand and pulled him to his feet. He was still a little shaky and coughing up a storm, but he was going to be all right and Jim would be forever grateful to Günter for that.

The German walked the boys back round the boat to the side door, as if he were showing his friends out of his home. The evening had drawn in and although the rain had stopped, the air outside was cold. Günter thanked them both again and there was much back-slapping and wishing of luck.

'Shall we bolt the door from the outside?' asked Jim. 'That way if anyone comes sniffing round they won't reckon anyone's hiding in there — because no one can lock themselves in from the outside.'

'Good idea,' agreed Bob, sliding two large iron bolts across the closed side door.

'Günter,' Jim called out.

'*Ja?*'

'We've locked you in. When we come back we'll knock three times like this…' Jim knocked on the door. 'That way you can tell it's us. If anyone else comes — hide. All right?

'*Ja. Dankeschön.* Thank you.'

The boys stole away into the evening shadows, up the rock steps, across the road and up the steep wooded bank to the fields on the top of Penlee Point. They hung back in the shrubs at the sea end of the field where they lay down in thick undergrowth, watching from a distance, hidden from view.

They had left it too late to get there before people showed up. The place was teeming. There were firemen and villagers everywhere. Jim's heart sank. How could they possibly get near enough to the plane to be 'discovered'?

The plane and the tree it had crashed into were still

smouldering at the far end of the field. The shell of the plane had remained pretty much intact, although the tree was very much worse for the ordeal and the whole place smelt like a bonfire.

A tall fireman came away from the plane shouting back to his crew. 'The cockpit's empty. Pilot must have bailed out. It's a single-seater so there'd only have been one.' The wind carried his voice towards the boys.

'Bailed out,' called another. 'Anyone see a parachute?'

'Everyone over here. I'll organise a search.' It was Old Thorny. The boys couldn't see him but they'd recognise that voice anywhere. 'There's a German out there and I'm going to 'ave him, if it's the last thing I do!'

'If you don't put the safety catch back on that shotgun, John Thornham,' Ma's voice came over loud and clear, 'I'll make sure it *is* the last thing you do! There's children running around all over the place and you're too trigger-happy by far. Put the darn gun down.'

The boys remained concealed in the brambles at their end of the field. 'Bleedin heck,' said Bob. 'How we gonna get anywhere near it?'

'It's all right,' said Jim. 'I've got a plan...'

He led the way, keeping low and out of sight in amongst the trees and bushes, until he reached the hedgerow that divided the field with the plane from its quieter neighbour. They stole a few yards up the edge of the dark hedge, before climbing over a five-bar gate into the second field. Jim had been right; no one was in that field. They stuck to the side of the field by the hedge, to minimise any tracks, and ran quickly and quietly up to the top, until they were near enough parallel with the crash site.

'Get down,' Jim whispered. 'And look like you've been blown up. Remember, we saw the plane come down, it exploded and this is where we fell — got it?'

Bob nodded. He lay down on the damp ground, his face resting on one arm, giving the impression he was having a nice afternoon nap.

'No you knucklehead — you're too obvious,' Jim hissed and kicked Bob's legs, knocking them until he thought they looked more realistic.

Bob moaned.

'You're meant to be unconscious,' Jim mouthed, stifling a nervous giggle. Then he ran ten yards further away and laid himself down, sprawling across the mud.

It was cold and wet on the ground. The mud oozed into his clothes and calmed his nerves. He wished Old Thorny would hurry up and find them.

Unfortunately Old Thorny couldn't have found his own arse with two hands, a compass and a map, and the boys had to lie there for another half an hour before the search party even ventured into their field.

Jim knew they were coming when the old gate creaked opened. Then he heard the pounding of feet and the distant sound of muffled voices. His pulse quickened. Would he be able to pull this off? Would Bob? It was too late to change his mind now.

'There's something over there!' someone cried out, and the whole group stampeded up the field towards the boys, flickering beams from flashlights lighting their way on the overcast, miserable, evening. Jim buried his face further into the long wet grass and braced himself. Panic set in and he couldn't control his breathing. Perhaps this wasn't such a good idea after all.

The search party slowed and stopped a safe distance away and waited for Old Thorny to catch up; the old farmer was wheezing and moaning and issuing instructions from the rear. 'Keep back, stand aside! He might be armed. Let me at him, I've got me gun.'

Jim lay motionless on the floor, ready with his fabricated story, which seemed all the more ludicrous when he realised he was going to have to claim that they had somehow been blasted through, or over the top of, a five foot hedge. It dawned on him how very, very stupid the plan was. How had he got himself into this mess?

He shut his eyes tight and held his breath. He could tell from the approaching footsteps that Old Thorny was heading to him first.

'Get your hands up, you Nazi scum!'

Oh God, he was going to be mistaken for the German pilot. He was going to be shot dead before he'd even had a chance to say, 'It's me!' Should he leap up and declare himself? He certainly didn't want to make any sudden movements, but he doubted whether he could have stood up, even if he tried, his legs were shaking that much.

Jim felt the shotgun's barrel jab him hard in the back.

'If you even think about moving I'll shoot your 'ead off.'

Jim let out a whimper. With the cold barrel of the shotgun shoved in his back, the time for plans and pretence was over.

'It's me. Jim,' he stuttered. He couldn't speak any louder, his voice was shaking too much. He knew Old Thorny wouldn't be able to hear him — he was deaf as a post.

'Nooooo!' Bob was up and running towards them.

Old Thorny spun round pointing the shotgun at Bob. 'Stop right there, Fritz!' he screamed.

Ma snatched a fireman's flashlight and ran forward, elbowing her way through the crowd. 'Bob! Bob! Is that you? For pity's sake what's happened?'

Old Thorny spun round again, this time sighting his shotgun on Ma.

The Fire Chief stepped forward and blocked the line of fire between Old Thorny and Ma. 'Calm down, John. That's Mrs Fox, she's come to help. She's not your German, you know that. And these two are boys — her boys. Come on, put the gun down. There are no Germans here.' He edged further forwards slowly and very deliberately with his arms raised.

'Gerrr away from me,' the old man cried. 'We're under attack. Can't you see? They're everywhere.'

Jim raised his head; Bob was stood next to him, blocking Old Thorny's line of fire as the farmer spun between them and Ma, his gun aimed first at Bob, then at Ma, then at Bob again.

'No, John. The German's not here. There's no threat here. Give me the gun.' The Fire Chief walked right up to the old man, his fireman's black uniform facing up to the green of the Home Guard. The Chief was half Old Thorny's age, taller, stronger and infinitely more in control. There was no competition.

Old Thorny spun round one last time and levelled his gun at Jim.

Jim thrust his face back down into the muddy grass, covered his head with his hands and prayed. He could hear Old Thorny wheezing, he knew he was taking aim, knew he would be easing back his trigger finger. He knew this was it.

'I don't think so,' said the Fire Chief snatching the shotgun out of the old man's hands. He broke it open and took the cartridges out before placing the unloaded weapon on the ground.

'There's a German out there. You're letting him ger away! Leave me alone and let me ger out there and look for him!' Thorny ranted. The Chief turned him gently around and escorted him back to the fire engine in the adjacent field. As he went he waved an instruction to one of his firemen, who ran forward to scoop up the gun.

'I want to speak to you boys later,' the Chief shouted over his shoulder.

Jim and Bob were both up and running to Ma's open arms.

'So do I!' shouted Old Thorny.

'And so do I,' added Ma, hugging them to her breast. 'I want you to tell me exactly what happened. And I can tell you already, I'm not going to like it one bit. And I suspect I'm not going to believe it either!'

Chapter 23

Saturday 2nd August 2014

The harbour was much busier than usual today. Callum moved out of everyone's way and leant against the window of the Post Office-cum-General Store, trying to catch his breath and work out what he should do next.

Over on the far harbour wall he could see Sophie fishing, her spiky red hair making her easily identifiable. Across the road, leaning against the war memorial, with his arms folded across his chest and one leg bent back at the knee, was Jim.

Callum whimpered. He couldn't run any further and there was nowhere left to go. He was beaten. He straightened up as best he could and flicked his long fringe out of his eyes. Jim strode across the busy road towards him, walking right through a child's buggy and a tourist's car. No one else flinched at this strange sight. Callum had to be the only person who could see him. And Jim had to be a ghost.

He didn't scream — he was beyond that. He just stood there, resigned to his fate. He remembered Jim's last words to him back at the bungalow, "You don't need to be scared and you don't need to worry." Man alive, thought Callum, I hope that's right.

'Come on,' Jim said, 'let's go have a natter.'

Jim walked further round the harbour and a very dazed Callum followed. They turned up a narrow cobbled side street flanked by quaint terraced cottages, stopping outside a rather chic café. Jim led Callum in and took the table in the bay window.

'You got any money on you?' he asked.

Callum nodded. Was he about to be fleeced by a ghost? What did a ghost want with money anyway?

'Great. Can I have a cup o' tea then? The one I left at Bob's was still hot. Don't y' luv a hot cup o' char? Nothing warms you like it.'

Bit bizarre, thought Callum. 'Can you drink it?'

'No, but I luv the idea of it.' Jim gazed out of the window, back across the road to the harbour and out to sea.

Callum popped up to the counter and ordered a tea for Jim and a coke for himself. The café was quiet after the clamour of the harbour, and the two waitresses were busy gossiping out the back about the loose morals of the deputy manageress and their latest body piercings. Callum was reassured they wouldn't be eavesdropping on his conversation — or listening to him talking to himself, if that was nearer the truth.

He slid back into the window seat and assessed the ghostly boy. Jim was wearing the same clothes as he'd had on yesterday and they didn't look any more sensible or any cleaner. They should have been a bit whiffy, but if anything there was a mild smell of roses in the air, nothing nasty at all. They sat in silence waiting for their drinks.

The waitress delivered a pot of tea for one and a coke, depositing them both in front of Callum in a rather slapdash manner.

Jim smiled as Callum pushed the teapot, cup and saucer towards him. 'Can you do the honours?' he asked.

Callum poured the hot tea and offered Jim milk. The ghost nodded and asked Jim if he'd pour some in the saucer, for old times' sake. Callum drew the line at that.

'Nana Jean always makes you a cup of tea, doesn't she?' he asked. 'Does she see you? Does Grandad? Does anyone?'

'No,' said Jim, warming his hands on the cup. 'No one's ever seen me. Well, not before you. But I think Jean can sense me. I think she's more open to it than most people. She can't see me or hear me, but she sort of knows I'm there, looking after Bob. Over the year's it's as if she's sensed that someone else wanted a cup of tea, and she always makes me one. She's a real trooper. I'm glad Bob married her. I'm not surprised though, she was a real beauty in her day.'

Callum spat his mouthful of coke all over the table. 'You fancy my Nan!'

'No! Of course not! But she was a good looking gal when Bob met her!'

Callum made a *yuk* sound. 'I've got no idea what you are talking about,' he spluttered. 'How could you possibly have known my Nan when she was that young?'

'I've been a ghost a long time… You do realise I'm a ghost, don't you?'

Callum shrugged. He supposed he did. But he didn't like it. Not one bit.

'I was your grandad's best friend before I died and I've hung around with him ever since.' Jim broke off and went back to staring out the window.

Callum's head spun. Could this be for real? Was Jim really a ghost, or was this some kind of massive wind-up?

He watched Jim closely. He looked harmless enough. And he seemed to be friendly. He was waving to a jogger coming down the road, in ludicrously high waisted shorts, the man waved back as he glided through a lamppost that got in his way. Then Jim looked over at the Ship Inn, where a group of lifeboatmen were laughing and slapping each other on the back as they headed in for a pint, even though the pub didn't open for another half hour — but then they didn't need the doors to be unlocked.

Jim nodded his head towards a small dinghy sailing into the harbour, carrying a rather damp fisherman who seemed very pleased with his day's catch. His boat sailed right through a larger, more modern vessel and docked alongside the harbour wall steps. Jim then pointed to a couple of pirates who were stood on the street corner arguing with each other, and a soldier and sailor in full World War II uniform sat near the base of the war memorial chatting away, without a care in the world.

'I'm a ghost, Callum,' he said with a broad wave of his hand. 'And so are all of them.'

Callum's jaw dropped open and the scales fell from his eyes.

'Well knock me over with an ambulance and re-programme my brain,' he muttered. 'No wonder it's so busy here today — you can barely move round here for dead people!'

Chapter 24

Friday 11ᵗʰ August 1944

The Fire Chief was the third person to turn up at the Foxes' cottage asking questions about the plane crash. He loomed large and threatening in his smart black uniform. He refused to sit down and stood bolt upright next to Ma's large wooden table, forcing the boys to jump to attention and stand for their interrogation.

'So boys, what were you doing yesterday, up at Penlee?'

'We was out walking,' Bob replied, a little too hastily.

Jim's shoulders slumped. They had agreed they wouldn't tell anyone about Günter. They owed him big time and they had agreed to keep him safe, but they weren't going to get away with it if Bob couldn't be more convincing. And anyway, it was too late to confess now. Ma had asked them about it last night, and if they were going to say anything that would have been the time. It would have been dead easy to tell Ma they'd seen the German running down towards the new lifeboat station.

But they'd kept quiet. The harbour had been awash with men out hunting for the pilot, and a tip off from the boys via Ma would have been all that was needed to send the military might of the Penzance District Home Guard storming into the new lifeboat station and then it would have been all over.

The boys hadn't said anything last night, they hadn't said anything the next day when Old Thorny had come round with his sergeant, and they weren't going to say anything this time either. Günter had saved Bob's life and they were going to save his. It was a pact the two of them had drawn up last night and there was no turning back.

But it wasn't convincing the Fire Chief. 'What? Out walking, in all that wind and rain? What kind of an idiot do you think I am?'

Ma spoke up, wiping a wet hand across her brow. 'I sent them up there; for rabbits. The meat ration doesn't stretch very far, and no one misses a few rabbits.'

Jim and Bob looked at each other and they both exhaled at the same time — breathing a silent prayer of thanks to Ma.

The Chief nodded. 'Alright, that's more like it. No need to cover up a little bit of light poaching. I'd much rather you told me the truth.' He smiled, like he was on to something. 'I can see why you might not want to mention that to Mr Thornham though, what with it being his field 'n' all.' He pulled out a chair. 'Right, let's all sit down and you can tell me exactly what did happen.'

There was a scraping of heavy wooden chairs on the slate floor as everyone settled themselves around the table and the Chief announced that he would like that cup of tea after all.

'We were up at Penlee, rabbiting, when we saw the plane,' Jim explained, leaning in with his arms resting on the table. 'It was in trouble all right. We thought it was gonna crash into the bank, but it didn't. It managed to gain enough height to make it up to the field next to us. Good God, it was low though — and awful loud. It tore up the trees and hedges and sort of slid all the way up the field. We ran towards it. Don't know why, we just did. Get a better look I suppose. Then it exploded.' He threw his hands up in the air to illustrate. 'Even though we was in the next field we was picked up off our feet and sent flying.' He brought his hands back down with a bang. 'I hit the ground real hard, sir. And that's it. Next thing I knows, I'm being attacked by Mr Thornham and his shotgun.'

The Chief thought about this while sipping his tea, scrutinising Ma and the boys in turn. He clearly couldn't tell whether he had heard the truth or not and he wasn't sure how hard he could push the boys in front of Ma. He told her she didn't need to stay if she had things to get on with, but Ma wasn't falling for that and the Chief was forced to carry on his questioning under her close supervision.

'Did you see the pilot bail out, before the crash?'

'No sir,' said Bob, a little too keenly.

'Could he of bailed out when he was over the sea?' suggested Jim.

The Chief scratched his chin. 'Do you think that plane could have gained the height to clear the bank and landed itself in that field, avoiding the coast, the cliff and the woods, all without a pilot? I don't think so, sonny.' The Fire Chief was no fool.

'Hadn't thought of that,' said Jim, staring at his shoes.

'Might o' done…' said Bob, more in hope than anything else.

The Chief asked more questions, but got consistently unhelpful answers from the boys and a few from Ma too. Eventually he gave up and left them in peace.

Old Thorny came back again the next day, this time alone. He asked all the same questions as the Fire Chief, but he wasn't as polite. He made no secret of the fact that he didn't trust the boys as far as he could throw them and he resented Ma keeping them at home on account of them 'being all shook up.' He told them that he thought they should be back up at the farm working and talking to him, away from Ma's protection. In the end she had to ask the old farmer to leave on the grounds that he was upsetting everyone.

But of all the questioning, Ma's grilling was by far the worst. It was constant and unyielding. She asked them directly about it at mealtimes, hinted at it throughout the day and was downright devious by the evening.

'So you saw the pilot bail out into the sea, you say?' she would drop into the conversation.

'Did we? Well no, I mean yes. I mean… ask Jim.' Bob was on the back foot and Ma knew it. She didn't let them out of her sight. She kept the boys trapped in the cottage, and by default, trapped Günter in the new lifeboat station on the other side of the harbour.

Jim began to worry. How long could you keep someone locked up in a shed without food or water? Bolting that door from the outside had perhaps not been such a bright idea.

On the fourth day after the crash Ma told the boys that the search for the German pilot had been called off. The general consensus was that he had either bailed out over the sea and drowned or left the crash site before the explosion and was miles away by now. Either way, the search was called off.

'Nothing to be worrying about any more,' she said. 'Might as well get back to normal,' and with that she released her two young tearaways back into the wild.

Jim and Bob raced up to their bedroom to grab the food they had been stashing, then shouting their goodbyes set off at a pace. They didn't go straight to the lifeboat station, in case they were being followed. Instead they took off southwards out of the harbour following the coastal footpath until it opened up on to a secluded rocky beach surrounded by high cliffs. They paused there to check if they had a tail. It didn't look like they did, so they doubled back, this time skirting round the edge of the village, across Treen fields, going north of Penlee Point before coming out on Cliff Road less than half a mile north of the new lifeboat station. They darted across the road, scrambled down a loose gravel bank to the tide line and then followed that round to the lifeboat station.

'Do y' reckon he'll still be there?' Bob asked as they started climbing the rocks towards the remote building.

'Dunno. It's think it's probably best if he's gone,' confessed Jim.

'Yeah, me too.' Bob took off his cap and stuffed it into his shorts pocket. 'What do you think would happen to us if Old Thorny found out we'd helped him?'

Jim had already given this a lot of thought. 'Reckon we'd be done for treason and shot,' he said, slowing up and looking at Bob straight. He needed to know what Bob thought and what he wanted to do next.

'Really?'

'Yeah — really. Think about it. This is Old Thorny we're talkin' about. He's more'n likely to shoot us if he even suspects we've done anythin' wrong.'

Bob shrugged. He weren't bothered. Jim took this as the all clear and led the way up the bank to the side door of the lifeboat station. He crossed his fingers, hoping that Günter had made a run for it. Any of the alternatives were going to be too awful.

They knocked three times, as they had said they would and pulled the stiff bolts back. The door slid easily on its well-oiled runners.

Inside, everything was quiet.

Deathly quiet.

Chapter 25

Saturday 2nd August 2014

Callum took the revelation that Jim was a ghost remarkably well. After all, it could have been far worse. The boy could have been an axe-wielding stalker and he himself could have been going bananas. The fact that Jim was a straight up, no nonsense ghost made perfect sense to Callum. And now that the two of them were sitting not drinking tea in a café in Mousehole, Callum's summer was starting to get a whole lot more interesting.

'So how long you been dead then?' Callum asked, between swigs of coke, as if asking a new friend at school which football team they supported.

'Since '44, about 6 months before the end of the war.'

'Cool.' Callum realised that that had been the wrong thing to say, but Jim didn't seem to mind. 'How?'

Jim shrugged. 'Long story. I was in a bust up. One minute everything is fine and dandy, the next minute no one can bleedin' see me and I find myself walking through stuff all the time and I can't pick a darn thing up. Couldn't bleedin' believe it, could I?'

'Yeah,' said Callum, as if he knew what Jim meant. 'Well, you wouldn't.' He took another sip of his drink, wondering what it would be like to suddenly find yourself dead and trapped forever in a place with as little to do as Mousehole.

They stared out the window. Callum looked at the people in the harbour and tried to guess who was a ghost and who wasn't. Jim laughed at him; it wasn't as obvious as he thought it would be. The ghosts appeared to be as real as anyone else. Callum would have expected them to be see-through, or floating, or making some sort of 'woo-woo' noise; but in reality they were... normal. The easiest way of identifying them, when they weren't walking through a wall, a car or a pedestrian, was by their clothing. They looked kind of out of place and old fashioned, like characters from a history book or actors on the set of a BBC Sunday evening costume drama — the sort of boring rubbish his mum liked to watch. They appeared to be stuck wearing the clothes they had on when they died. Mum might have called them vintage, but to Callum they were simply old.

'Fancy being trapped forever wearing flares,' Callum joked, as an old hippy went past the café with his trouser bottoms flapping in the breeze.

'Oh no. He's not a ghost,' said Jim. 'He just dresses like a chump for the fun of it.' They both laughed. 'I used to live in this house. It was your great grandma's then. Myrtle Fox. 'Ma' we used to call her. She was something else! She took me in when I was evacuated down here at the start of the war and then she let me stay when my folks died.'

'I'm sorry,' said Callum.

'It was a long time ago,' Jim replied.

'Did they die in the war?'

'Yeah. Me mam died in an air raid, when she was at work, in an airplane factory. I dunno what happened to me dad. He went to the front, then he was declared missing in action. He must have died over there somehow. Anyway, your great grandma, she took me in.' He looked around him at the familiar room. 'They've taken down a wall there,' he pointed to the middle of the café. 'This side of the room here, this used to be Ma's kitchen. Ma, Bob, and me, and Walter when he wasn't away at sea; we'd sit round a big table over there, putting the world to rights. She'd be spinning in her grave if she knew the kind of junk they churned out of her kitchen these days.' Jim was dragged back to reality by one of the waitresses trying to tidy up his tea cup.

'I'm still drinking that,' Callum protested.

'Doesn't look like it,' the tattooed girl drawled before scurrying away.

Callum studied the specials board. 'She wasn't one for goat's cheese paninis or couscous then?'

Jim smiled broadly. 'No. It was more rabbit stew and fish with Ma. Oh, her rabbit stew, it was to die for.'

'Perhaps it was,' suggested Callum. 'Can I see her? Is she here too?'

Jim ran his fingers through his thick dark hair. He shook his head. 'No, she moved straight on, none of this hanging around for her, and quite right too.' It was clear from the way Jim said this that 'moving straight on' was a very good thing to do.

'So even though we are in her house, she's not here.'

'No I told you, she don't like goat's cheese.'

'Be serious. Why's she moved on, when you haven't and they haven't?' Callum motioned to the two pirates outside.

Jim tried to explain the moving on thing. 'I don't know for certain. There's no manual and no one to ask. But as far as I can make out, if you die a normal death with no unfinished business, you move on straight away. That's what happens most of the time and that's what Ma did. No one knows where they move on to and I definitely don't. But if you die before your time, or if there's something holding you here or troublin' you, then you kind of get stuck until everything is sorted out.

'I've seen people stay a couple of months and then move on. Others stay for years, then something happens — I suppose something important's sorted out and then on they go. And I've seen people stay 'ere because they want to. Then there are some poor souls desperate to move on and they give it all they've got to try and sort their stuff out, but they can't and they end up hanging around for ages. I don't know what they are meant to do, or why they have to do it, and most of the time neither do they. But when someone does go, it's beautiful, mate, just beautiful. I've seen it loads of times. They light up all blue and sparkly and their face, it's beyond happy. They sort of glow, it must be the best thing ever.'

'That's deep.' Callum made a gurgling noise as he drained the last out of his can of drink. He leant back in

130

his chair and burped.

'So why haven't you moved on then?'

'That's my business, not yours. It's personal, so keep your beak out, all right?'

'Sorry,' said Callum, a little embarrassed he'd asked.

Jim didn't look offended so Callum changed the subject. 'Come on then; let's get out of here. Sophie's fishing over there. I'll introduce you.'

'Sure,' said Jim, grinning. 'I'd like to see you try.'

Jim melted through the glass door of the café. Callum followed and walked straight into it. The girls behind the counter burst out laughing. How embarrassing! He flicked his fringe, flushed bright red, opened the door and walked out properly. Jim was waiting for him on the pavement, bent double, laughing.

'Very funny,' Callum snapped, marching off.

'Lighten up, mate,' Jim shouted after him, running to catch up. 'I'd have opened the door for you, but I can't.'

'Yeah,' said Callum. 'About that. How does that work, then? Because I bet it was you that smashed that ornament at Grandad's house on the day I arrived. How did you do that if you can't open doors or move things? And you knocked my hospital papers on the floor last night.'

Jim put on his most spooky ghost-like voice and waved his arms above his head. 'I'm a poltergeist.' Callum stopped walking — was for real?

Jim sniggered and Callum wondered if this joker was ever serious. Based on the evidence so far, it didn't look like it.

Jim reverted back to his normal Cockney-Cornish

voice. 'We can't move anythin', but with enough effort — well, all our effort — we can nudge things a bit. That's as good as it gets. Last night, in the hospital, I was so mad I wanted to throw all your papers across the room, but all I managed was to knock one lousy sheet to the floor. Big deal.'

They started back around the harbour. 'When people think they've got a poltergeist, they've usually got a new ghost. One who's testing out how everything works, finding out what they can do and that. Once the ghost realises how bleedin' exhausting it is to move anythin' and how little they can achieve, they soon stop tryin'. Besides, no one wants to draw attention to themselves. That doesn't make for an easy life.'

'Or death,' Callum added, rather unnecessarily.

Jim shrugged. They started along the harbour wall, passing a long line of customers waiting for ice creams at the window of a tiny shop with a green and white awning.

'I knocked that ornament off Bob's shelf when you first got here because I was so upset to see him and Jean arguin' like that. I hates to see them argue. Bob hates it too, although he won't let on.'

'Why do you care?'

Jim took his hands out of his pockets and stood up straighter. ''Cos he's my best friend. Always has been. Always will be. I look out for him. Keep him out of mischief.'

'Good grief,' Callum mumbled. 'That must be a full time job.'

The boys slowed, then stopped as they reached Sophie, who was sitting on the edge of the harbour wall surrounded by fishing equipment: rods, reels, nets, tackle boxes and bits of angling equipment that Callum couldn't even identify.

'Hiya Sophie.'

'Callum, great to see you. I heard they let you out. You feeling OK?'

'Yeah, I'm all right.' Callum's confidence was beginning to slip a bit. How was he going to introduce Jim to anyone?

Jim sniggered. 'I'd best be off anyway. See y' around.'

'Yeah, fine, later then.'

'You're not stopping?' Sophie asked, assuming the 'later then' comment had been directed at her.

'No. Sorry. Yes. Yes; I was going to stop, if that's OK, for a chat.' Callum watched Jim's shoulders rise and fall, he was still chuckling away to himself as he walked back across the harbour wall and up Parade Hill. He turned back and waved to Callum before rounding a corner and heading out of sight. Callum waved back.

'Who you waving at?' Sophie asked.

'Well, that's quite a long story...' said Callum. And then went on to make an extraordinary shambles of explaining it all.

An hour later Sophie and Callum sat with their feet trailing over the edge of the wall, occasionally catching the spray off the waves. Sophie could not stop her giggles. Callum slung his arms up and over the protective metal rail that ran above their heads and leant forward looking down at the sea. In truth he was beginning to wish he hadn't told Sophie anything. It sounded pants in his own head; he dreaded to think what it sounded like to oh-so-smart Sophie.

'It's all true. I swear it.'

'You shouldn't have been allowed out of hospital.' Sophie concluded. 'You've gone mad in the head.'

'I'll prove it to you. I'm not sure how, but I will.'

'Course you will,' she said, rolling her eyes.

It was getting near to tea time and Callum thought he should be getting back to the bungalow. He offered to help Sophie pack up all her kit but she had no intention of leaving.

'I prefer it in the evening,' she said. 'It's quieter and the fish bite more. But if you're around tomorrow, I challenge you to prove that your Mousehole ghosts exist.'

'No problem,' Callum grinned back at her, getting up and brushing the dust off his jeans.

'OK then. Come round to the Tor Vista guest house tomorrow. I've got to help Mum with the breakfasts first thing 'cause Dad's away visiting Opa.' Callum looked confused so Sophie added, 'he's visiting my grandad. It eases up around 9.30. See you then?'

'Yeah, OK.'

Callum turned to go and then burst out laughing. 'Hey Soph, did I tell you that the ghosts get stuck wearing whatever they had on when they died?'

Sophie shrugged.

'Yeah, well they do. Anyway; looks like that guy bit the dust in the shower!'

Mousehole's only fully naked ghost spun round and

dropped his soap-on-a-rope for the first time in almost thirty years.

Chapter 26

Sunday 13th August 1944

The inside of the new lifeboat station looked and smelt the same as it had done when Jim, Bob and Günter had sheltered there after the crash.

The building was a brick shed 36 feet long, filled almost entirely with a 32 foot Surf Class lifeboat. It lay waiting, ready to be launched at any moment through the great red doors at the bow end, down the iron slipway and into the raging sea. Between missions, the blue and orange beast was hoisted back up the slipway and housed in the purpose-built shed.

The place smelt of oil and petrol, it was cold and damp and except for the distant sound of the sea below, it was completely silent. There were no signs of anyone having been there recently, and no sign at all of a German fugitive hiding out there.

The boys headed straight for the far side of the boat, expecting to find Günter camped out where they had left him, but the walkway was empty.

Bob threw his arms up in frustration. 'He's gone. He's darn well gone!'

'How? How could he? We locked him in, remember?' Much as Jim would have liked Günter to have escaped he knew in his heart of hearts he had to be in here somewhere.

'He wouldn't be on the boat, would he?' Bob asked, staring up at the underside of the hull.

'We didn't tell him he couldn't.'

The boys had sneaked into the lifeboat station on plenty of occasions, but they had never dared to board the lifeboat. Jim remembered the first time they had come here, to pinch some paint for their go-kart. That had been shortly before the boat and her crew had been called up for Dunkirk, to be part of the flotilla of little ships that saved so many Allies fleeing from French beaches. The lifeboat had limped back home to Penlee covered in glory, with machine gun damage to one of her two engines and her port side shot to pieces. The people of Mousehole had lovingly restored her. The irony of Günter hiding out on the heroic little vessel wasn't lost on Jim, but where else could the German have gone?

'Suppose he must be on it, then.'

The boys stepped backwards and craned their necks, trying to get a look at the deck, but from the walkway they could see nothing but the white painted underside of the boat. To view the deck they would have to climb aboard themselves.

They squeezed their way around the winch to a wooden gangplank that had been left propped up against the side of the boat. Bob stood with one foot on it and one hand on the chain link rope that ran alongside it, he turned to Jim for instruction.

'We'll check the deck and then get out,' Jim said, and Bob nodded.

The wooden gangplank creaked as they stole up it. Bob was first on deck. He called out in a stage whisper, 'Günter?'

Jim jumped down beside him and the two boys surveyed the vast empty space of the wooden deck. It was kept ship-shape and Bristol fashion, there weren't any cabins, not even a hold beneath the deck. The boat was nothing more than a large open floor space, with wooden benches running down the length of both sides, but fully loaded, as it had been at Dunkirk, it could carry fifty men.

The deck itself was clear except for a large polished wooden box that covered the paddle wheel, and a horseshoe shaped housing that sheltered the wheel. Bob walked around the box.

'There's nothing 'ere but a load of old rags,' he called back, kicking the discarded pile hard in his frustration.

'Ah!' A muffled cry came from the rags and Bob's face lit up.

'It's us. We're alone.'

The pile of rags said nothing.

Jim couldn't help noticing how small the bundle was. Could their friend really be in there?

Bob pulled the rags aside to reveal a shivering and half-starved Günter. He was in a bad way; the cut on his head must have bled for some time because he had thick black scabs all over his head and face. He looked dreadfully thin and his lips were blistered and cracked. He was a shocking sight.

Jim took one of Ma's pasties from his pocket and bending down he placed it into the German's hands. Günter struggled to lift it to his parched lips. He didn't even have the energy to eat.

Bob took out another couple of pasties along with a handful of apples, and handed them over too, putting them down next to Günter in his pile of rags.

'*Danke.*' Günter whispered, but they could barely hear him.

He was even smaller and younger than they remembered. His skin was grey, pallid and filthy dirty; his blond hair was now black with dried blood and his clothes hung off him. How could this transformation have occurred in only four days — how could this wretch have been the hero that carried Bob for all that distance?

But Jim knew why he looked like this. It was his bleedin' fault. He had locked him in here for four days and four nights without food or water. In his attempt to help Günter he had nearly finished him off.

'*Wasser? Wasser?*'

Jim and Bob stared at each other.

'Water?' Günter tried again.

'I'll get some,' said Bob, leaping to the gangway and running for the side door.

'I'm locking you in,' he cried shutting the door behind him, this time on both of them.

Great, thought Jim.

He crouched down opposite Günter. Just the two of them again, like it had been on the night of the crash.

Günter sucked at an apple, slowly and deliberately, savouring every drop of juice he could extract.

Jim tried to remember what the German had looked like on the night of the crash. He remembered he'd been small and thin, but they'd both been pumped full of adrenalin then. The man — or boy — that sat in front of him today looked far younger and much, much thinner. Could he have got this ill that quick, or had he been dangerously underfed before he even left Germany?

What had they done to the man they owed so much to? Jim apologised again and again for not having thought through locking the lifeboat station.

Günter said nothing.

Their silence was interspersed by the sound of Günter's stomach struggling to digest the food it so urgently needed but couldn't cope with. Jim soon realised that Günter wasn't being rude by staying silent; he simply didn't have the energy to talk.

'I knew you would come for me,' Günter finally whispered, his mouth so full of apple that he struggled to get the words out.

Jim smiled. 'I wouldn't of been so confident, mate.'

Keen to fill the silence, Jim told Günter about how everyone had been searching for the downed pilot and the interrogations that he and Bob had been through with the Home Guard, the Fire Chief and Ma. As Jim talked, Günter ate and Jim could see a little pink colouring return to his new friend's face. It was like witnessing someone come gradually back to life.

Bob burst back into the boathouse with a fire bucket he'd 'borrowed' from outside the Tor Vista Guest House, filled to the top with fresh cold water from the village pump. Günter cupped his hands and drank and when his thirst was quenched Jim used a little of the precious water to wash his face. The boys pulled Günter into a sitting position, leaning him back against the paddle box. They sat either side of him, propping him up, preventing him from slipping down and hitting the floor.

The three of them stayed there for hours, Bob and Jim chatting away about everything that had happened since the crash, Günter very slowly eating and drinking. Through a mix of broken English and hand gestures Günter asked whether his plane was still up in the field.

'It's still there, but it ain't ever gonna fly again, that's for sure,' Jim said, remembering the fireball that had been the FW 190.

Günter shrugged. He seemed more concerned about how much trouble the boys would be in if they were caught helping him than he was about the state of his plane. But Jim and Bob laughed and said they didn't care what happened to them.

'We owe you one, mate' Bob reminded him.

'*Nein*. No,' Günter shook his head. 'If someone sees you helping me, I get you in trouble. I do you no good. I must go.'

'You're not strong enough, not yet,' Bob protested.

This was undeniable. Günter wasn't even able to sit up unsupported, and that nasty cut on his head was going to need time to heal. He couldn't possibly go on the run at the moment. The boys had thanked him for saving Bob's life by locking him in the lifeboat station and nearly starving him to death. They couldn't send him out there, on his own, not yet.

Jim and Bob decided that Günter should remain in the lifeboat station until he'd regained his strength and then they would help him to escape. Through a series of charades and shouted instructions this plan was conveyed to the German.

Bob spat in his hand and held it out to Günter, who looked at it in disgust, with no idea what Bob was doing, thrusting his filthy hand at him. Jim nodded encouragingly and spat in his too. At last the German picked up on the idea and did the same. The three of them clasped their sticky hands together and the pact was made.

They would wait until Günter was stronger and then he would leave and make his escape.

Chapter 27

Sunday 3rd August 2014

Callum slept in until nine the next morning, giving Grandad the opportunity to go off on one about the laziness of the youth today. He wolfed down some cornflakes, made his excuses and ran out, leaving Grandad droning on about the importance of a proper breakfast, while Nana gently stroked her teapot, staring into space with a dazed expression on her face.

To Callum's disappointment, or was it relief, Jim was nowhere to be seen. Could it have all been a weird dream? He hoped so. The alternative was simply too complicated, although it would be a bit embarrassing to admit to Sophie.

It was less than a ten minute walk from Grandad's bungalow, to Tor Vista, Sophie's parents' guest house, and Callum suspected it would have been even quicker if he hadn't been following Nana's rather indirect directions.

Tor Vista was a large and impressive whitewashed

house with a grand entrance and wide bay windows that faced out to sea. A smaller back door on the road side of the building was wedged open, providing easy access to and from the car park. Callum popped his head round this to see if anyone was in.

A middle aged man with a bushy white beard and matching eyebrows was coming down the stairs in a hurry, dressed in old fashioned fisherman's clothing.

'Excuse me?' called Callum. 'Is Sophie in?'

The man stopped dead and stared at Callum. He checked behind himself to see if the boy was talking to anyone else, but he soon realised that he was alone and therefore Callum must be talking to him.

'Well, I'll be blowed.' He said. 'You can see me!'

Callum sighed. Guess it hadn't been a dream then.

'Well, well well. This is very useful, very useful indeed…' the man said, stroking his beard.

Callum could have kicked himself; he really didn't want to get mixed up with anyone else who wasn't fully alive and breathing. He'd have to get better at spotting the difference between the living and the dead — and soon, before all of Mousehole's ghosts worked out what he could do. He'd been up all night thinking through what it meant to be able to see ghosts, and he desperately wanted to discuss it with Sophie. He had to get her to believe him and then she could help him work out what to do.

Sophie burst into the hall, a door swinging open and shut behind her on a very busy dining room. She wore a blue and white striped apron and was carrying a large tray piled high with dirty dishes.

'Hiya Callum. Come on, you can give us a hand loading the dishwasher.'

He followed her into a large kitchen with the ghost of the fisherman following him, still droning on about how wonderful it was to have a living person to talk to and all the things Callum would be able to help him with, starting with sorting out the people in room number 5. Callum ignored him, in the hope that he would go away.

The kitchen would have had an industrial feel to it if it hadn't been so untidy, but the clutter piled high on every work surface made it more homely all round. Callum saw the bacon sizzling on the hot plate and regretted his meagre breakfast.

'You can start by putting this lot in here,' Sophie instructed, passing him her heavily laden tray and pulling down the door of a huge dishwasher.

'He will not,' said Linda, bursting in with another tray of dirty dishes and walking straight through the ghost, who was waving his arms at Callum in a very threatening manner.

'Oi, you great big lump of lard! Tell Linda the people in room 5 are nicking her towels!'

'Linda,' Callum stammered, 'as I came in I heard someone saying that the people in room 5 are nicking your towels.'

'I knew it!' she shrieked and took off at top speed.

The ghost came over to pat Callum on the back and he winced, expecting the affectionate slap to hurt his sore shoulders, but of course he felt nothing.

'Jack Holmes,' the ghost said, by means of an introduction. 'This is my guest house, or at least it used to be.

I like to keep an eye on it. Well, well, well. You being able to see me, that's going to be very helpful indeed. Very, very helpful. I think we can start by tidying up this kitchen. Tidy work place, tidy mind, that's what I say…' and he wandered off scratching his beard and working on a to-do list of ghostly interventions for Callum.

This was precisely what Callum did *not* want to happen. The more people and ghosts that knew what he could do, the more out-of-hand this was going to get. He didn't want to be haunted forever by ghosts trying to get him to do their dirty work — or their cleaning — and neither did he want people thinking he was some kind of freaky ghost whisperer. This was a status update definitely not for his Facebook wall: 'Callum Fox has started seeing dead people and they're getting him to do their housework!'

But he did need at least one person to talk to about all of this, and as he didn't know anyone else down here that someone was going to have to be Sophie. She had been there for him when he went into hospital. Now he needed her to believe him, about Jim, the ghosts and everything, and the sooner the better.

Sophie finished washing her hands and loaded up another tray with fresh plates of delicious cooked breakfasts. Callum wondered whether she'd be convinced if he told her about the ghost of Tor Vista.

'Sophie, guess what? You've got a ghost here too.'

She didn't look impressed.

'It's the ghost of the old owner, Jack Holmes. He told me about the towel thieves. He must have died when he was out fishing, because he's dressed like Captain Birdseye from the fish finger ads.'

She gave one of her exasperated sighs. 'Yeah right. Everyone's heard about Jack and his fishing accident. You're going to need a bit more than some Googled background on this place to prove to me that you can see ghosts!' and with that she flew out again to deliver her cooked breakfasts.

Before he could protest, Linda returned from the car park, with her arms full of fluffy white towels, an expression of quiet satisfaction on her face. She didn't ask Callum any tricky questions about how he had known, she was simply grateful to him for his help; so much so that she offered to cook him a full English as a reward. The food looked so delicious he didn't hesitate in accepting.

Callum wasn't sure where to sit. There was a large kitchen table but it was covered with piles of paperwork. Linda made some excuse about the whole place being messier than normal because Sophie's dad was still away. Then she pulled out a stool and pushed some of the mounds of paper to one side to make room for Callum's plate. There were stacks of magazines on hotels and hospitality and a few on fishing which Callum thought looked particularly boring. There were piles of bills weighed down by an assortment of paperweights and a collection of email printouts and hand written guest correspondence held down by an old tin compass.

The compass had flecks of green paint around the outside and the needle was in the shape of a small aeroplane. The plane rotated from a pin in its tail so that the nose always faced north. Callum picked it up and turned it around, it was cold, smooth and very old. There were four screw holes protruding around the outside and instead of E for East it had an O. Must be a typo, Callum thought, and placed it back on top of the stack of papers.

He was about to ask Linda about the compass when his breakfast arrived and being easily distracted by good food he forgot all about it.

He devoured his second breakfast of the day, thinking to himself that Grandad might have been right after all. Breakfast truly was the most important meal of the day.

Chapter 28

Sunday 20th August 1944

The boys took food to Günter every day for a week and each time the experience was like a real life *Boys Own* adventure. They stole around the harbour finding different routes to and from the lifeboat station in case they were being followed, and as they went they collected essential supplies: water from the village pump, a blanket from a neighbour's washing line and any old newspapers from the bins. They were on a vitally important mission and it was the most exciting thing they had ever done.

With each visit the boys could see Günter regaining his strength and improving his English. He appreciated everything they did for him and he was great fun to be with. He told them stories about Germany before the war and his short and eventful career in the Luftwaffe. Bob hung on every word he said, and whilst Jim questioned some of the details, he generally believed him too.

Günter told them he was seventeen. He'd been called

up on his sixteenth birthday and after a period of awful general training he had been assigned to the Luftwaffe, the German equivalent of the Royal Air Force. He said it was the best of the pretty poor options available to him.

'They trained me and I fly,' he told the boys proudly.

'Yeah; but not very well,' Bob sniggered.

Günter had to agree. 'That was my first flight. Not very good, eh? I was flying with lots of other planes. There was bad weather. I got lost. Then I had engine trouble. You are right, I'm not very good pilot.'

'You're a bleedin' useless pilot, mate,' Jim said, slapping him playfully on the back, and they all laughed until their sides ached.

Bob and Jim took it in turns to take the old fire bucket down to the harbour to fetch clean drinking water for Günter. Today it was Jim's turn. He was happy to help and was whistling a little ditty to himself at the village pump when Ma spotted him.

'What you up to?' she yelled across the road. 'Have you set fire to something again?'

Jim looked up alarmed and the pit of his stomach dropped.

'Err… Bob and me's washing the go-kart, Ma.'

'That old thing? You haven't had that out for years.'

'Yeah. We're doing some work on it.' He had to get away. He stopped pumping and ran off, the fire bucket swinging at his side and the cold water sloshing down his leg, soaking his shorts.

He felt terrible lying to Ma. He knew he had no choice, but his conscience felt as uncomfortable as his wet clothes. And it surprised him. He'd got so used to being around Günter that he'd stopped thinking about him as a German pilot on the run. The encounter with Ma bought back the stark reality of what they were doing. They were hiding a German pilot.

This wasn't a game and it couldn't go on. Sooner or later the lifeboat would be needed and then Günter would be discovered and that would be the end of it. They'd been lucky that there hadn't been a call out last week, but they couldn't count on that luck lasting much longer. Jim hadn't had to clean the cut on Günter's head for days. It must have healed up by now, and he was stronger and fitter. It was time to talk to him about leaving.

The preparations for Günter's escape began in earnest the next day. The first thing they had to do was get him out of his uniform and into some normal clothes.

Bob pinched a pair of his dad's old trousers and a shirt. He had been a little worried about the clothes being missed, but Jim insisted that by the time Walter got home he wouldn't remember what he'd owned before the war and probably wouldn't care. So they took the clothes, along with a piece of string to hold the huge trousers around Günter's tiny waist. The German certainly smelt better when he had clean clothes on and they all agreed he would be a lot less conspicuous.

Günter wanted to get to the nearest port. He thought his best chance of getting home would be to stow away on a boat heading to anywhere on continental Europe.

'That's never gonna work,' said Jim, sitting on the

wooden paddle box. 'You'd be better off getting to the narrowest part of the English Channel, stealing a rowboat and rowing across.'

'We could build you a hot air balloon,' Bob suggested, walking over and sitting down on the bench. He said it in all seriousness, as if that were the next logical step up from having built a go-kart. Jim sometimes despaired of him.

'Of course, why didn't I think of that,' cried Jim, throwing his arms in the air. 'Or we could go the whole hog and break into an RAF base, nick a Spitfire and pop him home on the next bombing raid!'

Günter put an end to their argument by saying that he would set off for the nearest large port and see if stowing away was an option. If it wasn't he would think again and make new plans as he went.

'That is what I shall do,' he announced. 'Tell me where the nearest large port is and how I get there?'

Bob suggested Plymouth, which Jim thought was the biggest. But as it was also a Royal Navy base he wasn't sure it was a very good idea. But it was the best plan any of them could come up with and Günter seemed set on it.

'I can get you a map,' Bob offered. 'I'll nick one from school.'

'That would be wonderful,' Günter declared.

Jim said it was quite funny that Günter felt he needed a map, because if he were any good at map reading he wouldn't be here in the first place.

'It is very difficult to read a map and fly a plane at the same time.' Günter protested. 'I will do much better on foot.'

'Then you'll need a compass too,' Bob suggested.

'There was a good one in my plane,' Günter said, getting up and stretching out.

'There's no way that'll still be there, mate,' Jim told him. 'It would have been burnt to a cinder, or pinched for someone's souvenir collection.'

Günter was more hopeful. 'There was a lot of smoke — *ja*. The engine was on fire — but not the cockpit. Bob survived, didn't he? I think it is time I went back to my plane — to see if there is anything there that will help me.'

The boys looked at each other and frowned.

'Ain't no point,' said Jim. 'It's too dangerous. It's out in the open, in one of Old Thorny's fields. The army will be up there any day to take it away. You can't risk being there when that happens.'

Bob agreed. 'We'll go; Jim and me. We'd go anyway, wouldn't we? See if there's anythin' up there for my collection. No point lettin' some other kids get it all. We'll go on Wednesday after we've finished up at the farm, and if we find the compass, it's yours mate.'

The German placed his hands on his waist. 'OK. I stay here until then. See if you can find a map and the compass and then Wednesday night I leave. Agreed?'

Günter spat in his hand and held it out. The boys spat in theirs and they all shook hands for the last time — the plan was made.

'Agreed!'

Chapter 29

Sunday 3rd August 2014

Sophie and Linda moved between the kitchen and dining room of the Tor Vista guest house like choreographed dancers, performing their well-rehearsed routine of cooking, serving and clearing breakfasts. By the time the residents had finished, Callum had scraped his own plate so clean that he'd almost taken the pattern off it. He stacked it in the dishwasher with all the others and Sophie switched it on with a satisfying clunk.

'Right,' she declared, taking off her apron and revealing a bright blue pair of short shorts. 'I'll go get my fishing gear.'

Callum groaned. All he wanted to do was to talk to her about the ghosts, and he didn't want to do that while she fished and he sat there like a spare part.

But Sophie had her own plans for the day. 'Come on then,' she said, 'I can't carry everything on my own,' and Callum was dragged to his feet to help.

Linda broke off from wiping down the hob. 'Oh Callum; before you go, I've got something of yours.' She foraged in her handbag to produce a broken and badly scratched old phone. 'Is this yours? It was found in the road after the ambulance drove off. It's in bad shape, but you can charge it up and hope for the best.'

Callum was delighted. He'd assumed his beloved mobile had gone forever, smashed to smithereens under the wheels of the ambulance. He turned it over. This phone had been such a huge part of his life before the accident, his primary source of communication with the world. Now that he could communicate with a whole new world it didn't seem quite as important as it had before. And it didn't look as smart either, but he was still very pleased to get it back.

Sophie lent over and examined it. 'That'll never work again,' she said; as ever, the voice of unbridled optimism. 'But you might be able to get the sim card out. Open it up.' Callum did and they both agreed it looked promising.

He thanked Linda for the phone and his breakfast and they set off with enough equipment to start up a small fishing business.

'Do we need all this?' he moaned as they squeezed through Sophie's garden gate on to the coastal footpath. He was struggling with two fishing stools, a windbreak and such a massive keep net that they would be perfectly OK even if they caught a whale.

Sophie insisted they would use it all and led the way, carrying two fishing rods, a heavy tackle box and a rather ominous bag of something live and wriggling. She set a cracking pace back towards the harbour but slowed as they went past the shops and stopped to say good morning and introduce Callum to everyone they passed.

'Hi. This is Callum Fox; Bob and Jean's Grandson... Yes it was him knocked over by that ambulance... yeah, they've let him out of hospital very early... too early I agree... he's a real mess.'

Callum wasn't required to add anything to these conversations, he just stood there like a complete numpty while Sophie had her moment in the limelight as the local know-it-all (not for the first time, Callum suspected!)

They were standing outside the gift shop during one such conversation with an old guy on a mobility scooter — who must have been shaken to pieces on the rough cobbled streets of the harbour — when Callum spotted Jim standing in a car-park space next to the ice-cream shop, appearing to stop any tourists from parking there.

'What about that space over there?' shouted a loud American in a flash convertible as it cruised past Callum and headed towards Jim's parking space.

Jim walked up to the car before it pulled in and, unseen by the driver and his companion, he passed through the body of the vehicle and right up to the unsuspecting driver.

'Nah,' drawled the man, shivering despite the warmth of the morning. 'Let's try somewhere else, I don't fancy that one.' He sped up and drove off.

A minute later Grandad and Nana pulled into the harbour and drove straight into the prized parking slot right next to the shops. 'Better to be born lucky than rich,' Callum heard Grandad saying to Nana as they disappeared into the store, delighted to have secured such a lucky parking slot.

Jim sauntered over to say hello to Callum with the air of someone satisfied with a job well done.

'Why on Earth did you scare the willies out of that tourist?' Callum demanded. 'You were deliberately holding that parking space for Grandad, weren't you?'

'Yeah,' shrugged Jim. 'Why not? I've got nothing better to do.'

Callum could think of a million better things to do with his time than help out his miserable old grandad.

'I think your friend is talking to himself,' the old man on the mobility scooter told Sophie.

'He does that,' she replied, raising her eyebrows. 'Come on, you.' She grabbed Callum's arm and pulled him after her.

Jim shouted his goodbyes and headed into the village store, presumably to scare any innocent tourists out of the queue for the tills. Callum wondered how Jim kept so cheerful if all he did every day was follow Grandad around, smoothing his passage through life. Callum could think of nothing more pointless.

He and Sophie left the far side of the harbour following the shoreline south towards a quiet beach which Sophie described as 'beautiful.' Callum said he wasn't so worried about the look of the place, but he did wish it had been a bit closer.

Several times during the long walk Callum thought he sensed someone behind them, and he spun round to catch the culprit out but he never saw anyone. Sophie was adamant there was no one there and said it was more evidence that Callum had lost it.

Perhaps I have lost it, thought Callum, hoisting the keep net higher up on his shoulder and running to catch up with Sophie. After all, I am carrying tons of Sophie's fishing equipment to a beach in the middle of nowhere. Who's the idiot now?

Chapter 30

Wednesday 23rd August 1944

Early that evening the boys headed up to the fields above Penlee Point. They hadn't been there since the night of the crash and despite having been keen before, Jim was feeling apprehensive.

'We're wasting our time and his! We should of packed him off last night, soon as you gave him the map. He would of gone too if you hadn't insisted we try and find his bleedin' compass first.'

Jim had a bad feeling about all of this. He had done since Ma had caught him at the village pump, it was as if he had a ticking clock in his head that was getting louder and louder, counting down the minutes until Günter was safely away and they were in the clear. He'd told Bob, but nothing ever worried him. Bob pointed out that they'd got away with it so far — why would an extra day make any difference? Jim cursed his friend's stubbornness.

'And there's no way that compass's is still gonna be

there,' Jim complained. 'Whatever didn't get burnt will have been nicked or requisitioned, for sure.'

'Well we won't know if we don't look,' said Bob, quickening the pace. 'And I want him to have everything he needs to get home; he'd do the same for us if it was the other way round. So stop your moaning and come on.' Bob grabbed hold of Jim's green jumper and hurried him along.

The boys turned into the big field where the plane lay abandoned in the far corner. The damage to Old Thorny's land and hedgerows was worse than they had remembered. No wonder the old fool had been whingeing about it. The plane itself was smoke blackened and badly bashed up, but it didn't look like anyone had tried to move it.

Bob jumped up on to the wing and stamped on it to check its stability. He lent down and offered Jim a hand up.

'Come on, mate, I ain't doin' this on my own, not this time.'

Jim clambered up beside him. From up on the wing he could see the extent of the fire damage. The nose of the plane, where the engine had been, was little more than a burnt out shell. Most of the plane's paint work had blistered off and what was left had been washed away by the rain. It made the plane seem less German and more neutral. The cockpit canopy had been left open, just as it was after Günter had pulled it back to rescue Bob. A pool of stagnant water had collected in the foot well and was giving off a foul stench.

Jim edged nearer to the cockpit.

Bob hung back. 'Tell y' what, I'll hold the canopy open and you get in this time.'

Jim didn't argue. He could understand Bob's reluctance to climb in again, after everything that happened last time.

Jim slid down into the pilot's seat. His hands instinctively took hold of the central control column, and his feet naturally found the pedals. It was as if the cockpit had been built for him. It still smelt of smoke and he looked behind him to check Bob had a firm hold on the canopy. He did.

'Ain't it something,' said Bob, pulling a screwdriver out of his trouser pocket and passing it down.

'Bloomin' marvellous,' Jim whispered, and for a brief moment it was him living out his dreams of boyhood adventures. He needed Bob to start shouting at him to remind him why they were there.

He studied the dashboard. There were several blacked out and broken instruments in front of him. Many of the smaller dials were set into the console and they weren't coming out at all. There were half a dozen larger instruments screwed to the outside of the dashboard and some of them looked more or less intact. He pulled down the sleeve of his shirt and used the cuff to scrape the soot off one of them. It didn't make any difference, he had no clue what any of the instruments were. This was going to have to be pure guesswork.

He picked one at random and got to work with the screwdriver. Four tight screws held the instrument firmly in place, and as it came loose it revealed a military green paint that had been damaged beyond recognition elsewhere in the cockpit. As the first instrument came free Jim passed it up to Bob and got to work immediately on the second and then the third.

He was unscrewing the fourth when Bob called out, 'Thorny. Quick! Get out!'

He left the fourth dial swinging on its last screw and was up and out of the cockpit quicker than a frightened rabbit out of a hole. The boys were back on the ground by the time Old Thorny got near enough to recognise them.

'You two! Stop right there!' He shouted, hurrying towards them. 'Might have guessed it would be you! What do you think you're doing with that plane? You shouldn't even be on my land.'

He was carrying his shotgun, as usual, the loading mechanism open with the butt under his armpit and the twin barrels resting over his right arm. His flat cap was pulled down low against the wind and his dirty waxed coat rustled as he walked.

'I said hold it right there, both of you.'

Bob slipped an instrument into each of his trouser pockets and thrust the third into Jim's hands.

Jim's pulse quickened and he took a deep breath to steady his nerves. They had done nothing wrong he kept trying to convince himself. But the ticking in his head was getting pretty darn loud.

'Hello, Mr Thornham,' said Jim. 'We were only havin' a look at the plane.' He kept it calm and conversational — or at least he tried to.

'Were you,' the old man replied, running his fingers

up and down the barrels of his gun. 'And what's that behind your back, you thieving little toe rag.'

'There ain't no rules to stop us collecting souvenirs,' Bob blurted out.

'Hand it over,' the old man repeated, glaring at Jim with the kind of revulsion that he should have reserved for the enemy at this time of war.

Reluctantly Jim held his hand out to reveal a small smoke blackened circular tin with four screw holes protruding at even intervals around the circumference. Old Thorny grabbed it and examined it intently, as if it would reveal the boys guilt in some way.

'It's shrapnel. A souvenir. You can have it if you want, Mr Thornham. We'd better be off anyway,' and with that the boys started walking away.

Jim checked over his shoulder to see Old Thorny remove his cap and scratch his head. 'That was close,' he whispered under his breath. 'You got the other two?'

Bob nodded, his legs moving as fast as they could without breaking into a run. 'Let's get straight to the lifeboat station and get him out of there. Come on.'

That had been the plan earlier, but since they had been seen by Old Thorny it didn't seem such a good idea. What if he followed them? Jim suggested going home first and lying low for a while. But Bob was worried that their friend would leave without them and without the two precious instruments which Bob was convinced would help him find his way home.

The boys compromised by hurrying towards their cottage, but when they got there, they only pretended to go in before doubling back on themselves and taking a very indirect route back to the new lifeboat station.

They were confident they weren't being followed and they knew that they had to get Günter away as soon as possible.

Chapter 31

Sunday 3rd August 2014

Sophie had chosen a beautiful secluded cove for their fishing expedition. It could only be reached by walking down a long stinging-nettle infested footpath and so they had the place all to themselves, even though it was a stunning spot on a scorching hot day.

Callum was busy rubbing his sore legs with what he hoped was a dock leaf, but suspected wasn't, and wishing he hadn't worn his shorts. Meanwhile Sophie was whining on and on about the art of sea fishing — Callum had the feeling that it was going to be a very long day!

Sophie showed Callum how to bait and cast the line, and he did try, but he was so hopeless that in the end Sophie had to do it for him, for her own safety as much as anything. He also refused to deal with the live bait — why anyone would touch those slimy squashy wiggling things was beyond him, let alone pick them up and stick them on the end of a hook. He gagged when Sophie did it.

When all the equipment was set up, Callum took to his unstable fishing stool, sat back and watched the lines, trying to look cool. But even this was tricky for somebody so uncoordinated, and he fell off the pathetic three legged seat so many times that he soon gave up on it and sat down on the rocky beach.

Sophie sat down with perfect ease on her three legged fishing stool — typical!

'Can we please talk about this ghost thing?' he asked, gazing out to sea and avoiding eye contact. This was going to be even more embarrassing than he had imagined. In the cold light of day it all seemed so cringe-worthy. His face coloured up and flashed like a Don't Walk sign at a pelican crossing.

'Do we have to?' she asked. 'Didn't you tell me everything yesterday? I don't want to make it worse by encouraging you.'

Callum flicked his fringe. 'Sophie, this isn't some kind of weird phase I'm going through. Something serious has happened to me, something inside me has changed and now I see things other people can't — and yes, I want to talk about it!'

She stared down at him from the lofty height of her fishing stool and he wished that he'd persevered with sitting on his. At least then he'd be the same height as her. Instead she looked down on him with an expression that said 'you've lost it — you've completely lost it.'

He ignored her and carried on. 'The ghosts have always been here, Soph. It's not like I invented them. But since the accident I can see them, even though no one else can.' He dug his feet and hands into the shingle. 'And

I'm worried. I mean it's a bit weird, isn't it?'

'Yes, of course it's a bit weird,' she said, throwing her head back and laughing a little too hard. 'It's a bit off-the-scale freaky… but I'll tell you what I think is even weirder? It's that you believe it so very much. Listen to yourself, Callum.'

She dropped her voice and spoke more gently. 'Look; this must be something you've made up, even if you don't realise you have. I can tell you won't admit it to yourself, but deep down you must know it's all in your mind. It must be a side effect of the accident, a kind of delayed shock. I'm going to Google it when I get home; see if it's normal, you know, after a head injury.'

Callum had expected this kind of reaction and had already thought through the 'it's all in your head' possibility. It didn't wash.

'But I couldn't have made up this amount of detail Sophie. Honestly I couldn't. I've never been this creative in my life. You should see my school report. My English teacher would be well pleased if I could make up even a fraction of this.'

He picked up a handful of stones and let them run through his fingers. 'I don't make stuff up — it's just not me. And besides, what about the hotel towels this morning? How could I have known about that if the ghost of Captain Birdseye hadn't told me? I couldn't see into their suitcases and I didn't see them packing, and they didn't walk past me saying: 'Oh great — we've got away with nicking some dirty old towels!' Only someone inside the hotel, that the guests couldn't see, could possibly have seen what they were doing, and that was the ghost of Jack

Holmes — not me!'

Sophie pierced another wriggling worm on to the end of her hook and then wiped her hands on her shorts.

Fishing, thought Callum, is absolutely gross.

She stood up to cast another line. Callum watched in silence, waiting for her verdict on his big speech.

'OK,' she said, moving her fishing stool out of the way and sitting down on the stones beside him. 'Tell me everything you've learnt about them so far and let's have a think about it.'

And so Callum did. He spoke as fast as he could, because he wanted to get it all out before she could ask him any tricky questions or criticise his theories. She listened to everything he had to say, nodding when needed, frowning a lot and occasionally playing with her fishing rods.

But did she believe him?

She interrupted him to reel in a spotted grey tiddler that had taken the bait, but on landing it she declared it too small and threw it back into the sea.

What was the point of that? The joy of fishing was lost on Callum.

'I'll tell you what I'm most worried about,' he carried on. 'So far only Grandad's friend, Jim, and Tor Vista's Jack Holmes know about this. Jim's great, he's not asked me to do anything and I don't think he ever would. But your Jack, he's already drawing up a task list for me. What will happen when all the other ghosts round here find out what I can do. Will they be queuing round the block wanting me to do stuff for them too?'

Callum lay back on the stones and looked up to

the blue sky. 'And then there are the people they've left behind, the living ones. If I'm not careful, I could end up with all the ghosts' families asking me to send messages to them, like one of those rip-off mediums you get on dodgy TV shows. I mean, I could end up as some kind of TV ghost whisperer, helping some Z list celebrity 'get through' to Michael Jackson or Amy Winehouse…'

Sophie held her hand up to get him to stop. 'Good grief, Callum — what are you talking about?'

Callum propped himself up on his forearm. 'Sophie, I don't want to be someone who talks to ghosts. I don't think that kind of thing ends well.'

'No, I shouldn't think it does,' she agreed lying back next to him and staring up at the cloudless sky. They lay there in silence for a while, deep in their own thoughts. Sophie got up, tended to her fishing rods and Callum watched her.

'Of course, it's most likely all a hallucination,' she concluded, coming back over and sitting down again. 'I mean it's got to be just in your head, it can't be real — so you don't need to worry about it.'

Was that honestly the best she could come up with? Callum had come here with higher expectations of her than that. He sighed out loud and sat himself back up.

'That's what I thought this morning. But when I got to your place and saw the ghost of Jack Holmes at your guest house, I knew it was for real — all of it. I wish you'd believe me.'

Sophie ran her hands through her short hair, making it even spikier. Callum could see she was thinking it through and struggling. It was as if she wanted to believe him, but the scientific whizz-kid in her couldn't accept it. 'OK. Let's see then,' she mused. 'Have you seen Elvis?'

Callum threw his hands up in despair. 'Elvis? Of course I haven't seen Elvis! For starters; he might not be a ghost. Then there's the fact that he didn't die in Mousehole, or anywhere near it. If he's haunting anywhere it'll be in America somewhere and anyway, if I'd seen anyone in a Day-Glo white and gold flared body-suit, singing *Viva Las Vegas* in Mousehole it would have been the first thing I mentioned, not something I might have forgotten to tell you about!' Then he added sarcastically, 'Oh mind you —hang on — there was that one time at the fish and chip shop...

'And before you ask I haven't seen anyone else famous either. Just Jim, some pirates, a soldier and a sailor from the war, a jogger wearing ridiculously stupid shorts, a naked guy with a soap-on-a-rope and an entire crew of lifeboatmen.'

Sophie's mouth fell open and an expression came across her face, the likes of which Callum would have only expected to see if he had insulted her, her parents and everyone she had ever loved.

His heart sank, he was in trouble now — and he had no idea why.

Chapter 32

Wednesday 23rd August 1944

Bob and Jim were both panting as they climbed the steep gangway up to the deck of the lifeboat.

'I tell you, we should of waited,' Jim protested, resting his hands on his knees, 'what if someone'd seen us?'

'Well it were fine, weren't it?' Bob snapped at him. 'And that's the last time we'll do it, so you can stop your bleedin' worrying, all right?'

Jim wiped the sweat from his brow and looked around for Günter, whom he found crouched behind the propeller box, folding away the blankets the boys had lent him for a makeshift bed.

'What is wrong?' he asked, standing up and stretching.

'We were seen — up at the plane, by the Home Guard. That's what.'

'So what?' cried Bob, throwing his hands up in the air. 'We was taking the instruments off the dashboard — well the ones that weren't all smashed up — when Old

Thorny shows up, yellin' and shoutin' like it's his plane.'

'Well it's in his bleedin' field,' Jim mumbled.

Günter looked anxious. 'You were caught?'

'No,' Bob snorted. 'We'd done nothing wrong. There's nothing he could do. Jim's nervy about it because he's got no backbone, that's all.'

Bob was right; seeing Old Thorny had shaken Jim up. But Bob wasn't the least bit bothered.

'Bring that bucket over here, mate,' Bob called out and Günter promptly fetched the old fire bucket, half full with yesterday's drinking water. Bob pulled out the two smoke blackened instruments that Jim had detached from the plane's dashboard, along with a large off-white cotton hankie and set about cleaning one of them.

'From my plane?' Günter asked.

Bob nodded as he methodically rubbed away at the soot caked onto the circular tin. Slowly the coating of grime began to thin and the glass of the instrument's face began to show through, revealing first some faint lettering on the dial beneath, then a miniature plane suspended on a pin, constantly bobbing around so that the nose of the plane always pointed due north.

Bob threw his head back and roared. 'It's the compass — we've only gone and got the bleedin' compass!'

'You jammy devil!' Jim couldn't believe it. Out of all the damaged instruments in the cockpit, the very first one they manage to salvage was the compass.

A broad grin spread across Günter's face. '*Danke. Danke.* Thank you. Thank you.'

Bob slapped Günter hard on the back, 'It's an omen. A good luck omen. You're going home, mate!'

Putting his squabble with Bob behind him, Jim pulled out his own hankie and set to work on the second instrument. This time, numbers around the edge of the face emerged from the blackness, along with a long white needle pointing to zero. Jim had no idea what he was cleaning but he rubbed it as hard as he could, in the hope of restoring something that would help his friend on his long journey. Bit by bit, more of the face became clear and flecks of green paint started showing through. It looked like a speedometer, but the numbers were too large for that.

The three of them sat bent over the bucket, with Bob and Jim polishing the instruments and Günter repeatedly thanking them.

Jim handed his tin to Günter. 'What is it?' he asked.

'*Höhenmesser*,' Günter said and without the English to explain he spread his arms out like wings and ran up and down the deck of the Lifeboat, with his body rising and falling like a plane taking off and landing.

The three of them laughed out loud. Jim and Bob had no clue at all what he was trying to say, but it didn't bother any of them; they had all got used to getting by on understanding most of what was said and not concerning themselves with any minor gaps in comprehension.

When Günter sat back down on the propeller box, he tried to return the Höhenmesser to Jim, but Jim refused, pushing it back into his friend's hand.

'As long as it helps you mate, you're welcome to it.' He pulled out a rather crushed pasty from the depths of one of his pockets and handed that over too.

Günter thanked him.

Bob gave the German a small bottle of milk and the compass, now sparkling like it was diamond encrusted. He'd scratched out the words 'Good luck, mate' on the back with his pen knife.

'Remember us, won't you? When you get home.'

'I will,' Günter said, fumbling in his pocket and pulling out two small pieces of cloth, one for each of the boys. He looked embarrassed; concerned that the badges from his old uniform might not make appropriate gifts, but it was all he had to give.

'Please', he said, passing them over awkwardly. 'To remember me.' And to Bob he added, 'for your collection.'

Jim studied his small piece of cloth. For something so small it weighed heavy in his hand, a reminder of their differences as well as their friendship. One thing was for certain — there wouldn't be many shrapnel collections in Cornwall with genuine Luftwaffe badges.

'Come on. Let's get you off then,' said Bob pulling them back to the business in hand.

'Got the map?' Jim asked.

'*Ja*,' Günter revealed the tip of a neatly folded map stowed away in his breast pocket and then he pushed the compass and the *Höhenmesser* into his trouser pockets too. 'I go now,' he said, throwing his arms around Bob and drawing him into a strong embrace.

'You will be careful, won't you?' Bob mumbled into the German's shoulder.

'*Ja, Ja*,' he beamed, releasing one boy in order to envelop the other.

Jim was reminded of saying goodbye to his dad all those years ago. The strength of his emotions took him by surprise. 'Hope you get home, mate,' he whispered. 'Hope you get home.'

'You too,' Günter replied, reluctant to release Jim and start his new adventure.

'Hold it right there, Fritz.' A fourth voice echoed around the lifeboat station. Cold, deep, disembodied and forbidding.

Jim's blood ran cold. He spun around, scanning for the source of the voice but could see nothing. Had he really heard it?

Bob had heard it all right. 'Did you hear…?'

'Put your hands in the air and move away from the boys,' the voice instructed — it was very real, and although he couldn't see anyone Jim knew exactly who it was.

Günter side stepped away from his friends and raised both his arms. 'Go,' he whispered to them.

But neither Jim nor Bob had any intention of leaving. They too stepped back, closer to their friend, shielding him from the threat.

'Go,' Günter told them again.

Bob and Jim ignored him.

'Thorny?' Jim whispered.

'Reckon so. But I can't see him, can you?'

'Oh yes!' Jim's mouth went dry. The double barrels of a very familiar shotgun were resting on the side of the boat, just above the gangway.

Of course it had to be Old Thorny. Jim could have kicked himself. How could he have been so dim-witted? The old bugger must have followed them from the crash site. His fear that they were being followed hadn't been paranoia, they actually had been followed! They'd made it so easy for him. How could they have been so stupid?

Old Thorny had repeatedly accused the boys of knowing more about the crash than they were letting on. He was going to go off the scale now that he had found them hiding the missing German.

The three of them had backed themselves up against the far edge of the boat. Opposite them Old Thorny and his shotgun blocked the only way down.

Think, Jim — think. How could he possibly talk himself, Bob and Günter out of this one? 'Mr Thornham, it's us, Bob Fox and Jim.' Jim could hear his voice wavering and he hoped and prayed Old Thorny didn't notice.

'It's all right,' Jim continued. 'This is our friend, Günter. He's one of us. He's helped us. He saved Bob's life. He did, honest.' Could he say enough to make Old Thorny stop and think, before he shot Günter dead? Or worse, all three of them?

'Yes, Mr Thornham, he saved my life. He did, I promise!' Bob's words tumbled out in a hurried mess.

'Don't be so darn foolish, boys. Move away from the Kraut.'

Jim and Bob edged even closer to Günter, they pushed their backs into his chest so they could feel the pounding of his heart. They shielded him from the twin barrels that were being waved across the deck, sweeping across them from left to right.

Old Thorny rose slowly from the gangplank. The whites of his eyes were wide and his face was set in a grimace of pure hatred. The old man hooked first one leg and then the other over the side of the boat. He landed with a thump on the deck, but his full-length wax coat got caught on the links of the gangway and for a moment he looked back trying to unhook himself.

Bob gave Günter a shove and whispered, 'Now!' and with athleticism that the boys hadn't seen since the night of the crash, Günter vaulted over the far side of the lifeboat and leapt down to the walkway below.

Old Thorny cussed and fumbled his way back over the boat's edge and stormed down the gangway, his feet thundering on the wooden slats.

Both Old Thorny and Günter were on the sloped walkway surrounding the hull of the boat. Jim and Bob ran to the bow and peered down on them. Old Thorny was between Günter and the door. The old man was closing the distance, shotgun raised, cocked and ready to fire.

Without a word the two boys flew down the gangway to help their friend. They raced up behind Old Thorny, who spun round, staggered to find the boys interfering once again.

Jim threw himself on to Old Thorny's back and pulled and pulled at him. Bob stood in front of him wrestling the old soldier for his gun. There were legs and arms everywhere. Old Thorny was swearing and spitting and no one could tell who was who or what was what. The old man twisted round with Jim on his back and Bob pulling at his gun. Günter joined in throwing a punch that hit Thorny hard on the side of the head. He staggered back but stayed on his feet.

Bob was yelling 'Günter, Go!' But Günter wouldn't leave the boys like this.

'Go!' screamed Jim.

Günter started to, but then stopped again, silhouetted in the doorway by the dim evening light from outside.

'Go!' Jim yelled. And with a last look of sympathy for the mess he was leaving his friends in, Günter turned and left.

Old Thorny twisted round again, desperate to ditch the kids and get after the German. He hurled Jim off his back and the youngster flew across the walkway, slamming into the wall. There was an ominous crack as Jim's head hit the corner of the doorframe. A white pain seared through him, sending his head, neck and back into agonising spasms.

He closed his eyes, 'Bob…'

Then the gun went off.

It was ear-shatteringly loud.

Too loud.

Jim felt both shots enter his chest. He felt the pain seep away from him through the gaping wound in his ribcage. He was pushed deeper into the wall by the momentum of the shot. His head filled with the smell and smoke of cordite, which made everything fuzzy. Good God, it was slow. Everything was so slow. His legs bent back on themselves in a way they had never bent before and he found he had time to think 'why are my legs bending like this?' They folded underneath him and he sank to the ground. His body crumpled into a tiny heap.

He couldn't hear anything. It was so silent, so bleeding silent — and very, very black.

He stopped hurting, he stopped feeling; he even stopped breathing. He kept his eyes clamped shut.

Something awful had happened, he knew it.
    He lay there, very still.
    Deathly still.

Chapter 33

Sunday 3rd August 2014

'That's low. That's really low.' Sophie leapt up to storm off, then seemed to change her mind, hovering over Callum glaring at him. For a moment he thought she was going to kick him.

He jumped up to defend himself. 'What did I say? What did I say?'

'You can't make jokes about the lifeboat, Callum. Come off it! What you said, that was really wrong.'

Callum reeled. 'I'm not making a joke! What did I say?' It was clear he'd said something that had made Sophie go off-the-scale ballistic. 'Look, I'm sorry if I've upset you, but I don't understand what I've done wrong.'

Sophie pulled the fishing stool back to its feet and sat down on it so quickly it wobbled. 'It's pretty low of you to use the lifeboat disaster to justify your ridiculous fantasy. I can't believe you used that to try and convince me about your stupid ghosts!' She gave up on the stool, stood up and this time sent the flimsy thing flying.

'I've never heard anything about a lifeboat disaster,' Callum said weakly. 'And if I did I wouldn't make things up about it. Be real! I'm simply telling you what I saw and I saw seven or eight lifeboat men, in full orange outfits, laughing and slapping each other on the back, going into the Ship Inn, the same as anyone else would. Well, except that they walked straight through the closed door instead of waiting for opening time. Sophie, I don't understand any of this. I'm not trying to be funny, or offensive. Please believe me.'

She glared at him, hands rooted to her hips, fuming. 'I don't believe you, Callum. I don't believe in your ghosts. And I don't believe you've never heard about the lifeboat disaster. I mean your mum lived here at the time; your grandad was one of the men who volunteered to step up and take their places — to make a new crew — when they didn't come home. You must know about it. It took eight men, all from round here. Everyone knows about it.'

'Oh God Sophie, I'm sorry. But I didn't! I'm not from round here. Honestly, I don't want to see any of this stuff, I don't!'

'I don't believe you see any of it,' she said and stormed off to the water's edge at the far side of the cove, as far away from Callum as she could get. She stood cooling her feet and her temper in the sea, letting the very tip of the waves run through the holes of her green crocs as she stared blankly out towards St Michael's Mount and beyond to the blue-on-blue horizon.

'What you need now my boy,' said a deep and husky voice that seemed to come from nowhere and frightened Callum witless, 'is something to raise your young lassie's spirits and prove to her that you're not a lying little scurvy dog.'

Callum leapt a foot off the ground. He had been convinced that he and Sophie were alone on the remote beach. He spun around to find a short fat pirate standing behind him. He wore a large floppy black hat which matched his entirely black outfit. He had a considerable amount of butch jewellery and carried an enormous great cut-throat sword.

It took all the effort Callum could muster not to cry out, but he knew that Sophie's mood wouldn't be improved any by him screaming and shouting at nothing but thin air.

'Go away,' he whispered through gritted teeth.

'Don't be foolish, me pretty boy. That's not going to be a helpin' either of us, is it?' The pirate raised his cutlass and held it to Callum's throat. If the sword had been real, Callum's throat would have been sliced open. He could almost feel the blood running down his neck.

'You can't touch me,' he croaked.

'Aye, you're right,' said the pirate, dropping his sword to his side and nodding in agreement.

It was a strange kind of truce; neither could physically touch the other and they both knew it.

'What you got there, Cap'n?' shouted a second gruff voice coming from across the beach. Callum turned round to find another pirate emerging from a cave at the bottom of the cliffs.

'This is me friend, Peg,' the pirate Cap'n said, pointing to the one legged pirate who was making his awkward way across the rocky beach towards them. He couldn't have looked more like a picture book pirate if he'd had a parrot and an eye patch.

'Peg and me's been watching you,' the first pirate announced. 'And we think having you around abouts here is very good news indeed — for all of us.'

Callum sighed. It might seem like very good news to the pirates, but he was pretty sure it wasn't good news for him.

'We can help you and you can help us. You scratch our backs and we'll scratch yours. That sort of thing. It could be to our mutual advantage.' The way he said "mutual advantage" made Callum feel very uneasy.

'There is no way I am ever helping you,' Callum whispered. 'And, let's face it, you can't scratch anyone's back. So, please go away.'

'So you want more time to think about it. I understand.'

Callum shook his head and started mouthing 'go away' again and again.

Peg hobbled closer to them, his broad smile revealing the worst teeth Callum had ever seen. 'Aye Aye Cap'n. This laddie can be our powder monkey and do our picking up and moving. Lots and lots of picking up and moving. We be back in the game, Cap'n. Back in the game!'

Peg drew his sword and thrust it at Callum's throat, as if checking to see if his would work when the Cap'n's hadn't. It didn't. But it made Callum leap backwards and shout out loud.

'Oi. You two. Leave the poor lad alone.'

Callum and the pirates spun round to see the naked man come striding across the beach towards them, one hand hiding his privates and the other swinging his soap-on-a-rope.

Good grief, thought Callum, there can't be a ghost

left in Mousehole that isn't trying to get in on this. Did they send out a bulletin?

'Stand back, Professor,' the Cap'n shouted, brandishing his useless sword. But the naked man strode right up to them, ignoring the sword as it sliced through his midriff to no effect whatsoever. The man had an authoritative manner. He was middle-aged, had short brown hair and the highest forehead Callum had ever seen. He swung his light green soap-on-a-rope casually from its twisted cord.

'Don't be silly Cap'n.' The naked man said, defusing the situation. 'Morning Peg,' he added. Perhaps an eternity spent without clothes would turn anyone into a diplomat.

'The boy's had a shock. Why don't we all give him a break?' Then turning to Callum he said, 'Hello, by the way.' He offered his hand to Callum who shook his head, horrified because it was no longer covering the man's privates. 'Professor Paul Robbins,' the man said, swinging his soap-on-a-rope into place to save Callum's blushes.

Callum heard him but said nothing. He stared, dumbstruck, at the naked man and the two pirates.

'Maybe now's not a good time,' the Professor replied. Then he turned back to the pirates. 'Why don't we leave the boy to spend some time with his friend here,' he suggested, nodding over at Sophie. 'There'll be plenty of time for talking later. I think he's had a bit of a shock and scaring him half to death isn't going to help anyone, is it?'

'Always used to work,' moaned the Cap'n.

'Yes, well, things have changed since the days when you could hit someone over the head and make them do your bidding.'

The ghosts went on to argue about how much Callum could reasonably be expected to do for any of them and how much time he should be given to get used to his new ghostly go-between status. Satisfied by the Professor's assurances that Callum wasn't going anywhere and didn't need to be pressurised into helping them this very minute, the Cap'n and Peg left the beach with much 'Aye-Aye-ing' and swashbuckling.

The Prof turned to a stunned Callum and tried to convince him that the pirates weren't all bad. It was just that they were very excited to discover his new talents. He assured Callum everything would be OK and then he left too, sauntering off whistling a happy tune to himself and twirling his soap-on-a-rope as he went.

Callum watched them go with dismay. This was what he'd been worried about: loads of ghosts competing for his attention, trying to get him to do their dirty work and Sophie thinking he was mad, bad or both. This day just kept getting worse and worse.

He dragged his sorry self down the beach and waded through the shallows to Sophie.

'You've been talking to yourself again,' she said without looking at him.

'Yeah, a bit. Sorry. Look; I don't know what else I can say. It feels real to me… I understand it doesn't sound good, but it is the truth.'

'I dunno…'

Callum tutted loudly. Whilst Sophie had her practical plastic beach shoes on, he had just walked straight into the sea, soaking his only pair of Converse trainers. He edged backwards out of the surf and promptly slipped on some wet rocks. He fell into the fishing lines causing the floats and hooks to come reeling in. One of the hooks whizzed in so fast it caught on his arm and he screamed as the sharp pointy bit cut him, with the worm still wiggling on the other end of it.

Sophie lent over and very calmly unhooked the barb from his arm, then took the worm off the hook and threw it out to sea.

Callum sat back with his bum squelching in a rock pool. 'I've had enough, Soph.'

She gave him one of those 'I despair of you looks' that he was used to getting from his mum and his teachers. He smiled up at her, looking pathetic. It worked and she offered him her hand and pulled him back on to his soggy feet.

'Sophie, I need your help with this ghost thing. More and more ghosts are realising that I can see them. They want me to do stuff for them and I don't like it. If I don't do what they want they're never going to leave me alone. But if I start helping them, where will it end?'

'What do they want you to do?' she asked.

'Oh I don't know. There's a couple of pirates who want me to be their powder monkey — whatever that means; a naked Professor who's being all friendly, but he probably wants something too. Then there's Jack Holmes back at your guest house working on his to-do list... I give in! It feels like they all want a piece of me and they aren't ever going to leave me alone until they get it.'

Sophie raised a quizzical eyebrow. 'Pirates? From Penzance were they?'

'I dunno — is that bad?'

She laughed. 'It's all bad, Callum. Whether it's real or in your head, one thing's for sure - it's not good. Come on; let's get all this fishing stuff packed up and get you back home.'

Callum agreed. He'd had it with the fishing expedition.

There was one positive though; at least Sophie was talking to him again and not accusing him of being an inconsiderate pig. And although she was very clear that she didn't believe in his ghosts, she was beginning to accept that he believed in them. And that was progress.

'OK, let's suppose Jim is real,' she said as they headed home, fighting their way back down the stinging-nettle path, weighed down by all their fishing equipment. 'I don't believe he is, but for the sake of argument let's pretend I do.

'If Jim were real, why would he spend his time looking out for your grandad? I mean, he's so horrible; I wouldn't go out of my way to help him if he was the last pensioner alive. So why does Jim?'

Callum nodded, he'd been bothered by that too. 'He says he was Grandad's best friend. And he's about twelve, so I think he must have died when he and Grandad were about our age.'

'Nah,' said Sophie laughing. 'Your grandad was never that young!'

Chapter 34

Wednesday 23rd August 1944

The silence in the lifeboat station was shattered by the sound of the shotgun crashing to the floor. Jim clenched his jaw tight shut, but inside he was screaming; for his mam, for Ma, for Bob. If he opened his mouth and let it out he didn't think he'd ever be able to stop.

He deliberately kept his eyes shut, not wanting to see his wound. If he saw it, it might start hurting and at the moment he felt nothing, nothing at all. He was numb.

There was someone beside him and he assumed it was Bob. He felt a large warm hand take his wrist and feel for a pulse. It was rough against his skin, so it wasn't Bob's, it must be Old Thorny's. The hand slid down his face, passing gently over his eyelids, as if closing them. Couldn't he see they were already shut?

'He's dead,' the old man whispered.

'No I'm not,' Jim's eyes flew open and he sat bolt upright. 'I'm bleedin' well not dead, you idiot — come on,

Bob, give us a hand up.'

But Bob didn't move. He slumped back against the side of the boat, his mouth wide open in his own silent scream. Jim staggered up and over to him. He placed a reassuring hand on Bob's shoulder but instead of being comforted Bob visibly shivered. He didn't even look up.

'You all right, mate?' Jim asked.

There was no reply.

'What's up?' Again there was no reaction. Bob sat motionless, frozen at the base of the boat.

'Come on, Bob.' Jim was getting worried. He reached out again, this time to shake his friend, like Günter had shown him on that first night after the crash. But he couldn't grip his shoulder, instead his hand melted through his friend. Jim let out a piercing scream and leapt back.

He flew round and glared at Old Thorny. 'What you done to him?'

Old Thorny said nothing; he seemed lost in his own thoughts. The old man was kneeling, hunched over the floor where Jim had fallen, the knees of his trousers damp from an ominous puddle of a dark sticky liquid.

'What's that?' Jim asked, half knowing, half not wanting to know. What had reduced Bob to a quivering wreck and diverted Old Thorny from hunting down Günter?

Günter? Could it be Günter in that pool of... blood? But the shotgun had hit him, not the German. Günter hadn't been there, he'd already gone.

Jim moved round Old Thorny to get a better look. In the dim light of the evening sun he could see a small body. It lay crumpled on the floor in front of Old Thorny, in a foul pool of blood and gore. But it wasn't Günter.

Any breath Jim had left was lost with the realisation. 'No!'

The sound escaped with the last of his breath.

It was his own broken body, sprawled across the floor, a vacant and abandoned vessel. The jumper that Ma had knitted for him had been blown clean off and the legs that poked out from his baggy shorts were bent backwards and broken. Jim was standing above himself, looking down at his empty body. His hands flew to his mouth; he bent double and retched from the very pit of his stomach.

Old Thorny was ranting. 'The German did it — right? Bob, get a grip, we'll say the German did it. Come on, boy, pull yourself together. We'll say the German wrestled the gun off me and he shot Jim.'

Bob didn't reply.

Jim couldn't bear it any longer. That thing on the floor, it wasn't him. It couldn't be. He was here. He looked down at his own feet, his own shorts, his own green sleeveless jumper — they were all fine, he was fine. The body on the floor, it wasn't real. He was real, standing here. This version of himself was the real one.

He didn't understand how, but this had to be Old Thorny's fault, it must be. The old man wanted to frame Günter: that's what this was all about. Old Thorny was framing Günter for something that hadn't happened.

Jim straightened himself up pulled his arm back and with a whirl wind of anger he lashed out at Old Thorny with a blow that should have sent the old man reeling.

Jim's fist flew through the air and travelled straight through the old man's head and out the other side. The sensation was terrifying. It clearly had no impact on Thorny whatsoever, but the momentum of the punch caused Jim to stumble and fall, and to his horror he fell into the old man, or rather right through him, and landed on the floor in the pool of his own blood.

He held his hands up in disgust, expecting them to be red and dripping, but they were clean. How? He put his right hand back into the blood and held it up to the light from the doorway. Still nothing.

He couldn't touch anyone — and nothing could touch him.

He was a ghost-like version of himself.

He was a ghost.

Chapter 35

Sunday 3rd August 2014

It was early afternoon when Callum arrived back at the bungalow. His shorts were still damp from where he had fallen into the sea and he was hot and thirsty too. He let himself into the porch, kicked off his soggy trainers and headed straight for the kitchen to find a cold drink.

He stopped abruptly in the narrow hallway. Something was wrong. There was too much noise coming from the kitchen, and it definitely wasn't Nana's TV or radio. It sounded more like a party. Droplets of condensation covered the door handle and Callum felt a chill in the air that shouldn't have been there on the hottest day of the year. His heart sank; that kind of cold could only mean one thing — ghosts. And lots of them.

He was about to leg it when he heard Nana talking to herself. He knew she was sensitive to this kind of supernatural thing. He couldn't leave her in there on her own. He took a deep breath and opened the door.

The kitchen was jam-packed with Mousehole's ghosts. The pirates were over by the fridge arguing over something pointless and the eight-man lifeboat crew were crowded round Nana's tiny portable telly watching *Cash in the Attic*. Jack Holmes, from Sophie's guest house, was sat at the small kitchen table trying to talk to the naked Professor with the soap-on-a-rope and they were both having to shout to be heard over all the other noise. The end result was a deafening uproar, in the midst of which poor Nana was wondering round in circles walking through ghost after ghost, complaining about the cold.

'Ah Callum, thank goodness you're back,' she cried. 'Could you go and find your grandad and ask him to come and take a look at the fridge, please? It must be on the blink. The kitchen is freezing, can't you feel it? He's in the shed.'

'OK.' Callum turned on his heels to make a quick exit.

'There he is,' called out the pirate Cap'n and as Callum started running they all followed suit. Callum ran barefoot through the house and out into the garden. By the time he got to the shed they were already there; several of them having taken the more direct route straight through the kitchen wall.

They were even louder out here, calling his name and shouting at him. It was like being hounded by a pack of ghost paparazzi.

'Leave me alone,' he shouted, stuffing his fingers in his ears. 'Will you all just leave me alone?'

It couldn't carry on like this. Every time he left the house more and more ghosts realised what he could do.

They must be telling each other, spreading it along their ghostly grapevine. At this rate, all of Cornwall's dead would have found out by the end of the week; it could be nationwide by the middle of August and global by the end of the holidays. Was he going to end up with all the ghosts in the whole world banging on his door? Callum buried his head in his hands.

'Shut the bleedin' hell up!' Jim yelled, emerging from the side of the shed. 'I SAID… SHUT UP!'

There was silence.

Callum peeked through his fingers. To his surprise the ghosts had indeed shut up and were hanging their heads like scolded school children.

'What the hell do you think you're doing to this poor lad?' Jim bellowed. 'My friend, Callum,' he put a cool arm around Callum's shoulder, 'he ain't nothin' to do with any of you. You've got no business being here. This is my patch and my business. Now ger out!'

The guest house owner, Jack Holmes, put his hand up to ask a question, his thick white beard bristling with self-satisfaction. 'But I've already spoken to the boy, Jim. He's already started helping me. I'm working on a list of things he can do.'

Jim gave Callum with one of those 'I despair of you' looks and Callum shrugged.

'OK, Jack, you go back to Tor Vista and work on your list. If Callum wants to help, he'll come to you. But he doesn't have to; all right. And he certainly won't if you carry on like this.'

'Aye, we've spoken to him too,' chipped in the pirate Cap'n, motioning to himself and Peg.

'Have you? I might of guessed!' Jim raised another eyebrow and Callum shook his head vigorously. 'Well, there's no way he's helpin' you. Clear off, and I don't want to see either of you back here again.'

The pirates sloped off, followed by Jack Holmes and the lifeboatmen, all of them making a long straggly line of chastised ghosts traipsing down the steep garden path.

'Oi, Skipper. Have you been haunting him too?' Jim called down the garden.

The oldest lifeboatman turned back, smiling. 'No, Jim. But we did want to see what all the fuss was about. See if it was true, you know how it is.'

Jim grunted an acknowledgement and the men carried on towards the gate.

The naked Professor with a soap-on-the-rope fell behind, standing a short distance away, his pale skin glowing in the bright sunlight, like a sheet of fresh white paper but with more hairy bits.

'For goodness sake,' said Jim. 'Can't you find something bigger than a bar of soap to hide behind?' The Professor side-stepped behind a waist high rose bush.

'Can I speak to the boy, please? Can I? It's ever so important.' He looked pleadingly from Jim to Callum.

But Jim was having none of it. 'Not today, mate, nothing's happening today, skedaddle.' And trailing his soap-on-a-rope along the top of a hedge the naked Professor joined the other ghosts filing slowly out of Grandad's garden.

Callum was beginning to realise that his new-found ability was as much a revelation to the ghosts as it was to him — which meant that they weren't going to leave him alone. He was their new toy and they all wanted to play with him. He was overwhelmed, and slumped to the ground defeated.

Jim sat down beside him, laying a cool hand on his arm. 'It'll be all right,' he said. 'Things'll settle down, you wait and see. Everyone will get used to it soon enough.'

'But I don't want everyone to get used to it,' Callum moaned. 'I want to be left on my own and for all of *them* to go away!'

At precisely that moment Grandad Bob burst out of the shed, in his baggy brown cardigan and outdoor slippers. 'What do you want to go away?' he demanded.

Callum sighed heavily. 'Nothing, Grandad.' He had no desire to discuss any of this with the old man. If Sophie had found it hard to believe, he didn't even want to think what Grandad Bob would make of it? Besides, if Grandad had any idea what was going on in his grandson's head he would have him back in hospital quicker than you could say 'hallucination.'

'Nana wants you in the kitchen,' Callum mumbled.

'Come on then lad; pull yourself together,' said Grandad, shuffling off across the garden.

Jim got to his feet. 'Bob's right you know.' He offered Callum a hand up which Callum refused, preferring to stay where he was, slumped against the shed, sulking.

It didn't stop Jim giving him a lecture. 'You've got to pull yourself together, lad. You can get through this, but you're going to have to pick yourself up and get on with it. Come on, worse things than this happened in the war.'

Callum didn't reply.

'Look, I'll go and have a word with the others, see if I can stop them telling anyone else. But nothin's gonna get done with you sitting round 'ere with your head in your hands. While I'm gone, why don't you speak to your grandad about it, he might be able to help.'

'Yeah, right! Like I'm going to discuss any of this with him!'

Jim wasn't impressed. He tutted loudly and flounced off after the other ghosts.

'Come on, son,' Grandad called up from the bottom of the garden. 'Up you get. It's not like anyone's died!'

Callum leant back and thought about what Grandad had said. 'It's not like anyone has died.' But Grandad had been wrong. That's exactly what had happened — people had died! All the ghosts that were following him, the lifeboatmen, the naked Professor, Jack Holmes from the guest house, the pirates, even Jim — all of them had died, and all before their time.

This was serious stuff. Dead serious stuff.

Jim had told him that to become a ghost you had to die before your time and with unfinished business. All these ghosts, who were haunting him today, were doing so because they all had things they still needed to do.

So, how do you get rid of a ghost with unfinished business? Presumably, you have to help them sort it out. And if Jim could stop the word spreading to any more ghosts, then he'd only need to help this lot - perhaps there was a way out of this mess after all.

Callum wondered what helping sort out the dead's unfinished business might involve. It didn't sound like the kind of thing he could do on his own. No, he was going to need help, and down here that meant only one person — Sophie.

So, first things first, he would have to get Sophie to

believe him. And in the meantime he most definitely needed to get out of these damp shorts.

'Coming, Grandad,' he shouted, standing up, brushing himself down and heading back to the kitchen.

He had a plan at last.

He was a ghost whisperer on a mission.

Jim and his friends needed help and Callum was going to give it to them and get them 'moving on' — whether they wanted it or not.

Chapter 36

Wednesday 23rd August 1944

Jim was in a hellish nightmare. He stumbled out of the lifeboat station and up the steps, screaming long and hard as he went. He had to get away, as far away from here as possible.

At the top of the road he stopped. Where should he go? What should he do?

A hundred yards away he saw Günter silhouetted, motionless, against the evening sky.

'Günter!' Jim called after him. 'Help me!'

Günter did nothing.

Jim ran right up to his friend and stood before him shouting in his face. 'Günter, you've gotta help me — please!' But Günter couldn't see or hear him.

Jim grabbed at his friend's clothes but his hands melted right through him.

He sobbed and yelled and beat his fists on the German, all to no effect.

Günter looked worried. Perhaps he had heard the shot and didn't know whether to go back to the lifeboat station or run away as planned. He seemed paralysed by his indecision. The sound of a car engine brought him back to his senses. He darted to the undergrowth at the edge of the road and hid.

Jim stood square in the car's path as it came around the bend. The bright bug-like headlamps of a Morris Eight moved steadily towards him, lighting up two streaks of tarmac. He held his hand up to draw the driver's attention.

'Stop, please. Stop!'

The car didn't slow down.

He was determined not to move aside. He held both arms out in front of him, closed his eyes and braced himself for impact. When he opened his eyes again the car was behind him. It had passed clean through him. He was untouched and unscathed. There had been no impact, no feeling, no pain. The car had simply driven straight through him.

The evidence was indisputable. He was a ghost.

No one could see him, no one could hear him. He was completely alone. He turned back to the lifeboat station where he'd left Bob in shock and Old Thorny cooking up some cock-and-bull story about how the German had shot him. What on earth should he do now?

There was a movement behind him and he spun round to see Günter emerging from the bushes. Checking the road he jogged off, compass and map in hand.

'Günter! Wait,' and with no better idea of what to do, he ran after his friend. They made their way north-west out of Mousehole and into the open countryside. They walked for miles and miles, over fields, down narrow lanes, up and down muddy footpaths and around silent farm buildings in the dead of night.

Jim found he had no limits to his energy. He didn't need to rest or sleep, he just kept going. It was strange to think that this was the fittest he'd ever felt.

There was no conversation as they travelled. As if chatting to Günter hadn't been difficult enough before the gunshot, it was out and out impossible now. But the solitude suited Jim and the walking and running distracted him. There were so many questions racing around his head, so much to think about. He concentrated on the simplicity of his next step and keeping up with Günter.

The one question that he kept returning to was whether or not this could be a dream. How could it possibly be real? He pinched himself to see if he would wake. He didn't. So he pinched Günter — and that had no effect either.

After several hours of walking and running, hiding, lying in ditches and running again they came to an old mine. Günter wanted somewhere to shelter and rest. He crawled through a fence and sprinted a long way downhill to the small mine shaft entrance. Jim wondered how Günter had known it was there and wondered if it had been marked on his map.

Checking again that the coast was clear, Günter disappeared into the shallow mine and crawled down it for several hundred feet, finally stopping in a large and circular cavern that formed a meeting point for several intersecting shafts. There, deep under the ground, Günter stopped and sat himself down to rest behind a cage lift.

'Günter? Can you hear me?' Jim didn't expect an answer, but he felt he had to ask the question one more time. There was no reply. They sat in silence, side by side, propped up against the cold rock.

Jim could see well enough in the dark and he watched as Günter took out and ate his pasty and drank Bob's milk. He pulled out the compass and the *höhenmesser* and turned them over in his hands. He was deep in thought and Jim wished he could ask what he was thinking, what his friend was planning on doing next. But he supposed that was obvious. Günter was planning on getting some rest and then continuing his journey homeward.

Günter nodded off into a fitful sleep, leaving Jim even more alone, with too much going on in his head to give him any peace of mind. He was cold. He was terrified and everything was strange and scary. He couldn't hold back the tears which streamed down his grubby cheeks, but no one heard his sobs and no matter how much he cried no trace of his tears were left where he sat.

The next morning Günter was even more focused. He smoothed out his clothes, pocketed the compass and drank the last swig of his milk. He set off back down the mine shaft leaving the *höhenmesser* behind on the floor.

'Oi, don't you want this,' Jim called after him. But he knew Günter wouldn't hear him.

It was clear to Jim that the *höhenmesser* wasn't as much use to Günter as the compass and Günter was travelling light.

Whilst Günter had slept Jim had realised that following him was comforting, but not a very good idea. Why would Jim want to follow Günter to Nazi Germany? That wasn't where he should be going. He needed to get back home to Bob.

Jim had spent the whole night thinking through the events of the evening before and he had considered all the options available to him in his current state.

It looked like he was a ghost.

If he was a ghost, then he must be dead.

But Bob wasn't dead, and he would need Jim's help and support now more than ever. Even if Bob couldn't see him or hear him, Jim knew he had to go back to Mousehole to help his best friend.

It wasn't much of a plan for an afterlife, but then he didn't have any idea how long this weird half-life of an existence would last. But as long as it did, he knew he wanted to be with Bob. He wanted to be there for Bob, like Bob had always been there for him.

Jim ran his fingers over the smooth glass of the tin instrument Günter had left behind. He reached out to pick it up but his hand passed straight through it. This inability to pick things up was going to be a total pain. The *höhenmesser* was his and he wanted to take it with him - but hard as he tried he couldn't pick the darn thing up.

Frustrated, he lashed out at it and somehow, miraculously, the little tin wobbled, nothing more than a tiny quiver, but it was movement. He tried again and again; at first nothing happened — his hand travelled clean through it time after time. But finally he nudged it with enough force to shunt it a short distance across the floor, to where it slipped straight down a large open drain.

Blast!

Jim lay flat on the floor of the dirty cavern and stuck his head through the narrow opening of the drain. It wasn't so much a drain-hole as a window onto another level of the mine, deeper and older than the one he was in. He could see the *höhenmesser*, caught a short way down, resting on a heavy wooden joist, high above the floor of the lower mine.

Jim stuck his arm through the hole. The wall surrounding the small opening offered no resistance to him and he could easily lean through it and touch the tin, but his fingers had no purchase and he realised that he would never be able to pick it up, the very best that he could achieve would be to knock it off the joist further into the mine. He gave up; there was nothing more he could do.

Annoyed with himself for losing the *höhenmesser* and frustrated with his new-found inabilities he stood up and went to brush the dirt from his shorts. There was no need, nothing had stuck to him. It was as if he didn't even exist — which, he supposed, was true; he didn't, not any more.

He crawled back through the narrow shaft that he and Günter had travelled down the night before and emerged into the bright sunlight of a new day. He was surprised how close he was to the sea and a cliff edge.

The sea and the coastline were rough and wild, leading Jim to suspect that he was on Cornwall's north coast, a long way from Mousehole. It was going to take him some time to find his way back to Bob.

He looked around at the grey brick buildings of the mine offices, the large steel headgear that dominated the landscape and the wooden black and white sign that read *Geevor Tin Mines Ltd*. He took a deep breath and strode right up to the mine's main gates and out onto the road.

It was time to go back home.

Chapter 37

Friday 8ᵗʰ August 2014

The weather kept getting better and better, and by Friday morning the tourists, or emmets as Sophie liked to call them, had descended en masse upon the West Country. At busy times like this none of the locals ventured out, preferring the seclusion of their own gardens to the heaving beaches and parks.

Callum and Jim were whiling away the morning sitting on top of Grandad's shed, looking out to St Michael's Mount and the sea beyond. Callum liked it up here, it was more interesting than sitting on the grass and Grandad and Nana left him alone — they said they couldn't find him, but he suspected they knew perfectly well where he was.

'I hear the Professor's been round again,' Jim said. 'Did he bother you?'

'Nah,' Callum flicked his fringe away from his eyes. 'He was fine. I reckon he's a good bloke. He wants me to help him so that he can move on, that's all.'

Since Jim's big telling off, the ghosts had more or less left Callum alone. Occasionally they would come by, and if Jim wasn't around to fend them off they would tell Callum about their problems and ask for his help.

'I don't mind so much when it's only one of them. It's when they all turn up at the same time that it scares me.'

Jim nodded. 'That's understandable. But you don't have to help any of them; you know that, don't you?'

'Yeah. But I was thinking... I think I'd like to, if I can.' He twisted round and smiled at Jim. 'I think it's the right thing to do. And if I help them sort their stuff out they can 'move on' and then they wouldn't be following me around anymore. It's a kind of win-win, wouldn't you say.'

'Good plan,' Jim agreed. 'But how easy is it going to be?'

Callum leant back, letting the sun warm his bare legs. 'Well, the naked Professor thinks that if he can get his theory to the right people then that'll be his 'business' dealt with. And Jack Holmes, he thinks he needs to get the Tor Vista guest house back to its former glory. I'm not sure how easy either of those things will be, but I'm working on them.

'And what about you, Jim? What do you need, so that you can move on?'

Jim ran a hand through his messy black hair, stretched out his pale and scrawny legs and rolled his long shorts up as high as they would go.

'Dunno. You could start by getting this awful jumper off me,' he laughed, tugging at his green tank top. 'You try wearing one of Ma's knits in August,' he sighed. 'But that ain't gonna happen, is it?'

'Come on, be serious. I'd like to help, if I can.'

'Well...' Jim shifted his position a little awkwardly. 'I suppose I'd like to see your grandad happier; that's all I've ever wanted. He's had such a tough time since... Well, let's just say he's had a tough time and I don't think I can move on until he's happy again.'

'Yeah, well, the Professor's idea for solving the world's energy problems is going to be easier to fix than that!' Callum laughed, and then stretched out and looked back at the horizon.

Jim scratched his head and pulled out a louse. 'It's a tricky thing, identifying what you *really* want.' Jim examined the nit. 'I mean; what do *you* really want?'

That was a good question. Callum thought long and hard and flicked his fringe twice in the process.

'I want someone who's still breathing, to believe me when I say I can see ghosts. And I think I want that person to be Sophie. We've been getting on OK, these last few days, having a laugh, that sort of thing. Then as soon as I mention you lot she gives me that look. The one that says: "shouldn't you be locked up for the good of the community?" It's not good.'

'Do y' like her?' Jim asked, with a mischievous grin.

'Not like that!' Callum punched Jim's arm — his hand sailed right through the ghost causing him to lose his balance and wobble unsteadily on the roof top.

'She's a friend — that's all. She's clever and witty and straightforward — I like that.' He blushed and hoped that Jim wouldn't notice.

Jim smiled. 'All right; but there are other people round here you could talk to. Have you tried talking to your grandad about any of this?'

Callum threw his hands up at the thought. 'Oh yeah! Because he's clever witty and straightforward — NOT!'

'He's not that bad,' Jim protested. 'I agree he's not clever, but he was a good laugh when he was younger and he's dead loyal. You'd have liked him if you'd met him before I died.'

Callum doubted it.

But it did make him wonder. Jim had died when he and Grandad were both twelve, the same age as he and Sophie were now. What impact would the death of your best friend have on you at the age of twelve? Was that why Grandad was always so miserable? Had it cast a shadow over him that he'd never been able to shift — from the age of twelve to eighty-two? Surely he could have put all that behind him at some point in the intervening seventy years?

But what if he hadn't? Was that why Jim hadn't moved on?

'Yeah, I probably would have liked him back then,' Callum acknowledged. 'But I don't think I can talk to him now. He's too awful.'

Jim was offended. It clearly bothered him that Callum had such a low opinion of Bob. They both stared out to sea, deep in their own thoughts until the sea breeze had blown any ill feeling away.

Jim sat up, a twinkle in his eye. 'What we need then is proof. We need something that will prove to Sophie that I exist — then you'll be happy; and if it proves I'm here to Bob at the same time, that's all for the better. And I think I might have just the thing!'

Callum liked the idea already. 'OK. What?'

Jim was grinning from ear to ear. 'What if I can lead you and Sophie to something that used to be mine? Something from when I was alive? Something that only I know about. Something that when you find it, it'll prove, beyond all doubt, that you must have spoken to me. It will prove that I exist!' Jim looked remarkably pleased with himself.

'And you've got something that can do that?'

'Yeah. Well, sort of. I hid it — well dropped it — on the day I died. Something from 1944. Your grandad'll recognise it, he'll be able to vouch for it, and when he does there'll be no doubt that I led you to it. Sophie and Bob will be convinced. Double whammy!'

Callum sat up. 'OK then,' he said. 'Tell me more...'

And while the sun beat down on the gardens and beaches of Cornwall, Callum and Jim sat on the roof of Grandad Bob's shed and made a plan to retrieve the *höhenmesser* from the crashed Focke-Wulf FW 190, the very one that Günter had left Mousehole with seventy years earlier. Jim knew exactly where it was, and now with Callum's help he was finally going to bring it back to Bob.

And if that didn't prove that he existed and cheer Bob up, Jim didn't know what would.

Chapter 38

Saturday 16th August 2014

Callum turned back to face the front of the bus, laughing out loud. 'I wish you could see what I can see,' he said to Sophie.

'I can't even begin to tell you how glad I am I can't!'

Sophie and Callum were on their second bus of the day, having already caught the Barbie pink village hopper from Mousehole to Penzance, where they changed at the seaside bus station to the Number 10 to Pendeen. They were now winding their way down ever more narrow roads, through a patchwork of ripe pre-harvest fields.

To Sophie the bus was almost empty; there were the two of them, the driver and a couple of old biddies sat up at the front, carrying heavy bags home from their Saturday morning shop in Penzance.

But to Callum the bus appeared almost full. Jim and the naked Professor with a soap-on-a-rope were sat behind him; Jack Holmes, the Tor Vista fisherman, sat across the aisle; the two pirates sat behind Jack and all of the lifeboat men were sitting across the back two rows, singing slightly naughty songs about a woman called Nell who liked rubber gloves and Pontefract cakes. Callum delighted in the silliness of it all.

'Sorry, mate,' Jim said, leaning forward and whispering into Callum's ear. 'They wanted to come along for the ride. They've promised to go off and do their own thing when we get there.'

Callum made no response. He was getting better at blanking Jim in front of Sophie. It was all part of the coping strategy that he and Jim had drawn up to help make Callum's ghostly experience seem as normal as possible, both for him and everyone else.

'Oi...' the driver called down the bus, taking his eyes off the road as they approached a hair raising hairpin bend. 'Did you say you wanted Geevor Mine?'

'Yeah, that's right,' Sophie shouted back.

'You know it's closed on Saturdays?' the driver told them, slamming on the brakes to avoid hitting a tractor that had pulled onto their road from a neighbouring field.

'Yep, that's why we're going. It'll be quieter.' Sophie shook her head. 'You sure about this?'

'Sure I'm sure,' Callum replied. 'Look, the worst case scenario is we have a nice day out on the north coast. But if all goes to plan, we'll have a nice day out *and* pick up Jim's lost tin.'

Sophie was intrigued. 'Ok, go on. Tell me what it is we're after?'

Callum grinned. 'Jim says it's a green tin instrument, circular, about ten centimetres across and four centimetres deep. He's doesn't know what it's meant to do. When I pushed him, he said it wasn't as useful as a compass.'

Callum lurched forward as the driver slammed on the brakes again. 'Mind you, lots of things aren't as useful as a compass, so that doesn't narrow it down much.'

'OK. So we're looking for a ten centimetre tin, of no known purpose, somewhere in the whole of Geevor mine, when it's closed!'

'Yeah, that's about it. You did say you'd give it a go — you didn't have to come.'

She shrugged. 'Suppose so, OK... How did it get into the mine then?'

'Dunno exactly. Jim said that on the night he died he followed another friend of his and Grandad's there, and that friend left it behind. Jim tried to pick it up but couldn't, what with him being dead and all. He says it's tucked away somewhere no one can see and it should still be there. And assuming it is, you'll have to believe everything I've been saying. And,' he added, 'I want a full apology, for you having taken the mickey out of me!'

'*If* you find it, and I very much doubt that you will,' Sophie said, waggling her finger at him, 'then I'll apologise. And I'll have an awful lot of questions too!' She delved into the pocket of her thin summer jacket and pulled out a packet of fruit pastilles which they shared.

'Did you see *Top Gear* on the telly last night?' she asked.

'No.' Callum groaned 'Did it clash with the *Antiques Roadshow*?'

The bus dropped Sophie and Callum right outside the main entrance of the mine in the shadow of the imposing Geevor headgear. The headgear is a massive pulley mechanism that looks like a tall tower of steel scaffolding, with wheels at the top and thick steel ropes hanging down. When the mine is working, it's used to winch miners up and down the mine shafts in tiny cramped cages.

Callum had expected a modern glass-fronted visitors' centre, like the ones he'd seen on visitor attractions in London, but there was nothing as flash as that here. Instead there were a series of grey concrete buildings that had previously been the works offices. Only a fresh lick of Trafalgar blue paint on their wooden doors gave any indication that the place was still in use.

He hadn't expected it to be so close to the sea either; he knew it was on the coast but this was right on the very edge of a cliff, it was a small miracle that it hadn't fallen into the sea.

Sophie explained that Geevor had been a working tin mine right up until the 1990s and it was now doing a roaring trade as a visitor attraction, although clearly not on Saturdays. Today the mine was absolutely deserted.

'It's popular with tourists because it's underground,' she said. 'It's what they call an all-weather attraction.' She held her hand out to confirm that it had indeed started to spit with rain. 'Oh great!'

The preceding few weeks of fabulous summer weather had been too good to last and the TV weatherman had predicted that Cornwall would be back to its wet and windy norm by the end the day. Callum looked out across the rough Atlantic Sea as the grey clouds approached with the promise of more typical British weather.

The wind was picking up and the rain was turning

to a constant drizzle. Callum pulled his hood up and his sleeves down. He wished he'd brought the raincoat that Nana had suggested that morning, but it was too late now.

'Right. Where to?' asked Sophie, drawing her jacket tighter around her and burying her hands deep into its pockets.

'This way,' shouted Jim, striding off to the right, around the perimeter fence of the mine buildings and towards the sea.

'This way,' Callum repeated and they set off after Jim.

As promised, the other ghosts didn't go with them, but instead set off for the visitors' block and the Hard Rock Museum. Fenced off areas and locked doors didn't slow them down at all and Callum was surprised how excited they all were about their day trip to the museum.

'Geevor's underground mines go on for miles under the sea bed,' Jim explained and Callum repeated as much to Sophie.

'Yeah, I came here on a school trip last year,' she told him. Not in an offhand snooty way like she might have done earlier in the summer before Callum had got to know her, but simply as a matter of fact. 'They used to have loads of pumps keeping the water out of the mines and when they failed any miners caught underground drowned.'

'Bit rough,' said Callum.

'That's right,' Jim said, talking to Sophie, forgetting that she couldn't hear him. 'If you remember, they've got a couple of big shafts below here; 'Victory' being the main one and 'Wheal Mexico' being the old nineteenth century one. Well, they use a network of tunnels off those to get to the mine face. They also have a number of adits — smaller tunnels — that were dug to remove the water that was pumped out from the major shafts.' Jim looked to Callum to relay his words to Sophie.

'Try and keep it simple,' he hissed under his breath, before summarising Jim's mini-lecture as: 'Err. There are big shafts and little tunnels.' Sophie was unimpressed.

Jim continued regardless and Callum started repeating as Jim was speaking, in an attempt to relay his words more accurately.

'Well, we are going in via the Deep Adit. That way we don't have to get into the visitors centre area, which is all fenced off.'

Callum stopped dead in his tracks and held his hand up, in a 'hold it right there' gesture. 'What? We're going down there, through a water tunnel? When the whole thing's closed — are you mad? You know I get claustrophobic!'

Sophie waited patiently for Callum to finish his argument, which as far as she was concerned, he was having entirely with himself.

'It's OK,' Jim assured him. 'I've checked the tides and we aren't going that deep underground. We'll be fine, honestly. I'm not going to take any risks, am I?'

'Yeah, well, you haven't got quite as much at stake as Sophie and me, have you? What with you already being dead!'

The discussion continued until Jim managed to convince Callum that it would all be OK, and then Callum announced to Sophie that it would be fine and there was nothing to worry about.

'Quite easily persuaded aren't you?' she observed.

Callum blushed. He knew how stupid it must look, to have an argument with yourself and lose. He pulled the hood of his sweatshirt closer around his face and walked faster.

It took a good half hour to reach the entrance to Deep Adit. They walked all around the mine and along the cliffs before reaching a rectangular hole cut into the red rock. At some point the entrance had been marked out and supported with wooden joists, but they had long since fallen down. Today it was nothing more than a dilapidated, narrow, man-made cave, slightly taller and slightly wider than a grown man. Rocks had fallen in and around the entrance and it all looked thoroughly neglected and very dangerous. It smelt of damp and clay, and when Callum breathed in he could taste metal in the air.

'Do you think it's safe?' Sophie asked.

'Yeah — if it was dangerous it would be sealed off. Anyway, most of the time the mine is open to the public, so it's got to be all health and safety checked.' He wasn't at all convinced by his own argument, but he didn't want to be a wuss.

'OK, but, I don't think the public use this entrance,' Sophie observed, leaning into the cramped tunnel. 'And don't you think we should have hard hats and pot holing equipment?'

'I've got a wind up torch,' Callum announced proudly, producing a tiny blue torch with a National Trust logo on the side. He wound the handle round and round and the place echoed with the loud ratcheting sound.

By now the rain was coming down horizontally and neither Callum nor Sophie wanted to hang around. Even the rather dodgy tunnel looked more appealing than staying out on the wet and windy cliff face.

'Come on,' yelled Jim. 'It's fine. These tunnels are used for pot holing all the time.'

Callum gave Sophie the final decision. 'It's your call, what do you reckon?'

'Let's do it,' she said. Callum beamed back at her, pleased and worried all at the same time.

He wound his torch up a bit more and set off after Jim, clambering across the fallen rocks, going further and further into the mouth of Deep Adit. Sophie followed close behind him, calling out every few steps, asking Callum to shine his torch where she was treading.

The tunnel sloped very gently upwards and narrowed as it went. Shortly after starting to dig the Deep Adit the original miners must have given up on creating a smooth ceiling, choosing instead to chip out just enough rock to fit themselves through. The result was like walking through a series of neatly fitted coffins. The space was wide enough for the shoulders of a man, tapering to fit his head, there was no room to spare at all. The grey sunlight back at the entrance made an eerie church window outline that glowed dimly behind them.

Callum's torch gave off a pathetic light; he pointed it ahead of himself but could only see more rough clay-like rock. He held his other hand out behind him and Sophie took it. They steadied each other as they tripped and stumbled down the narrow tunnel.

Chapter 39

Saturday 16th August 2014

Callum hated being in confined places, he always had. Now, as he trudged through the Deep Adit tunnel, he could feel his heart rate increasing and his breath coming in short sharp bursts. He took long slow breaths and tried to calm himself down.

'Not much further,' said Jim. 'And then this crosses both main shafts, that's where the *höhenmesser* is. I'm gonna go ahead; you keep following the tunnel. At the end you'll have to do some climbing, but it's only about six feet and there's plenty of footholds. It'll be easy. Wait for me when get to a big cave with the cage, all right?' and before Callum could say it wasn't all right, Jim shot off, his waiflike figure speeding easily down the cramped tunnel.

'Jim says it's not much further,' Callum relayed to Sophie — who ten minutes later accused Jim of being a liar in surprisingly bad language for a young lady.

After clambering up the six-foot wall, Callum and Sophie found themselves in an almost perfectly circular cavern as large as a house. The ceiling was roughly chipped out of the rock like a huge bowl. A cage lift was positioned in the centre and Sophie said that meant that they must be underneath the tall headgear they had seen when they first got off the bus. Half a dozen other tunnels came into this central point, at least one other small adit and several big mineshafts.

Sophie stood up straight and stretched. 'Weird being down here, on our own, isn't it?'

Callum nodded, 'Yeah. It doesn't feel right; I think we should go back.'

'Don't be silly, we've made it this far. We might as well have a look around. Can I have the torch for a minute?'

Callum handed it over, then had a fit when she turned it off, to see how dark it was — the answer was pitch black, like you've never seen black before.

'Sorry,' she said, flicking it back on.

Holding the torch out in front of her she went over to examine the cage. Callum followed her closely, not wanting to be away from her or the torch. They were right down in the bowels of the earth, entirely on their own. This was not good. Why had he ever agreed to do this and where was Jim anyway?

Sophie was peering down the main mine shaft when Jim appeared out of another smaller tunnel, with the ghost of a long-dead miner in full helmet, overalls and hob nail boots. Callum could tell he'd been down here for a very long time because his helmet was topped with a candle and the wax had run down and set all over it, as if a pigeon had pooped on his hat. Whenever this ghost had died, it had to have been before battery operated helmet torches.

'Callum,' Jim called out. 'I was chatting to Gorran here and explaining what we are up to.'

'Hi Gorran,' said Callum. The miner's eyes grew to the size of saucers, a brilliant white in sharp contrast to his dirt blackened face. He let out a stream of language so heavily accented that Callum couldn't tell if it was English, Cornish or anything else, either way he had no idea what the old miner was saying.

Jim laid a hand on Gorran's arm and he quietened. 'Right,' said Jim addressing Callum, Gorran and Sophie. He put on his 'this means action' voice. 'I was over here.' He ran to the far corner of the cavern.

Callum grabbed Sophie's arm and pulled her and the torch in the same direction. 'Jim was here,' he relayed to her, pointing to the exact same place Jim was pointing to. Sophie shone the torch at the floor and then in her own face so that Callum could see her expression. He didn't care.

'My friend; he was sat here.' Jim motioned to a small area tucked away behind the cage. Callum repeated it for Sophie — she'd come this far, he knew she was as intrigued as he was.

Jim carried on. 'And he left the instrument here.' He pointed his scrawny finger to the empty ground.

'And...' said Callum staring at him accusingly, hoping more than anything that that wasn't *it* and they weren't on a wild goose chase.

'And then he left and I tried to pick it up. But of

course I couldn't.' Gorran made sympathetic grunting noises and both Callum and Jim ignored him. 'I tried to pick it up and of course I couldn't. Eventually I knocked it, not a lot, but enough.' He turned to Callum, grinning madly, clearly still pleased with the achievement of his first physical movement as a ghost. 'Like I did to your nana's ornament and your hospital papers — remember? Because when you focus very *very* hard, you can sometimes make a tiny movement — not a lot, but just enough to nudge something.'

'And…' said Callum.

'And,' said Jim full of self-congratulatory pride. 'I knocked it down there!'

Callum didn't seem so impressed. 'Then he knocked it down there,' he told Sophie, pointing to the drain-like archway on the floor.

'Oh,' said Sophie. They were both disappointed. All this way to be told the thing had slipped down a drain. If that was the case why had Jim bothered to drag them all this way?

'It got caught on a wooden joist,' said Jim. 'And it's still there.'

Callum repeated this for Sophie and the two of them threw themselves on to the dirty floor, flat on their stomachs and peered through the small hole. It was an archway, about half a metre wide, cut into the red rock and showing a drop down to a lower shaft. Callum guessed that the arch was a drain, used if the cavern ever flooded.

He stuck his head through and his shoulders jammed on the sides of the arch. 'Can't see a thing,' he shouted back.

'Gorran's seen it,' Jim told them, almost jumping up and down he was so excited. 'It's there! He's seen it! It's caught on a ledge, about a yard down from here, high above the old Wheal Mexico shaft.'

Callum updated Sophie, who couldn't resist shoving Callum out of the way to have a look for herself. Sophie's slender body was an easy fit through the arched hole, and she wiggled through quite a long way, shouting back to Callum, 'hold my legs.' Her voice was all echoey from the depths of the cavern. Callum grabbed hold of her below the knees and held on tightly.

'I can see it!' she cried. 'It's like a large sweet tin, with bits of green paint — is that it?'

Jim couldn't contain himself, 'Yes that's it, that's it!'

'Cut me a bit more slack, I'm going to try and reach it'.

Callum held onto her legs as she shuffled further forward until her whole body had disappeared into the hole. It was dark in the cavern because Sophie had the torch. It gave off the merest hint of a dim yellow glow surrounding her outline.

'I can touch it,' she shouted. 'But I can't pick it up…' She had wiggled so far through the archway that no more than the back of her knees and shins were visible.

'I want to see,' shouted Callum, 'Jim, you hold her legs.'

'No, I can't. Don't be silly, Callum, you know…'

But Callum didn't wait, he crawled forwards to try and peer through the drain hole to look for himself, relying on Jim to hold Sophie in place.

It's difficult to say at which point Callum realised

that Jim was not the right person to be holding on to Sophie's legs. At first when she started to slip forward he assumed Jim was giving her some more room to try and reach her prize; she must have thought the same because she didn't call out until she was slipping too fast to stop, and by then it was too late.

'I can't hold her,' screamed Jim.

'Sophie. Stop!' yelled Callum — as if she had any chance of halting the slide herself.

And in the blink of an eye her feet slipped through the roughly cut drain and Sophie and the wind-up-torch were gone.

The cavern was plunged into total darkness.

Sophie's scream could be heard getting fainter and fainter until there was an ominous thud that echoed through the tunnels and the cavern.

Then silence.

Callum shook. He collapsed where he was and fear washed through him, wave after wave, each one worse than the one before. Sophie was injured at best, dead a real possibility. He called out her name. There was no reply. He called again and again. What should he do? He was stuck miles underground, he had no clue where she had fallen or how to get there.

'Sophie!' he cried again and again.

Chapter 40

Saturday 16ᵗʰ August 2014

This was his fault.

It was his fault that she was here.

It was his fault she had fallen. It was all his fault.

No one had any idea where they were. No one was going to come and help; this was where they would both end their lives. Down a Cornish tin mine, in the dark, alone. Callum's pulse raced and raced, he couldn't get enough air into his lungs, it was as if he were drowning, gulping and gulping for air.

The enormity of the situation flooded over him.

What had he done?

What had he done to Sophie?

Callum's head went fuzzy, his knees gave way and he passed out.

Chapter 41

Saturday 16th August 2014

Callum came to his senses to find Jim slapping him hard across the face.

'Get a grip. Come on Callum, get a bleedin' grip!'

If he'd been able to feel Jim's hand it would have hurt.

It hadn't been a nightmare. He was still in the deep, dark, damp mine — without Sophie. He could just about make out Jim and behind him the old miner, Gorran, the weak flicker from the candle on his helmet giving off the only light in the place. Further behind them he could hear other voices too.

'What's going on?' he spluttered.

Jim brought him up to speed. 'Gorran's found Sophie. She's on the floor of the old Wheal Mexico shaft. She's badly hurt, but alive. I've pulled everyone from the bus together and we're forming a rescue party — but we need you.'

'Where is she?'

'Down there,' Jim pointed to the drain. 'You remember; you dropped her down the drain?'

Callum felt as if the walls of the cavern were closing in around him. He remembered all right.

Jim pushed on. 'She's breathing — but not well. She's a bit… broken, but it could be a lot worse.'

Callum stared at him in wide eyed disbelief. 'How? How could this be any worse?'

Jim dropped his voice, so as not to offend the ghosts. 'At least she's not dead!'

Was that the best news he could expect? That she wasn't dead — yet? He staggered to his feet, rubbing the dust from his hair and face.

'Some of the lifeboatmen and their Skipper are with her. The rest of us are trying to work out how to get her out of here. It's lucky we've got Gorran, he knows where everything is, but we can't move her until you come to your senses.' Jim laid a comforting arm on Callum's shoulder. 'It'll be OK,' he said and then he turned to the old miner. 'Right Gorran, let's go.'

Gorran said something completely indecipherable and the group moved off at a cracking pace. Peg the pirate's wooden leg clomped on the rough stone floor sounding out a drum like beat to the procession. Jack Holmes from the guest house came over to check that Callum was OK, but Callum wasn't interested. He ran clean through the lot of them to catch up with Jim and Gorran and he hurried them along as they made their way down the steep sloping passage ways, heading further and further into the depths of the mine.

After about twenty minutes a small group came into

view, they were crouched on the floor ahead, wearing the reassuring blue and orange of the RNLI, and in between them sprawled across the floor was Sophie. Some of her spiky red hair visible in the failing light from her torch.

'She's still unconscious,' the Skipper reported to Jim and then to Callum he said, 'we need you to loosen her clothing, to help her breathe, then you can move her. Careful… we're worried about potential spinal injuries.'

Callum let his mouth hang open, staring at Sophie's crumpled little body. She looked awful. She had landed on her left side and her left arm and leg were sticking out at unnatural angles. She had a gash above one eye and there was blood everywhere. He bent down and wiped her face clean with the sleeve of his sweatshirt. He loosened her jacket and shirt, fumbling with the fastenings.

This wasn't right. None of this was right. Callum hadn't done a lot of first aid, but he knew that you weren't meant to move someone with suspected spinal injuries and he told the Skipper as much.

'How about I go up to the surface and get help. Then proper medics can come down and move her.'

The Skipper was looked offended.

'I mean proper, alive and breathing medics that can pick her up and move her, with a back board and stuff, like when I had my accident. That's what we need.'

'You're right, laddie. That is what we need — but the tide is coming in and the water's rising. We haven't got time to get you to the surface, let alone get any equipment down here.'

Water? What water? Of course; they were in a sea mine. He had come down some pretty steep tunnels on

228

his way to find Sophie. They must be at least at sea level by now. There was a distinct and ominous wetness to the walls. Callum's shoulders slumped further. This tunnel must flood with every high tide. They were never meant to be this far underground. His hands started trembling and sweat began to pour out of him.

The naked Professor came hurrying up from the far tunnel swinging his soap-on-a-rope. 'Skipper, the water's at the next bend. It's moving faster than I'd expected. I've re-calculated and I think we've got fifteen minutes before it reaches her.'

There was no doubt the Skipper was in charge. He stood tall and broad, looking the business in his RNLI overalls. 'Thanks, Prof. OK, we need to get her moved.' He called over to Gorran. 'You — we need one of those crates on wheels. The type of thing you use for moving tin to the surface. There's got to be one down here somewhere.'

'Argh urgh argh umm,' the old miner said in his unintelligible accent and Jack translated it into: 'There's one back the way we came, but we'll need young Callum to push it.'

'Shouldn't we move her a bit first?' Callum stuttered.

But the Skipper wasn't deviating from his plan. 'No point moving her a few feet – we've got to get her all the way out and soon. We've got fifteen minutes. Go get the skip.'

Callum daren't argue. He nodded to the Skipper and then he and Gorran raced off with Jack Holmes close on their heels. Fifteen minutes until the water reached her. Surely things couldn't get any worse.

Gorran had found an old wooden crate at the mine face a short distance from where Sophie lay. It was heavy, and the metal wheels had rusted almost solid. Callum heaved and pushed at it whilst time ticked by.

It didn't move at all.

'The water's reached her feet,' shouted the naked Professor, hurrying towards them ahead of a trickle of cold sea water.

'I can't move it,' Callum cried in desperation and the Professor, Gorran and Jack tried pushing it too. They were entirely ineffective but provided Callum with much needed moral support.

It started to roll.

It was like manoeuvring the heaviest and most misaligned shopping trolley imaginable, but somehow Callum pushed and shoved it through the rough tunnels until he was back with Sophie. The water was licking at her legs and a very desperate Jim was attempting to hold the water back without any success what so ever.

Callum grabbed Sophie's limp body around the waist and began to drag her towards the skip. Considering how slight she was, she weighed a ton.

He puffed and panted and pulled and heaved. He managed to lift Sophie over the top of the skip and allowed gravity to slide her body in. She folded up pretty much in half and fell into the wooden crate. If she didn't have a back injury before, she certainly did now!

'She's in the skip, Skipper,' he called out and a cheer went up from the assembled ghosts. The water was lapping around the wheels of the rusty old cart and the extra weight of Sophie's unconscious body made pushing it back up hill even harder work.

'Gorran! Lead the way!' cried Jim and they were off again, with Callum straining to ram the cart up the steep slope, over the uneven floor, and through the maze of tunnels. The ghosts crowded around, urging him on. The lifeboatmen lined up along both sides of the cart and ran alongside it, as if they were launching a boat into the storm.

Sophie's red hair bobbed up and down in front of Callum's face.

'How much further?' he yelled.

'Nearly there,' Jim replied.

The rescue party rounded a corner and slowed to a stop in the cavern with the cage. Callum skidded to a halt, ramming the skip clean through Jim and halfway through Gorran. They'd made it!

'Well done,' said Jim, giving Callum a hearty slap on the back. 'So… how we going to get her back down Deep Adit?'

Callum sank to his knees. He had clean forgotten about the Deep Adit. To get back out the way they had got in he would need to drop Sophie down a six foot vertical rock face and then drag her through the tunnel. It was way too narrow to accommodate the skip and even if he had the strength to carry her over his shoulders or in his arms there wasn't enough headroom for the two of them in the narrow adit. It was impossible.

The ghosts congregated at the edge of the cavern assessing the drop. A couple of lifeboat men jumped down and there was much muttering as they all worked on different theories.

'We can't go that way,' announced the Skipper, who had been deep in conversation with Gorran and Jack Holmes. 'I think we're going to need to use the cage. Gorran says it still works. I believe it's the only way to get the girl out.' He looked around for the people he wanted. 'Professor, Jack: you go up to the top and check out the mechanism.' He sent up two of his own men too.

Callum was so grateful the Skipper was there. It was a good plan. It meant he and Sophie were just a short ride in the cage from civilisation, a 999 call to the ambulance service and then safety. They were going to be all right.

Jack, the Professor and two of the lifeboatmen walked to the bottom of the lift shaft, saluted the Skipper and started to climb. The mine shaft was shored up with scaffolding girders; the ghosts made quick work of climbing it and were soon out of sight. Gorran muttered something in his own unique tongue and sped off after the advance party, leaving the others twiddling their thumbs at the bottom of the mine.

The ghosts talked amongst themselves while Callum tried to make Sophie more comfortable in her crate. He wound up the torch and took off his hoody to lay it over her and keep her warm. He tried to fold her arms over her chest, being as careful as he could with her left arm. It wasn't so much broken as pulverised. When he picked up her wrist the rest of the arm didn't follow it, leaving a wobbly bit of flesh sagging between the broken ends of her bones. It quite turned his stomach and he dropped it.

'That'll be fine then,' he muttered to himself and ignored the Skipper who was shaking his head and tutting at him.

Callum lowered his head to listen to Sophie's breathing; it was shallow, but steady. His long fringe flopped across her face and she stirred.

'Mum?'

'Sophie... Sophie. It's me, Callum. It's OK, I'm here.'

'Oh great!' she mumbled and passed out again.

Chapter 42

Saturday 16th August 2014

'Sophie, Sophie!' Callum wanted her to wake up again. In truth he wanted her to spring up miraculously and start looking after him.

He smoothed her hair and whispered to her, without any idea of whether or not she could hear him.

'Sophie, you've had a nasty fall, but you're going to be OK. We're in the mine — do you remember? We're waiting for the cage to come and take us to the surface.'

Sophie murmured something that Callum couldn't catch and the Skipper came over to see if he could help.

'Look, lad, you want to make sure her windpipe's not obstructed. Tilt her head up like this,' he placed his hands gently behind Sophie's head showing Callum how he would move her if he could.

Callum was in awe of the Lifeboat Skipper. He didn't believe for one moment that the RNLI trained their lifeboatmen in making people comfortable when they were folded in half in a wooden crate on wheels. But he assumed the general principles were all the same, so he adjusted Sophie's head as requested and then went back to trying to stroke her better.

'Do you think her breathing's OK?' he asked.

'It's getting better,' the Skipper replied. 'Not perfect, but steady. Do you have a first aid kit on you, lad?'

Callum stared down at his feet.

'Pretty ill prepared for today's adventure, weren't you?'

Callum needed no further chastisement. He knew he was to blame and that he would never ever be able to forgive himself for this.

'Here they come,' called out Jim and Callum saw the small group of ghosts climbing back down the lift shaft.

The Professor jumped the last few feet, caught his breath, positioned his soap-on-a-rope and addressed the expectant group.

'Right! The lift is operated by an electric winder that pulls the steel ropes attached to the cages. There's one cage at the top and one at the bottom. As one goes up, the other comes down.' The Professor pointed to the thick steel ropes that hung down the lift shaft to the cage and moved his hands up and down, demonstrating the alternating movements of the two counter-balanced lifts. 'They are pulled by the headgear above ground — that's the big tower.' There was much nodding and grunting from everyone.

'The winder machinery is locked away in a small housing next to the headgear; it's called the winder house. Gorran says the machinery still runs on special occasions, so we can use it — as long as we can get it going. Gorran's shown us the controls.

'There's a large red electrical switch that needs to be flicked to the 'on' position —that'll get the electricity flowing; then a big black lever that needs to be pulled down to free up the cages. After that the cages can be controlled by the buttons inside them. Callum can manage those buttons easily enough.

'The problem we've got is that we can't flick the electricity switch on or pull the lever. Callum could, but he won't be able to get into the winder house. You've never seen so much anti-vandal security. Multiple locks, bars over the windows — it's like the sea mining equivalent of the Tower of London.'

There was a lot of murmuring.

Callum put his hand up. 'Professor, is there any way I can break into the winder house? I don't mind doing anything illegal.'

'Clearly!' heckled one of the lifeboat men, with a snigger.

The Professor ignored him. 'Sorry Callum, but you won't be able to. We've checked out all the weak points, and — well, there aren't any weak points.'

Callum was having none of this. He took a deep breath and shouted at the top of his voice. 'This doesn't end here — you hear me? Sophie needs to get out of here *now*. So get your sorry arses back up that lift shaft and get doing your 'knocking things a little bit' all together and get that switch switched and the lever levered NOW!'

They all stared at Callum.

Sophie murmured, causing Callum to yell again even louder. 'I SAID, NOW.'

The Lifeboat Skipper stood forward. 'OK men, it's worth a try. To the winder house! COME ON!' And with a war like cry to action the lifeboatmen took to the scaffolding of the lift shaft and started to climb.

'Aye Aye Cap'n' shouted Peg and he and the Pirate Cap'n joined them, followed by Jack from the guest house and the naked Professor, who once again took his soap-on-a-rope between his teeth and started climbing.

'Callum, go with them,' Jim shouted. 'As soon as you're up there, you can call for an ambulance. I'll wait with Sophie. You go.'

Callum didn't move. 'But... Sophie will think she's on her own.'

She groaned in response to hearing her name and Callum leant over and wiped more of the blood and dirt from her face.

'You OK?'

'Yeah,' she grunted.

'I'm going to get the lift that will take you to the top. Jim'll be here with you while I'm gone and I'm leaving you the torch. OK?' Callum gave the battered old torch one last wind up and laid it in the skip next to her. 'Don't worry. Jim's here, he'll take care of you.'

'All right,' she mumbled.

Oh no, thought Callum. Had she bumped her head that badly?

'Can you see him?'

'No,' she said. 'But I believe you. All right. Please, just go get the lift.'

Callum was thrilled she was talking. 'Can you feel your legs?' he asked.

'Yeah — and they hurt like hell. GET THE LIFT.'

'She'll be fine,' said Jim.

Callum had to agree; and with that comforting thought he went to the base of the lift shaft and started to climb. The ghosts had made it look so easy — it most definitely was not.

The lift shaft had been cut vertically through the rock and the sides shored up by iron girders. Extra girders were zigzagged across the rough walls for more support making the whole structure relatively climbable.

Soon Callum's palms stung from clinging to the rusting metal and his knuckles were bleeding from where they kept knocking against the rock. His arms ached and his legs started shaking but he pushed on, getting closer and closer to the speck of light at the top.

Jack Holmes was waiting at the top and as Callum came into view he started cheering him on and offering advice on how best to manage the last bit of the climb. Callum threw his hands over the edge and pulled himself up on to the smooth flat surface of the floor, where he lay panting, trying to catch his breath.

'This way,' yelled Jack, not letting exhaustion get the better of Callum. He hurried Callum to his feet and out of the cages area, thrusting him into the daylight and rain.

Callum winced, shielding his eyes. He stretched himself out, to let the heavy rain cool down his shaking limbs. He was in amongst the mine buildings, behind the visitors' centre fencing that he had seen that morning.

'Come on, boy!' Jack cried from around the next corner. Callum staggered on and found him standing outside a small building, conveniently labelled for visitors and teenagers in distress as 'The Winder House.' Jack was peering into a small window, stroking his Captain Birdseye beard. Callum ran over to him and pressed his nose to the glass.

The inside of the winder house was like the cockpit of an old airliner. A tattered blue chair took centre stage, surrounded by a large white console with two huge dials tracking the position of the cages. There were a number of coloured bulbs and one enormous black lever, positioned bolt upright on the left of the winder driver's chair. The Skipper was sitting in the chair, his hand on the black lever — ready to give it all he'd got.

Meanwhile everyone else was crowded around a bank of switches on the opposite wall — and in particular the large red electricity override switch.

'One, two, three, pull…' they cried altogether. The effort that they were putting in was clear. Callum held his breath. Nothing.

'Come on!' he cried and a few of the lifeboatmen turned to give him the thumbs up.

'OK, let's try one at a time,' shouted the Skipper, leaving his chair and walking around the desk to the large red switch. 'With all of you pulling at the same time no one can get a proper focus on it.' The crowd stood back. The Skipper placed his hands on the switch, one resting on top of the other; he pushed down hard with everything he had. It quivered. It didn't flick to the 'on' position, but there was some movement — it was progress. Cheers went up from the assembled ghosts and Jack melted through the wall to join his colleagues as they slapped each other on the back in what Callum thought were highly premature celebrations.

He needn't have worried; the Skipper called them to order. 'It's not enough, we need the whole thing flipped over. Who wants to try next?'

A series of lifeboatmen stepped forward and followed their leader's example. Each time the switch seemed to move a little further, until a very burly lifeboatman stepped up for his turn, cried out: 'you beauty,' and pushed the switch all the way to the 'on' position. The whole place lit up. The lifeboat man had turned on Geevor's main electrics. There were cheers and whoops of joy from everyone.

'OK. Now for the cage lever,' cried the Skipper, trying to regain a little restraint in the winder house. The black lever had to be pulled down, like a giant gear stick. The Skipper was first to try. Again, nothing. The pirate Cap'n was keen and spent an age pulling, but to no avail. The burly lifeboatman, still panting from his exertions with the electricity switch tried — and it wobbled, but not enough.

'Argh, umm, oarrr, argh, urgh, errr, umm, errr.' Gorran said quietly to Jack, who held a hand up for silence and translated: 'Gorran used to be the winder-man here,' he told the group, 'before electrification. He's watched all the winder-men through the ages and he understands the process. He'd like to have a go. The last time he was in charge he failed to get everyone out, and he wants to put that right. If that's OK with you, Skipper.'

A respectful silence fell over the crowd as they parted

to let the old winder-man take his place. The Skipper patted him on the back.

Gorran positioned himself in the big seat, testing out the arm rests and stretching his feet under the desk. He took off his helmet and sat it down next to him. He surveyed all the monitors and ran a single finger across the line of flashing lights. He calmly put his left arm out to take hold of the big black lever. Focused on it with every fibre of his being and pulled down hard and fast until he had nothing left to give. The lever stuttered and then eased itself down, clicking into position.

The surrounding ghosts let out an almighty cheer that nearly took the roof off the old winder house, even with its steel bolts and bars.

'Arumph, ergh, umn, argh.' Gorran cried in triumph, pointing at Callum.

Jack stuck his head through the wall. 'Go!' he shouted. 'Callum, GO! The cages are free to move, take this one down and get Sophie straight back up here. Gorran will monitor the cages until you are both safe on the surface. I'll stay up here with him. GO!'

Jack was grinning from ear to ear. Gorran looked even happier. The lifeboat crew, the pirates and the naked Professor poured out of the old building, hurrying Callum along to the cages.

The Professor ran next to him. 'Phone for the ambulance — before you go down. That way it can be on its way while you are riding up and down in the cage.'

'But my mobile doesn't work!' Callum said, throwing his hands in the air.

As ever, the Professor had thought of everything. He pointed to an old landline phone housed at the back of the cage area. Callum picked it up and dialled 999.

The cage doors slid open onto the rain-soaked surface, and Callum pushed Sophie's skip out of the lift and into the daylight. The ghosts stood to attention, making a guard of honour for them, clapping, shouting and whooping. Peg stamped his wooden leg, the Professor swung his soap-on-a-rope around his head and Jack Holmes did a quick side-step in front of the Professor to save Sophie's blushes.

Jim had ridden in the cage with Callum and Sophie and he followed them out, mighty relieved to be on the surface again.

With his task accomplished, Gorran stepped out of the winder house for the very last time and took a bow, to great applause. He raised a hand in acknowledgment and with a broad smile faded away, waving goodbye as he went.

The crowd fell silent as the air around Gorran lit up with blue sparks of electricity.

'He's moved on,' Jim said quietly.

When the area where the old miner had stood stopped sparking and all trace of him had gone the ghosts broke into more spontaneous cheering.

'Do you know what Gorran means in Cornish?' Jim asked.

Callum shook his head.

'It means Hero.'

'It certainly does,' agreed Callum.

He pushed Sophie in her wooden skip right up to the gates of the Geevor Tin Mine. He couldn't get them open, but it didn't matter, they had come far enough.

In the distance a familiar sound rang out. It was the distinctive wailing of an ambulance. Callum positioned Sophie in her skip so that she could see out and rearranged his jumper to make a cushion for her head. He wanted her to be as comfortable as possible — which frankly, wasn't very comfortable at all.

The ambulance screeched to a halt on the other side of the gates. The passenger door flew open and a paramedic leapt out. As she ran towards the gates Callum raised his hand in a tentative wave. Oh good grief, he thought — it's the same woman.

'Not you two again!' she cried.

Chapter 43

Monday 18ᵗʰ August 2014

Jim said that although he liked Sophie very much there was no way he was going to visit her. He said that hospitals always gave him the heebie-jeebies. Callum pointed out how ridiculous that sounded, as he was already dead and therefore his health couldn't get much worse. But either way, Jim refused to go, so Callum set off for Penzance on his own.

He had heard, via Nana and Linda, that Sophie was going to have to stay in for another few days. She had four broken ribs, her arm had been re-set and her leg was broken in two places. But apart from that she was doing fine, and Callum thought that was a small miracle, all things considered!

Nana had also told him that he couldn't put it off any longer. He needed to get himself over to that hospital to see how she was doing and apologise.

On arriving at the West Cornwall Hospital, Callum

asked at reception where he'd find Sophie, and had a wry little smile to himself when he was directed to the same room in which he'd spent his own traumatic night. That had been the night when he'd first met Jim and refused to accept him as a ghost, probably because Jim was suffering from the heebie-jeebies, what with it being a hospital and all.

Callum hovered outside Sophie's door, a bag of sweaty grapes in one hand and some wilting yellow flowers in the other. Nana had given both to him when he'd left the bungalow this morning and neither had travelled well.

He knocked.

'Come in,' Sophie sounded her usual confident self.

Callum edged through the doorway and stood at the bottom of her bed, assessing for himself the state of her injuries. It looked bad. Nana, or Linda, or both of them, had underplayed it. She was a mess.

Her head was bandaged up so much that it was as if she had a badly fitted turban on; her left arm and leg were suspended from the ceiling in some kind of pulley system that kept them both raised up off the bed. She had two black eyes and cuts and grazes on almost everything that wasn't already bandaged or plastered.

'You look awful. Not just awful — off the scale terrible. I mean… man alive, you wouldn't think anyone could look so bad and not be dead!'

'Thanks! It's great to see you too.'

Callum flicked his fringe out of the way and started again. 'Sorry. How are you feeling? You look great, considering!'

She shrugged and beckoned him over to sit on the

chair beside her. He sat down sheepishly and clung to the grapes and flowers.

'I'm so sorry about everything.' He spoke to his shoes rather than Sophie. 'It was a stupid idea to go into the mine. I shouldn't have made you do it.'

'You didn't make me do anything,' she said, using her good hand to pluck the bag of grapes out of his lap. She went to eat one, but on a closer inspection thought better of it and popped them on to her crowded bedside table.

'Don't stress yourself.' She sounded more relaxed than he had expected. 'I was up for it all. I agreed to go. I wanted to try and reach the thing on the joist. I just wish I hadn't leant so far through that hole; I must have tipped the balance of my weight too much for you to hold. It's my fault not yours.'

Interesting, thought Callum. Perhaps she didn't realise that he'd let go and left Jim holding her legs — a ghost with an intrinsic inability to hold on to anything. Should he say something? Could he get away with this? Should he even try and get away with this? Would that be right?

'Is Jim with you?'

'No — he doesn't like hospitals.' He paused. 'Sophie, when you fell — did anything strange happen? I mean, have you seen anyone like… Jim, since, well, since..?'

Sophie beckoned him closer and Callum leant in. 'I thought I might have,' she whispered. 'Because the other night an old lady in a white gown came into my room moaning about how there's nothing on the telly anymore and how you can't buy salad cream and bloater paste anywhere. But then a nurse came in and said she was an escapee from the old people's ward. So no, I haven't seen anything unusual at all. I thought it would be cool if I had, but I haven't — it's been a bit of a let-down really.

'Mind you, when I was in the mine, waiting for you to get the lift, I knew I wasn't alone. I don't know how, but I knew Jim was with me.'

'He was,' said Callum.

'I know.'

They sat in silence for a moment. Callum was thrilled. She believed. Sophie believed him. He wasn't going mad; someone else knew what was going on and that he was telling the truth. He relaxed for the first time for weeks.

Callum offered Sophie the mangled flowers and she asked him to put them in a vase on the windowsill. As he did, she told him about her broken bones and how she'd need a sling and crutches for at least a couple of months, possibly longer, but after that she should be back to normal. She told him how fed up she was with being stuck in hospital and how awful the food was. Callum sympathised. It wasn't long before the conversation turned again to Jim. Now that Sophie believed in him she wanted to know more.

'What's he like?' she asked. 'Tell me all about him.'

Callum sat back down and made himself comfortable. 'Well, he's our age, but he looks about ten. He's small and scruffy, he wears long baggy shorts, a dirty shirt and a hand-knitted jumper without sleeves.' Callum rolled his eyes, as if it were a real fashion disaster.

Sophie tutted at him. 'That's a tank top, you numpty. That's what everyone wore in those days.'

'If you say so; I think it's pretty shocking. Anyway,

he's dead cheerful and everything. Well dead and cheerful.' He laughed at his own joke. 'He always sees the bright side of everything. And the other ghosts, they kind of respect him, because he's been around for such a long time and he's really clever. The pirates must have been around longer but they don't count because they're so stupid.'

'Was it his idea to go to the mine?'

'Yeah, I suppose so. I wanted to find something that would prove he existed, to show you. And he wanted to prove he existed to Grandad. And he thought that if we got the tin thing out of the mine it would prove everything. You saw it. Did it prove he existed to you?'

'Suppose it helped.'

'I wish you'd been able to reach it, I never did get to see it.'

Sophie straightened herself up in the bed. 'Oh, it wasn't anything special. It was a lot like Opa's compass, the one back at the guest house. Dad uses it as a paper weight. There are probably hundreds of them around. It reminded me of a speedometer or something. I think it would have taken more than that to convince your grandad.'

'Oh. OK then,' he said, not able to hide his disappointment.

The door opened and Dr Akbar strolled in. Callum thought she looked a lot less tired than she had done when he had been staying in this room.

'Hello Callum; I wondered when you'd show up again. I understand you are to blame for the state Sophie's in, is that right?'

'Yes, sorry,' Callum twisted in his chair. Evidently, being less tired didn't make her any nicer.

'Don't apologise to me, it's Sophie who needs the apology — and the police and the mine authorities, I should expect.'

'Yeah, they came round yesterday.'

Sophie gasped.

'It's OK. I apologised and Nana convinced them that we'd suffered enough. They're dropping the charges.'

'What charges?' demanded Sophie.

Dr Akbar was taking her pulse at the time, and judging from the expression on both their faces it must have been rising sharply.

'Breaking and entering, mainly,' Callum explained.

'Well I think it's fair to say that Sophie's suffered enough for the both of you,' said the doctor, laying Sophie's wrist back in her lap. 'How you got away without a criminal record is beyond me!'

Callum knew exactly how he'd got away with it. It was entirely thanks to Jim, who had freaked out the man from the mine authority when he was in the bungalow talking with Nana and Grandad. Jim had passed through the man a dozen times making him shiver like it was mid-winter despite the warm August weather. He'd knocked over his papers and his coffee; the man had been terrified and couldn't get out of the house fast enough.

Nana always said Grandad was very lucky. Callum was beginning to realise that Grandad's good fortune wasn't luck at all — it was the result of having Jim constantly by his side, nudging things into place for him, smoothing his journey through life. It wasn't luck at all, it was Jim's ghostly interventions.

'Once again you appear to have the luck of the Irish. Is there any Irish in you, Callum?' asked the doctor.

Callum shook his head.

'Mind you,' the doctor continued with a wicked grin. 'I wouldn't want to be in your shoes when Sophie's dad catches up with you.'

Callum gulped. He hadn't given any thought to how upset Sophie's parents would be. Sophie seemed to have forgiven him, but would her parents? And let's be honest, Sophie had only forgiven him because she didn't realise he'd actually dropped her head-first down the mine. Callum had walked away without a scratch but Sophie was laid up in hospital, black and blue and covered in plaster. What would any parent think?

'Is your dad home? I thought he was away.'

'Oh yeah, he got back a week ago. He's pretty keen to meet you.'

Callum swallowed hard.

'Sophie, see if you can persuade your dad to go easy on Callum,' the doctor gave Sophie a wink. 'The last thing I want to see is Callum back in here again, taking up another hospital bed.'

Were they for real?

Dr Akbar checked her watch and told Callum that visiting hours were over.

'I guess I'll be off then,' he said. 'But I can come back again tomorrow, if you like?'

'No need,' said the doctor, addressing Sophie directly. 'You'll be going home tomorrow. All you need is rest and sleep, and to be kept out of trouble.'

Dr Akbar turned to Callum. 'You'll be able to visit Sophie at home instead — and have that little chat with her father.' She stowed her pen in the breast pocket of her white coat and left the room, laughing out loud like a cackling witch.

'Come on Callum,' she shouted over her shoulder, 'your time is up.'

Chapter 44

Saturday 23rd August 2014

Callum had taken to spending all day in his bedroom, lounging around on his unmade bed, practising being a teenager. Sophie had been home for four days and he still hadn't been to see her. Now he felt guilty for not visiting, as well as for dropping her head-first down the mine and allowing her to think it was her fault. If he did visit, he was sure her dad was going to beat him to a pulp and frankly he knew he deserved it.

'There's no point moaning at me.' Jim protested, without looking up from his yellowing book of *Boys Own Adventures*, which Callum had retrieved from the living room and left spread open on the desk. 'I ain't helpin' you. Ask Bob.'

'As if!' Callum rolled over and stared at the faded flowery wallpaper. That was all Jim had said since Callum had got back from the hospital full of questions and worries.

'Jim, do you think I should tell Sophie it was my fault, or do you think that would make her dad even madder? It'd make her mad too, wouldn't it? Would it be the 'right thing' to own up, even if it meant me getting in more trouble? Do you think her dad would really hurt me? Do you think he would try and kill me?'

'I ain't helpin', ask your grandad... I don't know, ask Bob...' Jim's answers were getting repetitious and it was driving Callum nuts.

His guilt was getting worse and worse with each passing day. It lay heavy in his stomach, preventing him from eating and sleeping. He had to talk to someone and if Jim wasn't up for it there were no options left but to try Grandad.

'All right then' he shouted to Jim. 'And you see where it gets me!'

'About time,' Jim shouted at his back, making Callum slam the door so hard behind him that it warranted a telling off from Nana who was preparing another culinary disaster in the kitchen.

Callum found Grandad sitting in his favourite chair, alone in the living room, reading a book on World War II planes and being miserable. He was in his element. Callum flopped down on the brown settee next to the old man and put his feet up on the old wooden coffee table.

'What do you want?' Grandad asked with all his usual warmth and sensitivity. 'And get your bleedin' feet off the table!'

Here we go, thought Callum removing his feet and squirming in his seat. 'Can I ask you something, Grandad? Something serious?'

Grandad put his book down on table and looked up in surprise. Callum wondered when he had last been asked for his opinion on anything.

'Of course,' he said, sitting back, folding his arms across his chest and allowing Callum the time he needed to explain.

Callum struggled to find the right words and the words he did find came out a bit all over the place. 'Grandad,' he said. 'You remember when Sophie and I went in that mine…'

'Yes, I think I remember. Was that the time when I had to collect you from the hospital and then we had the police and that man from Geevor Mine round here trying to arrest you? Oh… umm… let me think. Yes… yes, I think I remember.'

Oh, this was going to be such hard work! 'Well. It was sort of my idea and… sort of my fault it all went wrong. And it's definitely all my fault that Sophie got hurt.'

Callum picked at a seam on the settee and Grandad watched him disapprovingly. Callum calmed his impatient fingers and carried on. 'Well, she doesn't realise that it was *all* my fault and I don't know if I should tell her, or if it's OK to leave her thinking it was her fault or just one of those things that happens. And my life is pretty complicated at the moment and she's the only person who understands.'

Callum thought back to when he had visited Sophie in hospital, he remembered how relieved he'd felt when she said she believed in his ghosts. 'I so wanted her to believe me, Grandad, and she does. But how would she feel if she knew that I was to blame for everything. And I feel *so* bad about it. And Dr Akbar says her dad's livid because he thinks it's all my fault — which it is — and when he catches up with me he's going to kill me.'

Yep, that about summed it up.

Grandad scratched his chin and let out a long 'ummm' noise to indicate how hard he was thinking. He stretched out his legs and uncrossed his arms, lining them up along the arms of his chair.

'OK. So let's see, then. Sophie's your friend — yes?'

'Yes.'

'Girlfriend?'

Callum flushed. Honestly! Why do grownups always think that? He was twelve, not twenty.

'No — just a friend. A good friend. We tell each other stuff and she believes me when I tell her... unusual stuff.'

'Ummm... I won't ask.' Grandad furrowed his brow and Callum dreaded to think what unusual stuff Grandad thought he might have been discussing with Sophie.

'But you've let her believe it was her fault that she fell head-first down the mine.'

'Yeah. That's not good is it?' Callum started plucking nervously at the settee seam again.

'No, it's not,' said Grandad. 'And stop pulling my settee to pieces.' Callum drew his hands in and placed them in his lap. Grandad carried on. 'OK. What do you think would happen if you told her it was all your fault and how sorry you were?'

'Dunno. I suppose she'd be mad and her dad would try and kill me.' Callum squirmed in his seat, flinching at the thought of what Sophie's dad might do to him and what Sophie might think of him if she knew the truth.

'I don't think her dad would do anything to you, lad. Worst case scenario he'll give you a hell of a telling off. But he can't be any madder with you than I was when I found out what you'd been up to — and you survived that.'

That was true. When Grandad had arrived at the hospital after the mine incident, it was like the arrival of a tropical thunderstorm — but with worse language. The car journey back to Mousehole had been rather fraught too, with Grandad yelling at the top of his voice about what an irresponsible fool Callum had been. But he'd survived.

Grandad leant in towards Callum and lowered his voice. 'I don't think you realise,' he said. 'But you're actually very lucky. You can still apologise to Sophie. You can go round to the guest house any time you want and explain what happened and ask her to forgive you. She might, she might not. Her dad might snap both your legs and break four of your ribs, then again he might not.' He leant back in his chair and closed his eyes, Callum wondered if that was it, but then he carried on. 'But she's still here; so you can apologise whenever you want. You don't realise how lucky you are.'

Grandad got up and walked over to the French windows. He stood gazing far out to sea, silhouetted against the bright daylight outside. 'I know what it's like when all you want to do is turn the clock back and *not* do something or at the very least say you're sorry about what happened.' His voice was very calm and had a faraway quality to it. 'You want to go back and do it differently, so it's not so bad and no one gets hurt, but you can't. You can't turn the clock back and say "let's not go into that mine" — but you can still say you're sorry for the consequences of your stupid decisions.'

He turned around and smiled affectionately at Callum. He'd never talked to Callum like this before. They were having a proper conversation. Not a rant or a telling off. For the first time ever, Grandad and Callum were talking, and Callum liked it.

He looked up at Grandad, shielding his eyes from the sun coming in through the window behind him. 'What do you mean, Grandad?' he asked.

'I mean, what if she had died and it was all your fault and you could never say how sorry you were? Have you got any idea how that would eat you up? How that destroys any happiness you could *ever* have?'

Grandad walked back to his armchair and sat down heavily. 'Every day of your whole life it would be eating you up. Because deep down you know that he should be there with you, but he's not and it's your fault.' Grandad wasn't looking at Callum anymore. He was staring out of the window, far out to sea.

'He?' Grandad wasn't talking about Sophie anymore. 'What do you mean, Grandad?' Callum shuffled forward so he was sitting right on the edge of the settee.

'I mean I had a friend, once.' Grandad snorted. 'The best friend in the world.' He took off his reading glasses and pulled at the saggy bit of skin between his eyebrows.

'We rescued a pilot from a plane crash — well he rescued me, saved my life. It's quite a long story.'

Grandad leant forward and opened the book on the

coffee table. It fell open to its usual page and he pointed to the picture of the Focke-Wulf FW 190 with the black arm of his glasses. Callum leant in and Grandad continued. 'That was the plane. The pilot was quite the character. Günter... his name was Günter.'

Callum looked from the book to his Grandad and back again. What was he saying? Was this Günter his friend? But Jim had always said he was Grandad's best friend. Grandad couldn't have had two friends — could he? It was a miracle he had any. Callum checked the plane again. It was definitely German. Would Grandad have rescued a German pilot? In the middle of World War II? He must have misunderstood.

'This pilot? He wasn't German was he?'

'Yes. But in a way he was one of us as well.' Grandad smiled at the memory and let out half a laugh. 'I now realise how very young he was. Back then all I knew was that he was lost and he wanted to go home. My friend Jim and I, we hid him in the new lifeboat station up at Penlee. He'd saved my life you see, when I'd been trapped in his plane... and Jim trusted him... and I trusted Jim. He was up there for weeks, we got real close.'

'You hid a German pilot in the Lifeboat Station, in the middle of World War II?' Callum couldn't get his mind round it. 'Wasn't that a really dangerous thing to do? What would have happened if you'd been caught?' Callum was beginning to sound like his mother. 'Did you get caught?'

Grandad sat in silence for ages before answering.

'Turned out it was quite dangerous.' He spoke slowly, closing the book and tapping it with the arm of his glasses. 'On the night Günter was going to leave, Jim and me were up at the crash site, unscrewing the compass and a few other bits and pieces from the plane — things we thought might help Günter get home. But we were seen by the Home Guard. A local farmer called Thornham. He followed us to the Lifeboat Station and then… and then… Jim died.' Grandad put his glasses down and closed his eyes, lost in his own thoughts and memories.

Callum wasn't sure he'd heard that right. Could that be true? Had Jim died while he and Grandad had been helping a German pilot escape? It was unbelievable. Of course Jim must have died during the war, he was a ghost dressed as a World War II evacuee, Callum understood that; but he had always assumed that Jim had died in a bombing raid. But then Mousehole probably hadn't been a major air raid target, not like London, which was why Jim had been evacuated down here in the first place.

Callum thought Grandad might be asleep, had this all been too much for him? Too personal. Too private. But he had to know more.

'Grandad,' he said, lightly shaking his arm. 'How did Jim die?'

A gentle clinking of china tea cups announced Nana's arrival and Callum budged up to make room for her on the settee. She didn't say anything. Grandad opened his eyes and smiled at her. When it didn't look like Grandad was going to say anymore, Nana answered Callum's question for him.

'The German killed Jim,' she said quietly. 'Mr Thornham brought Jim's body back down to the village and told everyone what had happened. There had been a struggle, the German pilot took Mr Thornham's gun off him and shot Jim dead. People talked about it for years. The wee lamb was only twelve. We think the German manipulated the boys into helping him, then when he had everything he needed he turned on them. It was a good thing Old Thorny got there in time, because he'd have killed Bob too, given half a chance. That might seem unlikely to you today Callum, but there was a war on. You can't imagine what it was like back then. Things were very different.

'But of course it was an awful shock for your grandad; he didn't say a single word for years. Shell shock they called it at the time. They'd have some fancy name for it today — they'd send him on a course of counselling and make him go on the Jeremy Kyle show — but in those days you simply got on with it.'

Nana poured out tea for everyone and Callum spooned half a bowlful of sugar into his without thinking. He was struggling to get his mind around everything that he'd heard. So, that was how Jim had died…

Grandad stared long and hard at his cup and saucer. 'It wasn't like that,' he said in a voice so timid that it sounded like a different person speaking.

'It wasn't Günter. He'd already left. It wasn't Günter.'

Nana put her cup back down. 'Don't be silly love. It must have been. Everyone said it was.'

Callum couldn't have been more captivated. 'What did happen, Grandad?'

Grandad took a long slow breath. 'Günter had gone. We told him to run for it and he did. Old Thorny was going to go after him and we tried to stop him. Jim climbed on to his back and I tried to get the gun off him.'

Nana's mouth fell open. 'You never said…'

A movement caught Callum's attention and he realised Jim was there, standing in the doorway. He came in and sat himself on the floor by Grandad's chair. He was as transfixed as Callum and Nana.

'I got the gun off Old Thorny but the safety catch wasn't on and I was holding it when the thing went off. It was so loud, so terribly, terribly loud. And hot, really hot. The recoil of it pushed me clean off my feet… Jim was hit square in the chest. No one could have survived it.' He took another deep breath and let it out slowly. 'When the smoke cleared it was me holding the gun. It was me… I'd killed him.' Streams of silent tears ran down his face.

'Old Thorny was shouting, "say the German did it, we'll say the German did it". I don't think he knew if he'd pulled the trigger or I had. He was covering his arse as much as mine. But I knew it was me. I was the one that was holding the gun.' Grandad struggled to get his words out. 'I'd killed my best friend… and that was the end of my world as much as his.'

Jim put his head on Bob's old and knobbly knee and held him.

Grandad's voice was shaking, 'I never even got to say how sorry I was.'

'I think he knows,' whispered Callum.

'Well I'll be blowed,' said Nana. 'And you've carried that guilt your whole life. Well that explains a lot!'

Grandad let out a wail that wrenched at Callum's soul. It was like he had seventy years of pain pent up inside him, pushed down deep within him until this very moment, when the valve flew off and everything started exploding out of him.

Callum looked from Grandad to Jim and back again. Jim was neither upset nor surprised. He was there comforting Grandad, helping him, supporting him, as he had done for all those years.

Jim was muttering to himself. 'It's all right... it was an accident... I always knew what had happened... it was an accident... you were trying to get the gun off Old Thorny... you didn't mean for it to go off... it weren't your fault... it don't matter anyway... you're the best friend anyone could ever have... I wouldn't change a thing, mate... not a single minute of it.'

Callum desperately wanted to tell Grandad that Jim was here with him, at this very moment and that he always had been. That he didn't need to apologise, Jim had never wanted anything except his best friend's happiness, and for him to stop feeling guilty and start living his life again. But how? What could Callum say to Grandad that Grandad would believe and that wouldn't result in Callum being rushed straight back into hospital?

Callum decided to touch upon the subject, to see what kind of response he got. 'Grandad, do you ever think that Jim's here with you?'

Grandad pulled out a huge cotton hankie and blew his nose on it very loudly. 'No lad. It's a nice thought, but no. I don't believe in ghosts or any of that new-fangled nonsense. And I hope you don't either.'

Nana got up, walked over to Grandad and perched on the arm of his chair. 'I sometimes think he's here,' she said. 'I've always said I think Bob's got a guardian angel and that's probably Jim. Sometimes, when it's just the two of us, I can feel him, it's like there's a third person in the room. I even make him a cup of tea.'

Grandad rolled his eyes and laid his hand on hers.

'Yes, but you've never been fully with it, Jean, let's face it.'

Callum sat a minute longer, taking it all in. Tears were streaming down Grandad's stubbly old chin. He wouldn't have thought that someone that old had that many tears left in him. He was being comforted by Nana and Jim who was kneeling on his other side.

He had so many questions to ask and there was so much he wanted to tell them, but he didn't know how, and this wasn't the right moment. He stood up, left them to it and went to make his bed.

It was time to go and see Sophie.

Chapter 45

Saturday 23rd August 2014

Much to everyone's surprise, Grandad offered to walk to Sophie's with Callum. Whether as moral support, a body guard or simply because the two of them were getting on better and feeling — well, like family — Callum wasn't sure, but he was pleased to have the company. So straight after lunch he, Grandad and Jim set off for Sophie's guest house.

Last week's rain had moved north and the summer holiday weather had made a welcome return to Mousehole. A warm afternoon greeted them as they stepped outside, and the palm trees that edged the road swayed gently in the sea breeze.

'Nervous?' asked Grandad, as they turned onto The Parade.

Callum nodded, wishing the massive knot in his stomach would shrink and that he would calm down. 'Do you know Sophie's dad? What's he like?'

Grandad stopped and leant up against the road side wall. 'I think his name's Thomas. Can't say as I've ever met him, but I've seen him around and only ever heard good things about him. He's not from round here. Came down on holiday soon after your mum moved up to London.'

They started walking again, Grandad forcing an even slower pace than before. Callum tutted, although Jim didn't share his frustration at all, the old man's doddering didn't bother the ghost at all. He must be very used to it by now.

'He was staying at the Tor Vista and that's how he met Linda.' Grandad continued. 'He took her off travelling, they got married abroad and then they moved back when the guest house became too much for Linda's parents. She's run it ever since and he comes and goes. I think he still works overseas somewhere.'

The guest house came into view and they made their way through the car park to the back door. Callum knocked and was startled when the old sea-dog, Jack Holmes, melted through it, inviting them in.

'Thanks, Jack,' Jim answered on their behalf. 'But they can't; they'll need the door to be opened properly.'

'Of course, of course.' Jack nodded to Callum and his Grandad.

Callum was doing his level best to pretend he couldn't see either Jack or Jim, but it was tricky. Jack was his usual exuberant self and seemed very excited about something.

'Jolly well done, Callum, on getting our Sophie out of that mine. You did a sterling job. First rate.'

Callum gave him the slightest tip of his head in an embarrassed acknowledgement.

'Look, Jim, there's something I've got to show you. Come with me.' And with that both Jack and Jim disappeared through the door.

Charming, thought Callum, as he and Grandad were left standing outside, waiting for someone who still had a pulse to come and answer the door.

'Coming.' Footsteps echoed inside the house and Grandad whispered, 'here we go, lad,' and squeezed Callum's hand.

Linda must have been baking because she had flour all over her apron and her hands were wet from where she'd washed them in a hurry. The smell of freshly baked scones wafted down the hallway.

'Hello Callum, my lovely, come on in. Bob! My goodness, what an honour!'

Whether the honour was good or bad, Callum couldn't tell.

'Come in, come in.' She ushered them down the hallway. 'Sophie's going to be so pleased to see you, and I know Thomas will want a word too.'

Callum gulped. 'We've come to see how Sophie is…'

'That's good of you. And Bob, what a nice surprise to see you as well; you will stop for a cup of tea won't you? There's a batch of scones in the oven.' Linda steered them into the kitchen and insisted that they make themselves comfortable at the table while she set about tidying up her baking things and making tea.

'Sophie and Thomas are in the office — they're on the computer. They won't be long.' Linda handed Callum a tall glass of cold tap water. He must have looked like he needed it. He swigged it down loudly, causing Grandad to tut.

Jack, the old guest house owner, and Jim were already in the kitchen, deep in hushed conversation. Callum tried hard to make out what they were saying but he couldn't hear them over Linda's excited retelling of Sophie's latest hospital visit, at which Dr Akbar had said she was healing well and there shouldn't be any long term complications.

Grandad gazed out of the large kitchen window, admiring the view, whilst Callum sat down at the messy kitchen table, trying to find the compass that he'd seen on his last visit, the one that Sophie had said was a lot like the thing in the mine. He found it, acting as a paperweight on top of a mound of email printouts. He picked it up and fiddled with it. It was about the size of an old-fashioned sweet tin, flecked with green paint and very old. Callum passed it from hand to hand and turned it round, forcing the little plane's nose to spin in dizzying circles.

Jack Holmes was pointing the compass out to Jim, waving his arms around and speaking in animated tones. Callum glanced up and saw Jim's eyes nearly pop right out of his head.

'Turn that over,' Jim shouted to Callum. 'Turn that over!'

Callum ignored him. He had no intention of making a fool of himself in front of Grandad and Linda by talking to a ghost at a moment like this. It's very distracting to have people talking to you that no one else can see or hear, and Callum wanted to make a good impression on Sophie's parents. He'd come to apologise and he wanted to concentrate on that, thank you very much.

He shot Jim a 'not now' look, said nothing and carried

on listening to Linda and Grandad, joining in with their conversation by making encouraging comments about Sophie's progress. Linda got out her mobile and showed them both photos of her daughter's X-rays. Perhaps a little bit too much detail, Callum thought, especially as he felt even guiltier when he saw the extent of the damage to Sophie's left arm and leg.

Meanwhile, Jim was hopping from foot to foot and wringing his hands. 'For goodness sake, Callum, turn the bleedin' thing over. Can't you see it matches the *höhenmesser* from the mine? This is important. Turn it over!'

The kitchen door swung open and Callum expected Sophie to come in, but instead a tall man with a mop of very light greying hair entered. He wore a pair of tan chinos and a black T shirt. He was older than Linda, but in good shape. Callum dropped the compass back onto the table and leapt up. He held his hand out but said nothing. 'Hello Sophie's dad' didn't sound right, he didn't know Sophie's surname and Thomas definitely wouldn't be right in theses circumstance.

'You must be Callum,' the man said, striding across the kitchen. He was imposing and sort of angular. Callum tried to assess his expression. He didn't look angry, but he didn't look pleased to see Callum either.

'I understand I have you to thank you for getting Sophie into the mess in Geevor, and getting her out again — is that right?'

'Yes — sorry. I'm really very sorry.' Perhaps he should call him Sir.

Linda interjected by calling out introductions from

her position by the Aga. 'Thomas,' she said, 'this is Callum and his Grandad, Bob, you'll remember, Jean's husband, from the bungalow up on Cliff Road.' Grandad dragged himself away from the view, shook hands with Sophie's dad, and Linda ushered them all over to the kitchen table.

Callum thought he saw Linda give Thomas a sort of 'be careful' expression, but he couldn't be certain, and if she was cautioning her husband against ripping Callum to shreds, then that had to be a positive.

Callum picked up the compass again, he was too nervous not to fiddle with something.

'What I want to understand,' Thomas said, 'is what you were doing down the mine in the first place.' He had an accent that Callum couldn't place; it was European but he couldn't say exactly where it was from.

Sophie and Callum hadn't had a chance to concoct a story together and Callum didn't want to tell her dad that they had been chasing ghosts. He had to think on his feet and hope that he didn't say anything that contradicted Sophie version of events.

'Show me the compass!' Jim was yelling at the top of his voice. 'Show me the bleedin' compass!' Even Jack was jumping up and down shouting. It was so off-putting. Callum desperately wanted to concentrate on talking to Sophie's dad. Why wouldn't the ghosts shut up so that he could think? He slammed the compass down on to the table. Thomas, Linda and Grandad Bob all gave him disapproving looks. Things weren't getting off to a good start.

'Jim told me about the mine and I wanted to see it for myself,' Callum began, rushing out his explanation without taking a breath. 'But when we got there it was closed, so we had a wander around, found the entrance to the tunnel and, well, it was raining, so we thought we'd have a quick peek inside to… you know… get out of the rain.'

He could tell instantly that this was not what Sophie had said. Thomas stiffened in his seat.

'Turn the compass over, please,' begged Jim.

Callum was worried Grandad was going to ask him who he knew called Jim. But he hadn't heard a word. He was leaning across the table staring at the compass, his forehead wrinkled and his mouth hanging open.

Callum gave in to Jim's cries and flipped the little tin over.

Jim, Jack and Grandad all moved in closer to examine it and there was a collective intake of breath from all three of them.

Grandad's age-spotted hand shot out and picked up the compass. He held it up to the light from the large window and ran his thumb over the faint lettering that was scratched on its back. The rough message was still visible, seventy years after his penknife had made the marks.

'*Good luck, mate,*' he read the words out softly.

There was silence. Everyone, dead and alive, stared at him.

'Where did you get this?' Grandad's voice trembled.

Thomas stroked his forehead. 'It was my father's.' He held out his hand and Grandad reluctantly gave him back the compass. Thomas turned it round and round until the nose of the plane pointed to the 'N' on the dial. He held it steady in that position and talked to the compass rather than Grandad.

'He always had this on his desk at home. When I went travelling, after university, he gave it to me, because he said it was very lucky and it would see me home safely.'

Callum looked from Grandad to Jim and back again. The colour had drained from the faces of both.

'On the back,' Grandad said, as Thomas turned it over to examine it. 'On the back, it says '*Good Luck, Mate*'. I wrote that.'

Linda put the tea tray down on the table with a jolt. Tea spilt from the spout of the pot and she made no attempt to mop it up. Instead she pulled out the chair next to Grandad's and sat down, staring across the table at her husband.

'Thomas…'

Everyone wanted him to explain.

'Your father?' Grandad Bob asked.

'My father, Günter Neumann. It was the compass from his plane.'

Grandad gasped and Callum thought he could have had a seizure at any moment. Linda laid her hand on his back and asked him if he was all right. He nodded, but couldn't say a word. Behind him Jim had fallen over and Jack was trying to sit him back up, propping him against the kitchen units and fanning his face ineffectively.

'Hold on,' said Callum, addressing Thomas in a stunned awe. 'Hold on; you're saying that your dad, Sophie's grandad, is Günter, the German, that saved my Grandad's life by pulling him out of the plane and that Grandad Bob and Jim then hid in the lifeboat station…

That's your dad? Come off it! What are the chances of that?'

Thomas put the compass in the centre of the table with the faintly scratched words uppermost for all to see; he took out a hanky and wiped his glistening forehead.

'But why didn't you say anything before?' Bob raised his hand, waggling a finger at Thomas. 'He must have told you…'

Linda was worried for him. 'You don't have to say anything Thomas, not if you don't want to…'

Thomas cleared his throat. 'My father told me stories when I was a child. Wonderful stories about Mousehole and how he sheltered here after his plane crashed.' He steadied himself with both hands on the table. 'He used to say he was the world's worst pilot. Only one flight and he managed to get lost and crash.'

Grandad smiled. 'He was a terrible pilot.'

Thomas seemed surprised by the warmth of Bob's reaction. He took a deep breath and carried on. 'He said some local children helped him, brought him food, blankets and clothes. Helped him improve his English and build up his strength, even went back to his plane and rescued this compass… to help him find his way home.'

He fell silent and everyone sat patiently waiting for him to continue as soon as he could.

'It was the story of my childhood. It was the only story I ever wanted to hear. When my education was finished I left Germany to travel and part of my tour was, of course, to come to Cornwall and to visit this Mousehole that I had heard so much about.'

Thomas reached across the table and took Linda's hand. She stroked it, and the empathy between the two of them was tangible. Callum glanced over to Jim; he wanted to be sure the ghost was hearing all of this. He was.

'Mousehole is so beautiful isn't it?' Thomas said. There was general agreement.

'And the people I met were wonderful too. I stayed here, at the Tor Vista and I met Linda. I told her and her parents all about my father and his stories — I promise you I did!'

Linda nodded in his defence.

'But they had a different version of the story. They told me that it was common knowledge that a German pilot crashed here, towards the end of the war, that he used two young boys to run his errands and when he was done with them he shot one and would have shot the other if the Home Guard hadn't arrived in time.'

Thomas released Linda's hand and sat back, bracing himself for the deluge of anger that he fully expected to receive from Bob. But Grandad said nothing, sitting back stunned by Thomas's revelation.

Callum couldn't bear it any longer. There was so much guilt tied up in all of this. Grandad had felt guilty his whole life because he'd accidentally shot Jim. And here was Sophie's dad, Thomas, feeling equally guilty because he thought his father had committed the same crime.

'But it didn't happen like that,' Callum cried out. 'Grandad, tell him! It didn't happen like that; did it?'

Thomas shook his head at Callum's outburst and carried on with his story, calmly and apologetically. 'It was the war. It was a different time. I always believed my father's story, but Linda's parents made it very clear to me that people round here would not remember it that way. And they were very convincing. They suggested we tell no one, and we haven't.

'Equally, I haven't told my father what Linda's parents said. He would be heartbroken to think people here believed him capable of such an abomination. I told him there was no one here who remembered the crash and he didn't have any reason to think I was lying.

'Mr Fox.' Thomas asked. 'Were you one of the boys that took my father food and blankets, all those years ago?'

Good grief, thought Callum, Grandad's going to start crying again! But to Callum's relief, the old man held it together.

'Günter was my friend,' he whispered. 'When I was no older than Callum here, he pulled me from a burning plane. It was an honour to have helped him. I scratched that message on the back of the compass myself and I meant every word of it. But Thomas, I must tell you, your father didn't kill Jim, I know he didn't — I was there.'

Thomas and Linda looked at each other.

It was Grandad's turn to explain. 'It was an accident… Günter had already left. Jim and I were fighting with the Home Guard… because he was going to go after your father and he'd have shot him first and asked questions later. Anyway, I tried to get the gun off him, but when I did, it went off; the rest is history. The Home Guard said let's blame the German and I was too shocked to say anything else. I'm so sorry I didn't stand up for your father.' His voice gave in and he could barely be heard.

'Goodness Bob, you were twelve.' Linda put an arm around him. 'You'd just seen your friend die. This Home Guard, he was the responsible adult, he's the one who should have taken the blame. Not you.'

But Grandad didn't care about anything except finding out about Günter. 'Your father, is he still… with us?'

Thomas smiled and then picked up the tea pot and poured tea for everyone. 'Yes, he is most definitely still with us. And not in bad health considering he's eighty-seven. Don't start him on the subject of his medication though, he'll talk for hours — there's nothing wrong with his lungs, that for certain.'

'So Günter is Sophie's grandad?' Callum sat back and scratched his head; she's never mentioned having a German grandad.

'We call him Opa,' Linda explained, 'it's German for grandad.' She picked up the sharp knife on the tray and cut some of the scones in half, took the lid off a pot of clotted cream and opened the jam, handing dainty cake plates round to everyone.

'My friend Jim gave Günter a second instrument,' Grandad told them. 'I've looked it up in several books. It was an altimeter, it told the pilot how far above the ground he was. Your father called it a *höhenmesser*. Have you got that too?'

Thomas said he hadn't heard about a second instrument and before he could stop himself Callum blurted out: 'Jim says Günter left it in Geevor mine, when he hid there the night he left Mousehole — the same night he was shot. Sophie saw it when we were in there but when she leant through the hole to pick it up, I let go of her legs and she fell, and the altimeter fell with her and now it really is lost.'

There was a stunned silence around the room.

'And Jim told you that?' asked Grandad in amazement.

'Yep. Sorry.'

Thomas was getting more and more concerned. 'How could you know that? My father did spend his first night on the run in a mine shaft on the coast. I think it probably was Geevor. But how could you possibly know that?'

Callum flicked his long fringe and turned to Jim for help. Jim raised both hands — he had no advice to offer.

'Grandad, when I asked you earlier if you thought Jim might still be here with you, it was because he is. I've seen him. I can talk to him.'

Everyone was stunned, including the two ghosts.

'Don't be foolish Callum,' Grandad said, but Callum couldn't be stopped.

'Ever since I was hit by that ambulance, I've been able to see… ghosts. I've seen Jim following you everywhere, looking out for you, looking after you. He never left. Then there's Jack Holmes, he stays here at the guest house, mostly moaning that Linda doesn't keep the place tidy enough…'

'Bleedin' cheek!' exclaimed Linda.

'Sorry,' said Callum.

Grandad was terribly perplexed. 'You've seen Jim?'

'Yes. He's around all the time. About so high: dark hair, scrawny, bright green sleeveless jumper, permanently cheerful. I think he needs to know that you're going to be OK, Grandad, before he can move on. He needs to see you happy again, not beating yourself up all the time about an accident that happened seventy years ago. He knows it was an accident, he's known since the day it happened, it's never bothered him and he wants you to realise that too!'

Grandad's mouth fell open and his eyes were agog.

'He wants you to be happy again, Grandad.'

Callum turned to a very confused Thomas. 'I'm sorry I dropped your daughter down the mine. It was entirely my fault and I'm very, very sorry.'

'It's all right,' said Thomas. 'She survived. I appreciate your honesty, and yours Bob. I can't tell you how much it means to me, to hear what actually happened to my father, all those years ago.'

But Grandad wasn't listening. He was in a stunned world of his own, processing everything that Thomas and Callum had said.

At that precise moment the kitchen door swung open again and Sophie hobbled in on her crutches, complaining about all the noise that was coming from the kitchen.

'Opa's on Skype,' she announced. 'Anyone want a word with him before he logs off?'

'I think I know somebody who might…' said Linda.

The whole party moved to Thomas's office, where Grandad was given pride of place in the swivelling office chair behind a large and cluttered desk. Thomas leant in front of Grandad and spoke quickly, in German, to his father who was live on Skype. Then with a click of the mouse he increased the sky blue Skype box to full screen and stepped back so that Grandad Bob and Günter were face-to-face for the first time in seventy years.

Grandad leant forward and ran his fingers over the computer monitor. The face in front of him was unmistakable; older, strangely healthier, greyer, but with the same twinkling eyes and smile — it was Günter.

'Bob, is that you?'

Grandad was amazed. 'Günter? How the hell did you find your way home?'

Günter chuckled. 'Well, I got a little lost…'

Pretty soon the two of them were laughing and chatting as if they had talked to each other only the week before.

'I was caught quite close to Bath.' Günter explained. 'I was taken to the Ashton Gate Prisoner of War Camp near Bristol where I stayed until the end of the war. Then I was brought back here to Germany. After that I went to university and then became an English teacher, like my father.'

'Bath!' Bob laughed out loud again. 'Bath, you were meant to be going along the south coast to Plymouth. There was no point getting you that map at all, was there?'

'Bath was very beautiful though,' said Günter and everyone in the room agreed. 'How is Jim?'

Grandad paused and looked over to Callum.

'He's fine,' Callum said glancing behind him to see what Jim was up to.

Jim was grinning from ear to ear, his face alight with happiness. Why wouldn't he be; Bob was laughing and smiling with his grandson, reunited with his old friend Günter and he knew Jim was there with him and that Jim had forgiven him.

Jim's work was done. He started to spark, to light up all over in a brilliant shimmering blue. He was smiling and waving and fading away.

'He's moved on,' Callum told everyone. 'He's moved on.'

Chapter 46

Sunday 31st August 2014

Callum's bags were packed and waiting by the front door.

'Callum, love,' called Nana from the kitchen. 'That was your mum on the phone; she's stuck in traffic. She's going to be at least another hour.'

'No problem. I'll pop down to the harbour — say goodbye to Sophie. Call me when she gets here?'

He patted his pocket to check he had his new phone. It had been an early and very much appreciated birthday present from his grandparents. He still couldn't get a signal in the bungalow but that hadn't been such an issue since Grandad had come home from Skyping Günter at the guest house and gone straight out to buy himself a brand new PC. The bungalow was now on-line and Callum was back in contact with the real world — RESULT!

'Hey, Grandad, Mum's running late — I'm going out to see Sophie.'

Grandad glanced up from his computer desk in the

conservatory and waved. It was his new favourite place to sit.

'Send her my love too,' called Günter, from his sky blue box on Grandad's monitor. He was sitting in the corner of Grandad's screen so often these days, it was as if the elderly German had moved in with them.

'Will do,' Callum shouted back, pulling on his trusty trainers and heading out into the sunshine.

He broke into a jog going down The Parade and then slowed as he rounded the corner into Mousehole. He cast his eyes over the broad harbour walls, looking for Sophie's tell-tale bright red hair. There she was, right at the far end of the left hand wall, sitting on a plastic chair with her crutches on the floor beside her and a fishing rod in her good hand.

'Shouldn't you have gone by now?' she called out as he approached.

Callum settled himself down next to her, so close to the edge that his feet hung down the side of the wall, catching the spray from occasional larger waves. He wrapped his arms over the metal bars and explained the delay.

Callum and Sophie had seen each other the night before, at the guest house. Linda had thought it would be nice to have all the Foxes round for a family supper before Callum went back to London — and it had actually worked out OK. Grandad had gone on a bit too much about how wonderful his new computer was and how brilliant Callum had been at setting it up, but they all agreed he'd taken to the new technology better than anyone could have expected and it gave them something to talk about.

When Grandad left the table, Callum told everyone that Nana was the real IT whiz of the family. He'd set her up on Facebook and Twitter, where she already had 850 followers and she'd been invited to a rave in Billericay next Saturday.

Sophie poked him with one of her crutches. 'Come on then. How's life in the bungalow without Jim?' She was clearly as pleased as Callum to have this extra chance to catch up on the kind of news that they hadn't been able to discuss last night in front of the adults.

'I miss Jim, but I don't think Grandad does. I mean, he never knew he was there until he was gone. He's asked me all about it and I think he believes me.' Callum paused and stared out to the horizon. 'He's ever so grateful that Jim had stayed with him, and he's pleased for him that he's been able to move on, but he doesn't miss him like I do.

'Nana and I think Jim was able to go as soon as he saw Grandad happy again. And he certainly is happy. In fact, I think he might be too happy!' Callum groaned. 'He keeps bursting into song and slapping me on the back and saying, 'This is the life, Callum. This is the life!' I think I preferred him when he was miserable… can't wait to get away.'

'Liar,' said Sophie, smirking.

She was right, of course. Life at the bungalow was great now, he could email all his friends, play computer games with Grandad and see Sophie whenever he liked. He couldn't believe it was time to go home already.

'Anything to report on the other ghosts?'

Callum snorted. 'The Professor came round yesterday

and I typed up his theory for him. He owes me big time for that, it took forever and was possibly the most boring thing I've ever done.'

Sophie reeled in her fishing rod and asked Callum to pass her up another worm. He handed her the bucket with a distasteful look and Sophie took great delight in waving the revolting creature at him.

'How you going to explain that you have found a physics Professor's theory — on your grandad's brand new PC?'

Callum grinned, 'I've thought of that,' he boosted. 'I've printed it off, soaked the papers in Nana's old tea and burnt the edges with a match. It's worked a treat!'

Sophie howled. 'It's a theoretical physics paper, not one of your pirate's treasure maps! You're about three hundred years out.'

Callum shrugged. He didn't care — it was the best use of Nana's tea he'd found all holiday.

'I'm going to give it to Mum, to pass on to her eco-friends back in London, the Professor thinks that'll be him sorted. There's not much else to report really. Your Jack Holmes is still busying himself around the guest house, the pirates are giving me a bit of a wide berth because I've refused to go hunting treasure with them and the lifeboatmen are as happy as ever, they don't want anything at all, they just like hanging around Mousehole.'

A flurry of orange and navy caught his eye as the lifeboat crew came into the harbour. Callum gave them a wave and they all waved back, before slipping in to the Ship Inn for a pint.

'Are you going to come down again next summer?'

Sophie asked and this time it was her turn to blush.

'Hope so,' he replied, kicking his heels against the side of the harbour wall, 'Christmas too. Mum called the other night and agreed that as Grandad, Nana and I are getting on so well we could have a proper family Christmas together, down here. Nana's over the moon about it. She posted it on Facebook, did you see?'

'No. Missed that one.' Sophie laughed. 'I absolutely love her updates though. You know, if she's going to become an internet sensation, you're going to have to tell her to stop writing everything in capital letters.'

'I've tried' Callum groaned. 'You tell her.'

He knocked his heels against the side of the wall a little harder and yelled as one of his trainers fell off and plummeted down into the sea. It bobbed about on the surf like a tiny boat decked out in Converse colours.

Callum hopped about one footed, struggling to hook it out with the keep net while Sophie cried with laughter.

He was putting his soggy trainer back on when his mobile went off. It was Nana saying Mum's car had pulled up outside. She hadn't *got* mobile phones; she shouted so loudly that he would have heard her if she had simply opened the door of the bungalow and yelled down to the harbour.

'She does her phone calls in capital letters too,' he sighed. 'I've got to go. Will you text me?'

'Yeah, I want to hear all about the London ghosts and what they're like. But I'll see you again at Christmas, won't I?'

'Of course you will,' he said, bending down to whisper a last goodbye and kiss her on the cheek.

She flushed the same colour as her hair and Callum felt his cheeks rising up to a matching red.

'Bye then,' he said, flicking his fringe and grinning.

He gave Sophie a last long wave from the end of the harbour wall, headed back past the car park and onto the main road. He had one foot squelching in his wet trainer, the other walking on air. Grandad and Nana had turned out to be terrific grandparents after all; Mum would be waiting for him back at the bungalow and he'd just kissed Sophie. He didn't think life could get any better. He took out his mobile and a text flashed up. It was from Sophie: Ambulance!

What? Callum looked up; he'd drifted into the middle of the road without realising. He leapt back on to the pavement a mere second before the green and yellow blur of Mousehole's one and only ambulance whooshed past him, horn blazing.

Callum let out a long and thankful sigh. Perhaps some of Grandad's luck was finally rubbing off on him.

He sent a message back to Sophie:

Thanks ☺